Praise for *The End of Getting Lost*

"*The End of Getting Lost* is a beautifully written love story with plenty of twists and turns. I adored going back to a time when we could actually vanish without an electronic trace. And what better place to do so than the shadows of Europe? Robin Kirman is wonderfully deft with suspense and plot. This is a true dark delight."

—Katie Crouch, *New York Times* bestselling author of *Girls in Trucks*

"*The End of Getting Lost* will draw you in, the story will surprise and captivate you, and you will be delivered from the concerns of your current life (at least for a while). This book just might provide the escape you need (as it did for me). So if you're considering what to read this week, think about escaping into *The End of Getting Lost*."

—Chris Schluep, *Amazon Book Review*

"A story line that offers an intriguing mix of romance, psychological thriller, and travelogue. Think *Before Sunrise* if Patricia Highsmith had had a story credit."

—*Time Out*

"Kirman's investment in well-placed twists and several surprising revelations uplifts the couple's story."

—*Shelf Awareness*

Also by Robin Kirman

Bradstreet Gate

The End of

Getting Lost

a novel

Robin Kirman

Simon & Schuster Paperbacks

new york   london   toronto   sydney   new delhi

Simon & Schuster Paperbacks
An Imprint of Simon & Schuster, Inc.
1230 Avenue of the Americas
New York, NY 10020

This book is a work of fiction. Any references to historical events, real people, or real places are used fictitiously. Other names, characters, places, and events are products of the author's imagination, and any resemblance to actual events or places or persons, living or dead, is entirely coincidental.

First Simon & Schuster trade paperback edition February 2023

SIMON & SCHUSTER PAPERBACKS and colophon are registered trademarks of Simon & Schuster, Inc.

For information about special discounts for bulk purchases, please contact Simon & Schuster Special Sales at 1-866-506-1949 or business@simonandschuster.com.

The Simon & Schuster Speakers Bureau can bring authors to your live event. For more information or to book an event, contact the Simon & Schuster Speakers Bureau at 1-866-248-3049 or visit our website at www.simonspeakers.com.

Interior design by Ruth Lee-Mui

Manufactured in the United States of America

1   3   5   7   9   10   8   6   4   2

Library of Congress Cataloging-in-Publication Data is available.

ISBN 978-1-9821-5985-6
ISBN 978-1-9821-5986-3 (pbk)
ISBN 978-1-9821-5987-0 (ebook)

For Emmanuelle

The End of

Getting Lost

One

It was the end of getting lost—a moment when travel could still feel like taking leave of the familiar, before there were ten different means for a person to be reached in almost any corner of the world in which she might be standing, when letters and postcards would still follow slowly on the heels of a young couple moving across Europe, and two people in love could escape their old reality a little, experiencing the world before them like a shared dream.

The year was 1996, the month June, when Gina and Duncan arrived at the Walensee, a lake less than an hour's drive from the clinic near Zurich where she had spent the past two weeks. She'd come there to recuperate from a head injury she'd suffered from a bad fall in Berlin. The injury hadn't been a small one, rehabilitation was required, but now that Gina was well enough to do without doctors and nurses, she and Duncan had escaped to the Swiss countryside. The scenery around Lake Walen was possibly the loveliest and most peaceful that she had ever seen: small villages

1

of white, red-roofed houses, lush fields of wildflowers and, across the still, blue water, green mountains topped with milky clouds. They'd spent three days there in a small guesthouse, hiking and biking among the villages, or boating on the lake. Duncan didn't usually swim, and the lake water was cold, but Gina liked to jump in anyway in the hours when the sun was strongest. After she'd tired herself with laps, and as the light began to weaken, she'd leave the water to go inside and dress, and then they'd bring their chairs down to the grassy banks to take in the sky and lake, lit pink and gold by the setting sun.

During this quiet hour, Duncan, who was a classical composer, listened to music with headphones on his Discman, and, beside him, Gina read—Fitzgerald's *Tender Is the Night*, which Duncan had bought her that week as a gift. He'd been aware a Zurich clinic featured in the story, otherwise under the impression that it was a romance about a glamorous American couple traveling in Europe. The day after Duncan gave Gina the book, her doctor at the clinic had remarked on the Swiss sanatorium, and Gina had been forced to tell Duncan that it wasn't a happy story, that the wife in the novel was mentally ill.

"Oh God, forget it, then," Duncan had pleaded, but she'd made clear that reading it didn't upset her. On the contrary, it soothed her to return to a novel that she'd read before and remembered—in better detail than she possessed regarding her own recent life.

In the last weeks, Gina had often felt like she was crazy—though the doctors in the hospital in West Berlin and at the Zurich clinic had made clear that what she'd experienced was entirely a physical trauma. She'd suffered a concussion and intracranial swelling, and no one could predict what sort of recovery she'd make. The consensus by the end was that she'd been lucky. Her sight and hearing were normal and she had no speech difficulties, no aphasia. Her mind was sharp, her reasoning was good, and her moods were stable. Her dizzy spells were now gone, her balance and motor coordination perfectly restored. In fact, only two weeks after her injury, she was taking runs through the Swiss woods.

The only significant loss in functioning involved her memory. She couldn't recall anything of the accident or of the months leading up to her trip. Beyond that, there were stretches of experience that remained missing, which she didn't know she missed—her dance performances that year, the departure from New York of their two close friends—until Duncan would refer to these and nothing would come to mind.

At the same time, there were also many things that she did remember that before she'd forgotten. It was as if her mind had been shaken during the impact, and material that had been buried cast up to the top again. Scenes from her childhood, for instance, a trip she'd taken with her parents to Italy when her mother was still healthy. Gina could see her mother quite clearly, as she'd looked on that visit—in a white dress walking barefoot on the beach, her dark curls to her shoulders, her smile wide and bright as the pale sand—looking, Gina realized with a pang, very much the way she herself looked now.

Her recent brush with death had brought her closer to her late mother, and closer too to Duncan, who had hardly left her side since the accident, except to see that she received the best possible care. Unimpressed with the medical standard in Berlin, where she'd been hospitalized first, he'd proposed moving her to the clinic just outside of Zurich, where the techniques for physical rehabilitation were more advanced. Gina was a dancer, he let the doctor know, and therefore required special treatment.

The Swiss clinic had been state of the art, and during her stay there, Gina often wondered how all this would be paid for. She had a hefty inheritance from her mother, but Duncan had always refused to touch it and insisted she keep it in an account separate from him. He preferred to live frugally from what they earned, though in this case he insisted on sparing no expense.

"I'd pay any amount to have you back as you were again."

She'd grasped then how much the prospect of losing her had undone him. In some ways, her accident had been even more frightening for Duncan, as the only one who could recall it.

She'd asked him, once, to describe that day for her: They'd been in Berlin almost a week when Gina set off for a morning walk around the city. Duncan would have joined her, but that morning he'd been struck with musical inspiration he wanted to get down onto paper. As Duncan worked, morning turned to afternoon, and Gina still hadn't returned. He was beginning to grow nervous when the phone rang in his room. A hotel receptionist was calling to relay a message from a local hospital. Gina had suffered an accident.

Duncan had rushed over to the address that he'd been given: the Charité Hospital on Luisenstrasse. There, the doctor presiding over Gina's case told him what had happened, that Gina had been found at a construction site at Potsdamer Platz. It seemed she'd gone poking around one of the sections that was off-limits and that she'd slipped along the way and hit her head on a piece of exposed pipe. Tourists had discovered her, unconscious, and called an ambulance. Inside her pocket was a hotel key with her room number, and this was how she'd been identified and

Duncan had been reached. Her prognosis was still uncertain then; the doctors didn't know what state she'd be in when she awoke.

"I thought I'd lost you," Duncan told her. "I lived it in that hospital that night, life without you. You were gone."

In moments when she caught him looking at her, she could see that this was true—he seemed not to trust that she was real, as though at any instant she might disappear.

"Still here," she'd tease him, smiling reassuringly, but hiding her private thoughts—she was mostly there, sure, but what parts of her were lost?

She'd asked Duncan to fill in any large events of the last year. He insisted her life had gone on much as before. She'd continued dancing with the same experimental company, and Duncan continued to play piano there to accompany rehearsals. They collaborated on their own work: Duncan composed music and she choreographed dances to go with it. The biggest change was that Duncan had landed his first significant commission, which enabled them to afford this trip, their belated honeymoon. She and Duncan had been married for over a year; they were the only couple that had married among their young friends. But since then, they hadn't been able to find the time or funds for such a frivolous excursion. And now, here they were.

Their travels, Duncan told her, were to last the whole summer, starting in Berlin and moving west. They'd planned on heading to either Munich or Vienna, but they'd changed their minds on the day that Gina was released from the clinic in Zurich, after they'd sat down in a café and she'd noticed a discarded *International Herald Tribune* left behind on a chair. America was gearing up for an election in the fall: Clinton against Dole. In Russia, the first presidential election was also underway, with Boris Yeltsin struggling to maintain power. Also that spring, Bosnian war criminals were ordered by the UN to stand trial; a bombing by the IRA in Manchester had injured two hundred people, and, back in America, a man named Ted Kaczynski had been identified as the Unabomber and indicted. As Gina read, her heart started to thud—the sheer breadth of what she'd missed, the many events unfolding that she knew nothing about. After that, they'd agreed on stopping at Lake Walen: a place with no one around to prompt her thoughts besides a landlady who came to drop fresh daffodils inside their room, a place where it was easy to forget the larger world, and so forget what she'd forgotten.

Now, on their fourth and last day here, she and Duncan planned on renting the landlady's car to visit the Churfirsten mountains, where they would hike to the Paxmal, the famous monument to peace.

They left after breakfast and drove out to the bottom of the mountain to begin the long, steep hike. The way up was difficult, and Gina found herself thinking of the man who'd made this trek on his own hundreds of times in order to construct the monument: a rectangular stone building with thick columns, a reflecting pool in front, and, along each side of the pool, stone walls decorated with mosaics. According to the guidebook, all this work had been accomplished by a single artist, and had taken him twenty-five years of grueling effort. The story moved Gina—the solitude in which this man maintained his vision. She wrapped her arms around Duncan and leaned into him, holding him tight. She'd always longed for an artistic life, but feared its loneliness. What a gift to have Duncan, her husband and a composer, a man she could both love and create with, sharing in beauty together.

The hike down the mountain was quicker, but still, by the time she and Duncan returned to the guesthouse for lunch, it was quarter past two. The cook was upset over having to put out food so late, since lunch service, she reminded them, was officially meant to end at two.

"I guess it's not just a cliché," Duncan muttered under his breath, "the Swiss and time."

As a punishment, the cook brought out the same food she'd served for lunch the day before: reheated salmon and potatoes.

As Gina picked at a spongy bit of potato, Duncan pushed his plate away. "Forget this, we've got the car all night. Let's drive somewhere and get a real meal."

After the lunch, which the cook frowned to see they hadn't eaten, they stopped at the reception desk so that Duncan could tell the owner of the guesthouse, Ms. Arner, that they wouldn't be around for dinner.

"I think my wife and I could use a night out."

My wife. The description sounded alien to Gina; *wife* and *husband* were terms they'd used only in private, when they didn't need to hide how much those archaic, yet still fresh, titles thrilled them.

They returned to their room, where Gina pointed out that there was enough sun left for a swim. At the lake, Duncan splashed around up to his waist, while Gina jumped in with a shout and swam laps in the cold water for as long as she could stand it.

When she emerged, shivering in the last rays of sun, Duncan

was waiting for her with a towel. He wrapped himself around her, containing the warmth between them. When he spoke, chest pressed to her bare back, his words seemed to vibrate within her. "This might be the happiest that I've ever been."

Around six they started getting ready. Duncan whistled as he dressed in a yellow linen suit that he'd gotten before they left Zurich. He hadn't brought many clothes with him on the trip, preferring to travel light, picking up what he needed as they went. Gina put on a blue dress, then searched for the silk satchel that contained her jewelry.

Inside, there wasn't much: a pair of diamond earrings that she'd received from her grandparents at her high school graduation, an anklet she'd bought in college, on a trip into the city with her best friend, Violet. Her most cherished piece was a ring she'd been given by her mother, a yellow stone, not precious, but exotic: it had functioned as an engagement ring until Duncan could afford a proper one—what little money they had they'd spent on simple bands. Hers hung a little loosely on her finger, she'd noticed; apparently she'd lost some weight from the stress her injury had caused her.

Feeling around in the satchel for her mother's ring, she found a chain caught among some threads at the bottom. She pulled it out: a silver bracelet with a turquoise stone at the center. It must be from her father or other family in Santa Fe, she thought, but when she turned the piece over, she noticed an inscription on the back: *For My Love.*

"Did you give this to me?" she asked Duncan, thinking that he knew her taste too well to choose a piece that was so bland.

He laid the bracelet in his palm and took note of the

inscription. "It's from an aunt of yours. Some sort of family heirloom."

Could she have forgotten such a thing? She felt a moment of unease at her failure to recall, but told herself not to dwell on such details. Did she really need to know the story behind every small object in her possession—the countless bits of information that we all carry with us and let shape, in some cluttered and arbitrary way, our sense of who we are? There was something freeing in forgetting, she'd discovered, as if all these tiny accretions were like layers of clothing that kept you from feeling the air, the night, the life that was cloaked around you.

She looked over at Duncan, seeing him almost freshly then, with the years together stripped away, revealing the qualities she loved in him: his gentleness, his intelligence, his delicate dark features and the green eyes that always had a slightly distracted look about them, like he was listening to some inner song only he could hear.

He turned to take her arm then, and she stepped out into the cool Swiss evening, with the sounds of crickets and lapping water and a man beside her with a mild voice and smiling face who'd stood by her and loved her since she was nineteen.

The drive to the restaurant wasn't an easy one. The roads were dark and curving, the signs difficult to spot. She and Duncan had to pull over twice to consult a map before locating the simple stone building with a restaurant in the back. The room was rustic but elegant, with exposed wooden beams, red tablecloths, and candles.

Duncan pulled out Gina's seat for her and, as she thanked him, she almost called him by the wrong name. "Graham—" she began, and stopped herself, puzzling.

Before she could remark on it, Duncan rushed to speak. "Supposed to be classic Swiss cooking, this place."

"I don't think I know what that is."

"Well, the guidebook says we need to get the cholera."

"Like the disease?"

"Exactly." He described for her what he'd read: "During the epidemic, since people were afraid to leave their homes, they'd throw everything into a pie."

"Desperation casserole." She laughed, and she could see how much it pleased him, since the accident, to see her having fun.

They turned to study the menu and Gina noted the prices. "Duncan, it's too expensive."

"Oh, it's fine. One plate of cholera won't kill us."

"I'm serious. The way we've been spending, and we've still got months ahead—"

"We're fine," he insisted, and reached across for her hand, just as the waiter stepped up to pour their water and describe the evening's specials. Gina tried to listen, to let her concerns go, though she couldn't quite believe that Duncan, who'd worked sometimes for free as a composer, had suddenly been paid enough to afford all this. As she wondered, she became aware of another distraction: a man was watching her from across the room. She looked away, concentrating on her order, but when the waiter left, the man was still staring. He was heavyset, with receding white hair and a pink face.

Meanwhile, Duncan had begun to speak about their itinerary. "Plus, later in the summer it will be packed, which is another reason to start there."

"What's that?"

"The South of France."

"Sorry, I wasn't listening," she admitted, and, leaning forward, added more softly, "There's a man over there who keeps looking at me. Do we know him? In the corner, with the white hair."

Duncan turned in his chair to check, and Gina saw the man lower his eyes.

"Never seen him. But he looks pretty harmless to me."

After a moment, the man went back to staring, and Gina began to fidget in her seat. She'd been out in public so little since her accident, and some of the effects of her injury had made her self-conscious. She felt a sudden urge to study herself in a mirror, so she stood and told Duncan she was heading to the bathroom.

In the mirror above the sink, she confronted a woman of twenty-five, her curly auburn hair cut shorter than she recalled wearing it, which made her look younger than she was. Nothing showed of her injury but the remnants of a scrape across one cheekbone. She smiled, just to make sure her smile was even, as it had not been in the first days at the hospital. This small change, temporary as it proved to be, had terrified her. She'd found herself thinking of her mother—after her stroke, her smile had never been the one in the pictures from before.

When Gina stepped out into the dining room again, Duncan wasn't at their table. She spotted him in the corner, speaking with the man who'd been staring at her. Catching her eye, Duncan abruptly excused himself to meet her back at their table, settling into his seat just as she settled into hers.

"Did you find out who he is?" she asked him.

"A German tourist. He said he'd seen you performing in Vienna."

"*Really?*" She supposed it was possible: she had spent two

summers in Vienna, dancing for an international festival, though her parts hadn't been large ones. "I'm surprised anyone would notice a single dancer in a group."

"*I'd* have noticed you," said Duncan, smiling.

The food arrived. Gina had ordered the *pastetli*, a meat pie, which she no longer felt like eating. She was agitated, suddenly, restless in her chair. Her first Vienna tour, as magical as it had been, had also directly preceded her mother's death. She'd had the call from her father about her mother's final, fatal stroke a week before she was due to return home.

She felt a sudden pang—homesickness, she thought. Now and then she'd had the impulse to call her father, though Duncan had reminded her of the risks involved in that. Her father was bound to panic at the news of the accident. After his wife's stroke, Mr. Reinhold never remarried. Gina became his everything. It would terrify him to learn his only child, so far from home, had suffered a brain injury of all things, and, even if her not calling might cause him worry too, nothing could be worse than his reliving some version of her mother's decline, noting minor gaps in Gina's awareness, or some way in which she might fail to be the person that she'd been before.

"Are you all right?" Duncan asked, peering up from his plate.

"I'm fine." She saw no point in spoiling things with her grim thoughts. "Go on with what you were saying."

"Our itinerary." Duncan hesitated but, after a short pause, went on. "I'd been thinking France, I guess, along the Riviera. There are some quieter spots, and better to visit now than in July or August, when the whole region is packed. Plus I speak French, so we can navigate more easily. What do you think?"

She hadn't given much thought to their travels, though now that

Vienna had been mentioned, she felt she'd like to go there again. And she'd intended to drop in too on her friend Violet, in Prague.

"If we're heading west, doesn't it make sense to visit Vienna and Prague first? I'd like to visit Violet for a day or two at least."

Duncan raised his glass quickly, and wine spilled onto his upper lip. "You don't remember what happened with you two? That argument you had?"

No, she didn't have the slightest recollection of any fight with her best friend, though it wasn't inconceivable that it could happen. She and Violet both had strong opinions, about their work and about Duncan—whom Violet had never liked—and it was a function of their loyalty to one another that they hadn't butted heads more often. "When did we fight?"

"It was after she'd moved to Prague. Over the phone. I guess she'd been dismissive about a piece I'd written. Nothing new, but this time she'd gone too far and you were really shouting, said you'd had it, you were done with her."

Violet putting down Duncan was plausible enough, though Gina didn't see much point in staying angry when she'd forgotten why she was.

"In that case, I think I should definitely call her. Take the chance to repair things while I'm here."

Duncan took a bite of his casserole and chewed it before responding. "Right, sure you should. Though I don't see any reason to put yourself under pressure right away. Plus, Prague isn't a simple place to get around, so maybe better to start with Vienna?"

She pictured Vienna then, recalled the nights she'd spent there on her first visit. She and her fellow dancers had performed at the Volkstheater, a grand building on the corner of Arthur-Schnitzler-Platz, stretching out backward, like a crouching animal. There were two tiers of columns at the entrance, but the relative modesty of the exterior gave little hint of what lay inside: red velvet seats and curtains, crystal chandeliers, a fresco on the ceiling. Perhaps it was the sheer beauty of the place that caused her to put more into her dancing in Vienna than she ever had before. Her limbs felt more powerful, her instincts freer. She'd had the thought that this was her apotheosis, the moment when her talent as a dancer reached its peak, and she would look back on those nights, years later, and recall that fleeting bliss.

"Yes, right. I think Vienna would do me good."

"Great, then we're decided."

Duncan clinked his glass against hers and Gina took a sip of wine. Soon she began to relax, to enjoy the food, the cozy room—until the man who'd been staring at her before rose from his table. She watched him lay his napkin down, squeeze by another diner, and make his way toward her. For a moment, she thought the stranger might say something, but when she looked up he turned away, disappearing out the door into the darkness.

The next morning, a vision struck Gina as she woke from sleep. She was in a gallery, in a white and airy space, with paintings on the walls. She crossed the room and came to stand in front of a portrait of Duncan and herself. This was a painting her father had done of them for their wedding. She stood there, facing the portrait, in an atmosphere of sadness, and then a tall, sandy-haired man stepped up alongside her. He leaned over and whispered something in her ear that made her start.

She sat up sharply, there in the bed she shared with Duncan. He was awake, looking at her.

"A bad dream?" he asked her, rubbing her back.

"No, just a thought . . . nothing." She lay back down beside him and felt his hand stroke her thigh under the sheet.

He'd been especially hungry for sex since the accident, and she'd been too, maybe for the connection it gave her to him, or the grounding in her own body. She was young and healthy, alive, his touch reminded her, and she curled under him as he began to kiss her, her cheeks, her neck, lifting up her top to bare her stomach.

She looked down at him, at his smooth shoulders, that transfixed expression he always wore when he was aroused, moving in a daze but deliberately, a mood of sex he'd absorbed from her, years ago, but which had since become a state evolved together— their style of movement, their patient tangles. Arching up over her, he reached for the nightstand drawer. She drew him back to her.

He hesitated, about to say something, until she reached for him by the hips and drew him inside her. She looked him in the eyes so he could read her desire, then pulled him closer so that his face was at her ear and she could hear the sounds he made, deep and adult one moment and in the next just like the eager boy who'd been almost a virgin when she first led him to her bed.

"I love you," he told her after, dropping behind her and pressing her up against him so she could feel his heart going fast.

"I love you too."

They lay there like that, in the quiet morning light, until Duncan finally stood and announced he'd take a shower.

"Want to join me?"

She did, really; he looked sweetly boyish standing there, with his face flushed, naked before her. But then she recalled her vision that morning and felt an urge to write it down. Had it been a dream? Or a flash of memory, like she sometimes had now? She wanted to collect these impressions that came to her, usually when she wasn't hoping to have them, when she wasn't trying to remember anything at all.

"You go ahead. I'll have a last dip in the lake before we go."

He nodded, disappointed, but she rose and kissed him again before he turned toward the bathroom and she moved to the desk. As the shower ran, she jotted down what parts of the image she could recall—*large gallery, Dad's show—Santa Fe? Stranger with blond hair.* She supposed she might ask her father to tell her if such a show had taken place, but these were just the sorts of questions that would make him worry. How frustrating it was not to be able to simply pick up the phone and have some answers.

Their room seemed smaller and more confining now. Crossing to the suitcase, she rummaged for her swimsuit. As she did, she came across the pad of stationery she'd brought with her, along with matching envelopes.

If she couldn't call her father, why not at least write him a letter? In a letter she could craft precisely what she wished to say. Crossing back to the desk and pulling out a fresh page, she began:

Dear Dad,

I'm writing to you from the countryside not too far from Zurich where Duncan and I have been resting up after Berlin. Berlin was thrilling and exhausting. I'm sure you'd be inspired by it. Everywhere the past is being smashed and rebuilt. Imagine a whole city intent on erasing history, reinventing itself according to new possibilities. It's like an art studio twenty miles wide.

She thought of other details she might invent—going to one of the nightclubs that had sprung up in old industrial sites, drinking with East Berliners and hearing their stories of childhoods filled with longings, disloyalties, and daily duplicities. Instead she caught herself, feeling guilty for enjoying the fiction a bit too much. Staying on course, she considered what else she should say. She ought to tell her father how to reach her, but the letter would take up to two weeks to arrive in Santa Fe, and then his reply would take as long to cross the ocean again. By that time she had no idea where she and Duncan might be.

Vienna will be next—Duncan and I leave today—though after that, nothing has been planned. I'll have to phone at some point when our itinerary is more solid, but in the meantime, I hope you're staying cool in the Santa Fe summer. Wear a hat—maybe I'll pick one up for you, something stylish from Paris or Rome. Miss you, Daddy, and love you.

Your girl,
Gina

She was signing the letter as Duncan stepped out from the bathroom in a towel. She folded up the paper and slid it inside an envelope. Duncan mentioned that they had stamps at reception. "I'll bring it down later with the luggage," he offered, bending to kiss her, brushing back the hair that clung wetly to his face.

Checkout wasn't until one, so Gina went to take her final swim while Duncan finished packing and settled the bill. Leaving out a change of clothes and putting on her bathing suit, she walked barefoot to the lakeside, which was grass nearly to the edge. She jumped into the water to avoid stepping on the pebbly bottom, and as she did another memory came to her—visiting Abiquiu Lake as a small girl. This was in the years before she could swim, before she was long and strong, when she would cling to her mother's warm body, lacking the courage to let go, the faith that, alone, she wouldn't just sink and sink and sink.

Now she swam hard, as if swimming against her own fear and confusion, the quiet terror that not knowing parts of her past still caused her. She swam for so long, in fact, that her lips began to quiver from the cold, and she worried that she'd be late to leave. Hurrying onto the grass, she raced up to the room to get changed.

Dressed again, she went to the reception room, spotting Duncan with his back to her. He was speaking into the desk phone.

"Yes, it all came through, thank you. I just wanted to add, I hope you know I never meant to hurt you."

She stopped herself, hearing these words. She'd assumed he was dealing with something practical, a reservation or an incorrect bill.

The landlady, Ms. Arner, called to her from across the desk and Duncan turned too, facing Gina with a casual expression in no way suited to the tone in which he'd just been speaking. Putting his hand over the receiver, he mouthed to her, "My mother."

"Ah, right."

She backed away, not to intrude. It was unfortunate how little interaction she and Duncan's mother had with one another, but she'd come to accept that this wasn't likely to change. Mrs. Lowy had been born a Jew in Alsace-Lorraine during the Second World War and, from the moment she'd heard Gina's last name was Reinhold, she'd regarded her with suspicion. Gina could only imagine what the woman would make of their visiting first Berlin and then Vienna.

"We'll need to talk about this another time, okay? I'm sorry. I promise I'll call again." Duncan hung up the line, shaking his head.

"Is everything all right?" Gina asked him.

He didn't answer right away. The call seemed to have unsteadied him. "Just had to check in, let her know we're okay."

"And apologize?"

"For leaving her behind, taking a trip, leading our own independent happy lives." He smiled, but Gina was still bothered.

"You didn't tell her we were headed to Austria?"

"No, God no. She thinks we're in London. She sent us letters there, apparently. I had to pretend we'd gotten them."

Regrettable as it was, she understood that lies like these couldn't be avoided. She and Duncan were both obliged to lie about this trip, in different ways, to protect their parents' feelings. She thought about the letter to her father, which she spotted atop a small pile of letters on the table behind the desk. Ms. Arner was standing by the table, copying something into a ledger.

"Thank you," Gina called to her. "For everything. It's been perfect here, really."

"Oh, it's been my pleasure," said Ms. Arner. "I wish all my guests could be this nice; I wish all couples could be so cheering as you both."

Gina smiled at the woman and then at Duncan, who was still watching the phone, distracted. When he noticed her looking at him, he quickly warmed, wrapping an arm around her waist. "There's a one o'clock train from Zurich to Vienna," he announced. "I've called a car to take us to the station."

Despite her unease that morning, she couldn't help but be excited that they were off to Vienna. Soon she'd be seeing that lovely city again: the fine, pale buildings tiled in bright orange or domed in verdigris; the rows of trees, the fountains and the statues, the monuments that peered out in the distance, extravagantly lit. She hadn't gotten to visit nearly enough of it during the rush of the festival, night after night spent dancing in that glittering theater, then spilling, drunk from motion and exhaustion, onto the vibrant streets. She'd made a mental list of all that she meant to see once the performances were done, but circumstance intervened, a dreadful call came from her father, and so those sights remained unreached: the Tiergarten, the Prater, the Hotel Sacher—all penetrated by a deeper yearning that made her wary of visiting without Duncan there too.

She leaned against him, thinking of how he'd held her after the flight home from Vienna—he'd arrived for her mother's funeral ahead of her, and was there to greet her when she stepped, in a daze, from the plane in New Mexico. Her Duncan. Her home, wherever in the world they might be.

Two

Duncan // Vienna

June 1996

Vienna was aglow. It was as elegant as Gina had described it after her first return, a time that had once felt far in the past, but which, in the last weeks, felt strangely near. It had been a shock to realize that time could be erased in this way—that Gina could suffer a fall and suddenly he was faced with the woman she was a year ago. He kept trying to imagine himself in Gina's place, waking up in a foreign country with no idea how he'd gotten there, and only one familiar face to rely on as a guide.

Now Gina was enjoying the chance to play guide for a change.

She sat beside him, rapturous at the taxi window, pointing to the buildings she still recognized.

"That's the Kunsthistorisches Museum," she said, "and there's the Hofburg Palace. And that one, over there, that's the Staatsoper." She pointed to a building in the distance, intricate and lit bright gold, like an immense filigreed treasure.

He forced himself to smile so as not to reveal his alarm: if she could recall the buildings in Vienna, what else might she soon recall?

They were approaching the Danube River now, the shining city reflected in the water, and Duncan did his best to relax into the ride. The car radio played and he focused on the music—he'd have preferred to hear classical while exploring this city, home to Strauss and Schubert, and the stomping ground for so many others of the world's greatest composers, Beethoven, Haydn, Mozart—but the taxi driver preferred to play American pop songs. "Don't Speak" came on, and Duncan hummed along, waiting to see if Gina did the same. All spring that song had played back in the States, and yet Gina didn't know it—he watched her to be sure, to see if the words didn't rise to her lips unbidden. Her silence calmed him. He exhaled and turned back to the window, relieved. No, she did not remember, not the faintest note.

The car crossed the bridge and headed up a wide road, Praterstrasse, on the way to their hotel. Together he and Gina had chosen a hotel not far from the train station and in the same area as the Prater, Vienna's famous amusement park. The room cost a third of what they'd pay in other parts of the city, both of them agreeing that the money they saved on the hotel could be spent elsewhere. He wondered if Gina regretted this decision now, leaving behind the charm of the other districts. In Praterstern, the main square was plain, with a few trees and a gangly-looking column. The streets were darker and more deserted. A cable car ambled behind them. He hoped she wasn't disappointed.

Their hotel on Walcherstrasse was even more dismal than Duncan feared. The lobby was old-fashioned, with a green carpet that looked mildewed, and a chandelier with many of the glass pieces missing. The man at the desk wore a suit with a bow tie;

his thinning hair was combed sideways and his lips were so red it seemed as if he were wearing makeup.

"*Willkommen*. The Lowys, yes?"

"That's right." Duncan came to the desk and he and Gina set down their bags.

"Your room is ready. I'll just need to see your passports." The man took Gina's passport first, then Duncan's, which he lingered over for some time, copying the details into his ledger, then pausing to study the picture.

"Could we just have those back, then?" Duncan reached to take them.

"All for you, Mr. Lowy." The man smiled. "That name, it's Jewish, is it?"

Duncan was at once unnerved and relieved—was that it, then? The man's curiosity was over the Jewish name? He hesitated, not sure how to take this, but the clerk rushed to reassure him.

"I like Jews very much!"

Gina pinched Duncan's arm, and they proceeded to the elevator, while the desk clerk lingered behind with their luggage. Once the elevator door had shut, Gina jumped onto her toes, her eyes wide with disbelief. "He likes Jews very much!"

"Right, we're his favorite after schnitzel."

Her laughter stopped; she was looking at him seriously. "Are you uncomfortable here?"

"Of course not." Though he had to wonder if it might be true; he was plenty on edge already.

His anxiety was twofold—compounded by guilt over how his mother would suffer to see him here. The farthest his mother had ever agreed to travel during his lifetime was to Florida, to visit a cousin in Miami Beach. Not once had she returned to her birthplace

23

in Alsace, an oft-disputed part of France bordering on Germany. She'd survived during German occupation in the care of a Catholic family, while her parents fled across the Alps. What family was left after the war moved to the US, and Duncan's mother had never had a good word to say for Europe. Growing up, Duncan ate exclusively American meals, and when the only languages offered at his school were German and French, his mother harangued the principal for weeks. European music she wasn't able to renounce, but she did everything else she could to forget the Continent, which remained dangerous to her, treacherous, and would always be, no matter how much history elapsed between the present and those events that had shaped her earliest perceptions. As Duncan grew older, he'd sought to escape the confines of his mother's fearful judgment, but being here, in Hitler's native country, he couldn't help but feel the shame he already carried with him deepen.

Naturally, he could never tell his mother the details of this trip.

As far as she knew, he was in London—that part of what he'd told Gina was the truth, though he hadn't relayed the rest of the story that he'd given his mother: that he was pursuing a professional opportunity through his college roommate, Blake. Such stories were nothing new. Duncan had survived his childhood by telling his parents what they wanted to hear. His father, mild and appeasing, could tolerate the truth, but not the pressure of hiding it from Duncan's mother, for whom the truth was mostly overwhelming. So from an early age, Duncan had learned to hide any aspects of reality that might distress those he loved. He supposed that a kind liar, the sort who omitted and elided to please others, was at least the better sort of liar to be.

"I'm very glad we're here," he said, as he and Gina headed down the dark hotel corridor. "No one who cares about music should miss Vienna. Plus, you love it here, and anything you love, I want to be a part of."

He stopped to kiss her just as the clerk from reception appeared behind them, carrying their luggage.

"Oh, excuse me," said the clerk, lowering his eyes.

"She's also crazy about Jews," said Duncan, and Gina had to stifle her laugher while the clerk opened the door, handed them the keys, and left.

Their room was dim and musty: dark lampshades choked the meager light and the walls were done in textured wallpaper that had faded unevenly. Though it was after ten and they were too tired to wander far, neither Gina nor Duncan felt like staying in. They hurried through the lobby to do some light exploring. There were restaurants by the train station, but these looked seedy, so they walked the other way and settled on a corner restaurant, where they ordered goulash and strudel and a carafe of wine. Gina was tipsier than Duncan when they got back to the room, and by the time he'd brushed his teeth, she was already curled up in bed, asleep.

Seizing this opportunity for privacy, he went down to the lobby and asked the desk clerk to point him to the nearest public phone.

"You might use ours here, sir."

"A little air would be nice," Duncan said.

The clerk looked disapproving. "There are phones by the train station. But at this hour, I warn you, you'll find all sorts."

"All sorts is perfect," said Duncan and, with a wave, he stepped outside.

The train station was well lit but mostly empty at this hour.

A few homeless people lay on blankets in one corner and, on the other side, where the buses came in, three young men with shaved heads were talking loudly, drunk. The scene was hardly different, Duncan thought, from the sort he encountered on his block back in the East Village. Once, in the first year he and Gina lived there, he'd nearly been mugged at the entrance to his walk-up, but what had scared off his assailant was a rat scurrying across the man's foot. The memory of this now distant life caused Duncan to shiver.

At last he found a working phone, and searched his wallet for the number of the answering service that he'd hired in Zurich—such were the methods for staying connected before cell phones were common. A service was safer, he'd decided, than messages on a machine that someone else might try to retrieve.

He dialed, and a woman soon informed him he had six new messages.

"You'd like to hear them?"

He wasn't sure he would, no. He couldn't imagine any of the news would be good. Still, he supposed that he'd better learn what he could about the mess accumulating in his absence. "Yes, please, thank you."

"Okay, then. Ms. Smyth from Carter Properties said that you're behind on rent. And there was a call too from your bank."

"I've been remiss with bills, since I've been traveling," he began and stopped. This stranger, he had to remind himself, wasn't owed an explanation. "Thank you, what else, then?"

"An Esther Lowy left a message too, wanting to know why she can't reach you in London. She says that she tried your friend Blake, but that he said you'd left. And then there was a message from a Blake Flournoy asking why your mother thinks you're in London with him."

In the silence that followed, Duncan wondered if the woman was hoping he'd respond, if she'd begun to take an interest in the story, to become curious, herself, how the pieces fit together.

"Any other calls?" he pressed her.

"Yes, sir. Another message from a Frank Reinhold, saying he needs to speak to his daughter, and if you're with her, to please call him."

Gina's father—this message troubled Duncan most. Any parent whose child was out of contact would be worried, and Gina's father was especially possessive. For this reason, he'd never been in favor of her relationship with Duncan and had grown, over time, increasingly mistrustful of him. The man must be itching for a word with Gina, whom he typically called several times a week. Duncan ought to find some way to explain her silence and reassure him she was well—and quickly.

"Sir?" The woman on the line interrupted his thoughts. "You still have another message."

"Right, yes. Go ahead."

"From a Graham Bonafair. He says to tell you that—"

"That's fine." Duncan stopped her there. He was feeling suddenly that he couldn't handle any more.

"You don't want me to read the message?" The woman's voice was grave; she seemed concerned. "I think maybe you ought to hear it."

"No, no, that's fine. I'll look into it," he said, feeling he'd made a mistake letting a stranger in on his communications. "I think I won't be needing your services any longer."

"Is there a problem, sir?"

"Not any problem, no. You can redirect my calls back to my line. I'll just call into my machine from now on." He took a breath, minding his manners. "And thank you. I'm grateful for your help. I really am."

He hung up the phone and stood a moment, considering what he might do next. The drunken men were laughing. A cool wind blew, and Duncan hadn't worn a jacket. All he wanted was to get back upstairs to Gina, to put his worries behind him, but he knew he ought to deal with at least some of these messages while he had the chance. Since it was already eleven at night in London, whereas in New York it was only six, he chose to make his first call to Blake.

Blake Flournoy had been Duncan's college roommate since the start of freshman year. They'd been placed together randomly by the school—certainly Blake hadn't been the type that Duncan would have chosen to live alongside. He had a smug look about him, shrouded in polo shirts and an eternal tan, his dark blond hair effortlessly upright off his forehead, swept sideways, in the style that boys less suave were struggling at that time to achieve with mousse. He gave off a general impression of indifference, skated through his classes, and kept their room a mess; his voice had a deliberate flatness to it, as if nothing were worth placing strain on his vocal cords.

"Yup." Even in a single word, Blake's tone was unmistakable, the blunt voice that many others found rude, but which gave Duncan permission to be his less polite, less cautious self. It was something he'd gotten used to, becoming close friends with Blake during college and remaining so after, even once Blake had moved to London.

"Hey, it's me."

"Duncan, holy shit. I've been trying you. Where the hell are you?"

"And a holy shit also to you."

"Your mom called yesterday, you know that? I'm assuming you're calling because you know that."

"Yes, I know, and thanks for handling her." He had no doubt that Blake had dealt with his mother well. During college, on mornings when Duncan slept in, Blake was always there to make up a story for his mother when she called. More than anything, it was Blake's lying to his mother that had forged the trust between them. Before meeting Blake, Duncan had borne the weight of his lies in secret, guiltily, but Blake's laxer conscience had lightened Duncan's too.

"And I guess you also know," Blake continued, "that she thinks you're here with me, applying for a job."

The job bit he'd improvised at the last minute. As long as he was already lying to his mother, he figured he might as well tell her something she'd like to hear: like that he was finally reconciled to the idea of a regular, well-paid corporate job. "I'm sorry, I should have told you I was using you as an excuse. Honestly, I never thought she'd follow up. I'm not sure why she did."

"Well, I am," Blake announced, and then said nothing, waiting for Duncan to ask. In small ways, Blake often insisted on having the upper hand—a quality Duncan had overlooked until Gina pointed it out, with obvious distaste.

"You're going to clue me in or what?"

"Some guy called her, asking after you, which got her all nervous."

At this, Duncan's pulse jumped. He must calm himself: of

course there were several possible explanations. He didn't need to think the worst. "This guy give a name?"

"She didn't tell me. But she seemed concerned that you might have gotten yourself into trouble."

"Shit. Okay." He was thinking of his mother, of the anxiety that must be suffocating her. He could hear her voice, the voice from his childhood that met him at the door if he was even ten minutes late coming home from school: *Someone could have taken you! A car could have struck you! Do you know what agony you've put me through?*

What reaction would she have now that he was across an ocean, unreachable, while she received alarming phone calls from strangers—saying what? He cringed to think.

"Duncan?" Blake was speaking to him again. "*Are* you in some sort of trouble? Is it a money thing? You need to borrow?"

"It's . . . it's nothing you need to worry over. I should just call my mother, reassure her."

"But Duncan, where are you? How can I reach you?"

"I'm, uh, moving around between hotels."

"Which hotels? Where?"

"Thing is, I can't really predict."

"Christ, Duncan, just tell me where you are, man! City? Nation? Continent?"

He felt a sudden urge to give in, to confess everything to his old friend, but his better judgment intervened. If there was one area where Blake had failed him as a friend, it was in his attitude toward Gina. To cynical, pragmatic Blake, Gina was a deluded romantic, and a dangerous one at that. To Blake—and come to think of it, to his mother too—it was Gina who'd led Duncan astray in his life, her fault that he'd forgone financial success for artistic failure, and now, whatever trouble Duncan might be in, Blake would assume this must be her fault too. So Duncan resolved to admit nothing. "Gotta go, then, Blake. More soon."

He could hear an exasperated Blake shouting at him as he hung up the phone.

Before dialing again, Duncan paused a moment, hand on the receiver, head bowed, bracing himself for his mother's panic. She picked up on the first ring.

"Mom," he said casually.

"Duncan, thank goodness! You're alive!"

"Of course I'm alive." He was having that feeling he often did when phoning his mother—at once sorry that he hadn't called sooner, and sorry that he'd called at all. He could hear the TV in the background, the six o'clock local news, which his parents watched nightly, and which always seemed to enumerate the dangers lurking just outside.

"Where are you?" she demanded. "Blake told me you'd left London for Wales."

"Yes, right, on a brief visit. A small reward."

"Does that mean the interview went well?"

"Hard to say, really, just have to wait." He could hear, through her anxiety, a note of hope. He wasn't sure if he felt better or worse for having offered it to her, though if she was thinking about the job, he supposed this was a good sign—that whatever else she'd heard about him hadn't left her too distressed. "While I've got you, Blake did mention that you'd had a call from somebody asking about me."

"That's right. A friend of yours. He said he needed to get in touch with you and asked if I knew how to reach you. He said it was important."

"And did he give a name?"

"Graham Bonafair."

A sour feeling came over Duncan, though he could hardly call himself surprised. It was to be expected that Graham would reach out to anyone who might have contact with Duncan. At least it appeared that Graham hadn't told his mother much, had in fact shown great restraint. For now. But perhaps behind this call was a tacit threat, a way of making clear that Graham could always reach out to those Duncan was close to and tell them as much as he pleased. And what could Duncan say or do to protect his mother, or anybody, then? Nothing. All he had in his power to do was to cheer her in the moment, to offer his mother whatever empty promises she needed: yes, he'd call again in a few days; yes, he'd be on a flight home soon; yes, he was hopeful about the job, felt his luck was due to turn.

"I'll call you again soon, Mom. And I don't want you to worry about me. I love you. I'm okay. You can trust me."

Three

Their first morning in Vienna was a lovely one, the sky blue and the sun warm, and Gina suggested she and Duncan take the train to Stephansplatz to enjoy a long walk through the center of the city. They began at St. Stephen's Cathedral, a Gothic building with a roof of patterned multicolored tiles. The last time she'd seen this church, its roof had reminded her of a snake. She supposed it was a reflection of the guilty mood dogging her on that trip, of her unease recalling the company she'd been in.

She'd left Duncan behind in New York then, and during the two weeks she was in Vienna, she'd felt terrible for doing that—thinking of him stuck in the heat in their apartment with the air conditioner that sputtered only lukewarm air. Meanwhile, she was visiting this remarkable city and in a grander style than she'd ever enjoyed. The dancers were put up, just two girls to a room, in a very good hotel in the MuseumsQuartier, where nearly all of the festival was scheduled to take place. Throughout the week, she'd been entertained by supporters of the festival; she'd been escorted by a Viennese politician to the Rathaus; she'd visited the Schönbrunn Palace; and was invited to watch the horses perform at the Hofburg within the Spanish riding school. That afternoon, one of the festival's board members, a Frenchman with dark hair to his collar who smelled of cigarettes and cologne, had taken a special interest in Gina and had invited her to visit the Staatsoper for a performance of *Aida*. Later, the same Frenchman had taken her walking precisely here, to Stephansplatz. She said nothing of this to Duncan now, only suggested they move onward, which they did, stopping for a visit at the Hofburg Palace, then walking through the lovely, expansive park along the palace up to the opera house.

Today, Gina found the Staatsoper less dramatic than it had seemed, lit up at night, when she'd visited with the Frenchman, but here in the daylight with Duncan, she could appreciate the finer details: statues under the arches of the second level, the bronze horsemen charging on either end of the roof. A crowd had gathered around the corner to observe a group of street musicians: a man with a violin and a female singer. They were performing lieder, and Duncan was familiar with the song, one by Strauss, mournful and haunting. They stood listening, Duncan's arm around her shoulders, and she was calm again.

From the opera house, they wandered into the Hotel Sacher, Vienna's most famous hotel, a tan five-story building occupying the whole block. Gina wanted to have a look inside, though she assumed tourists were discouraged from doing so. The best way to avoid being asked to leave, Gina suggested to Duncan, was to appear as if they had a purpose, to look as if they were there to meet a guest.

"Therese said in the lobby, didn't she?" she said to Duncan loudly as they walked past a porter at the door. "Or was it the dining room? Maybe we should have a look in there?"

She was heading for the dining room when one of the bellhops approached her asking if he could help her. "We're meeting friends," she told him.

"Which friends are those, madam?"

"The woman is Therese," she said, and turned to Duncan. "Funny, I don't think she gave her last name. But she'll be down soon." She smiled now, at the bellhop. "We're expected."

"Perhaps if you would wait by the doors, then."

"Of course," she agreed, but, not to be thwarted, started off anyhow. "I'll just run to the bathroom first, if that's all right."

Gina hurried away, hoping she hadn't left Duncan in a rough spot, and that he, like her, could seize on an excuse to quickly tour around. Moving past the bathrooms, she peered into a dining hall—the walls, curtains, and carpets a rich forest green. There was a second dining room, done entirely in red, and then another room, a bar, whose walls and velvet chairs were all deep blue. When she returned to reception, Duncan was nowhere to be found. Possibly he'd been embarrassed and had moved outside. She was heading for the exit when the same bellhop who'd approached her before stepped up to her again. "Your husband found those friends of yours you were looking for."

"Did he?" She smiled, though she couldn't imagine what could be meant by this, how Duncan could have given that impression. The bellhop gestured ahead, and she followed the line of the man's sight over to a spot in the lobby next to a large painting of a ship at sea. Duncan was standing with a very distinguished older couple. They were chatting together, their behavior so jovial that she also would have assumed they knew one another. But the couple struck her as unfamiliar.

The man had a baggy face but a warm smile. He was dressed with flair, in a white blazer and white pants, a pale orange scarf around his neck. The woman beside him was tall and thin, with white-blond hair, a high forehead, and slightly bulbous eyes. She wore a long, high-collared dress and heeled boots that made her taller than the man. She studied Gina with not entirely friendly attention.

"And she's back," Duncan announced, as Gina came to stand beside him. "This is my wife, Gina."

The man took her hand and introduced first himself and then his partner. "Riccardo Bianchi and my fiancée, Astrid Du Bellay."

"Riccardo is the director of the Teatro alla Scala in Milan," Duncan explained. "And Astrid is one of the program directors for the Salzburg Festival. They're here in advance of that."

Gina shook hands with the couple, caught off guard to hear they were so prominent, and surprised too that Duncan would know them. She'd been the only one to visit Vienna, after all, the only one who'd received such introductions.

"And are you also in Vienna ahead of the festival?" Astrid addressed her with a thin smile. "You're a dancer, isn't that right?"

Gina was startled too to find the woman knew this. "I am, that's right. But I'm not dancing now."

"We're on vacation," Duncan put in. "A sort of belated honeymoon."

"Lovely," said the woman stiffly.

"And how do you happen to know each other?" Gina asked, unable to contain her curiosity.

"Duncan was friendly with my daughter," said Astrid.

"Actually," said Duncan, "Gina and Marina were closer friends."

Were they? Gina couldn't place the name, though for the sake of appearances, so as not to offend the girl's mother, she pretended to recall.

"It was a while ago," Duncan continued. "She and Gina met during Gina's first summer in Vienna. Marina said she was thinking of moving to New York."

"And how's Marina now?" Gina asked Astrid, searching for something to say to indicate her interest in her daughter.

"Still in New York. Still working on her film, but I assume you'd know that. She hasn't said much about that lately, but Marina doesn't tell me everything."

Duncan nodded, smiling. Gina noticed his jaw tightening.

He put out his hand. "It was so nice to run across you both. I think Gina and I should get moving. We've got a packed day."

Astrid seemed prepared to see them go, but Riccardo wasn't quite. "If you're staying in Vienna, we'd love you to join us for dinner. Some friends will be here at eight thirty. Festival people, mostly."

"Oh, no," Astrid shook her head, chastising him. "Don't put them on the spot. They don't want to attend some dinner with a bunch of dreary people with white hair." And then, a conspiratorial smile. "Young couples in love have better ways to spend their time."

"Ordinarily we'd be happy to," said Duncan. "But I'm afraid we can't."

Gina looked over at him, unsure of what was happening. Influential figures like these were the sort of people that Duncan ought to be scrambling to join for an evening. Why was he instead in a hurry to escape? But then, perhaps this interaction fell under the category of those made uneasy simply due to her lapse in memory. She held her tongue. Duncan thanked them for the invitation and stepped away, steering Gina through the lobby and outside.

"Why *not* join them later?" she asked him, once they were out in the open air. "They seemed like interesting people, people we know, apparently. And maybe helpful to you too."

"I don't think that's very likely."

"Why not?"

"I doubt Ms. Du Bellay's my biggest fan. Things got a little awkward with Marina."

"Awkward in what way?" She was trying to sound relaxed, and yet she felt a knot growing in her stomach.

"Artistic differences. Personal differences. She'd hired me to do the score for her film and it just didn't work out." He shrugged, clearly wishing for her to drop the subject, but his reluctance was only arousing her need to know more.

"Why are you acting so uncomfortable about it?"

Duncan halted where he stood, concentrating on his words. "You're right, I don't like to talk about it." He sighed, mussing his hair. "Marina came to New York a year after you'd met, saying she was in film school and working on a first feature. You introduced me and she hired me. I wasn't sure about the project, but the money she was offering and my knowing who her parents were made it hard to walk away. Anyway, in the end I never did finish the piece for her, and still she offered to pay me." He looked away as he continued. "I didn't deserve it, but I felt I needed the money. So I took it."

She was piecing it together: this story and the mysterious

commission Duncan had been reluctant to discuss. "Did you need it for this trip? Is Marina's money paying for this trip?"

He nodded, still looking off into the distance, sheepish.

Yet she relaxed. This was a story she could believe—he felt guilty for running into the mother of the girl whose money he was spending to be here, especially because in some way he'd failed Marina. "I get it. Though I don't think you should feel guilty for being compensated for your work. God knows you've done work you weren't paid for, so you're owed money for work you didn't do."

"Thank you." He leaned down and put his hands on her shoulders, his forehead to her forehead. "I felt ashamed to tell you. But it's a relief, really, that you know. I hate having secrets between us."

"How many more are there?" She smiled, trying to make a joke of her misgivings.

She wanted to believe that the issue had been settled, and yet a feeling had been roused in her that she couldn't place, but which she knew must be tied to events she'd forgotten. As she blinked, she pictured a woman roughly setting down a wineglass. It was only the glass Gina saw, not the woman or her surroundings, nothing else to provide a hint of what this could mean.

They'd begun walking again, leaving the Hotel Sacher behind as they proceeded along Kärtner Strasse. The sky was growing darker, and the lights were coming up inside the shops along the street. Gina had walked this street before, during her Vienna tour, and soon sharper memories crowded out the vaguer ones. Kärtner Strasse was a favorite destination with several of the dancers, who'd go peeking into the designer shops selling dresses or shoes or bracelets for thousands of shillings. The girls would go in, and soon an older gentleman with an interest in the arts would go in after them, and some minutes later, the girls would come skipping out again with their shopping bags. Gina had tried to be broad-minded, to not judge these girls, many of whom had almost no money, not enough to buy themselves a gift, not even enough to buy gifts for friends and family at the holidays. Her own money had spared her the temptation to exploit admirers, but she knew for others it was harder. She thought now of Duncan—of how much shame he must have felt over taking money from a girl with more cash than talent, to compromise himself this way, all so that he and Gina could have this trip together.

She took his hand as they walked on, feeling her suspicion dissipate. She knew how it pained Duncan to be reliant on what money she had, how much he must have wished to treat her for a change. Whatever had enabled them to travel, here they were, and she would try to be grateful for it. Turning from Kärtner Strasse, Duncan steered left, onto the Graben, another of Vienna's central streets: six-storied white buildings lined the way in neat, stately rows, and at its end stood the copper-domed St. Peter's Church.

After a visit to the church, the time was six and Gina was feeling hungry. She and Duncan hadn't given any thought to dinner, but she proposed they pick a place along the walk. The area was crowded and cheerful, with restaurant after restaurant open onto the wide street, their tables nestled under smooth square umbrellas, tan and red and green. They chose a spot not far from a large Gothic column topped with gold and ordered meat and dumplings and sauerkraut and beer. The beer was served in immense steins but, to her surprise, Duncan finished his when they were just halfway through the meal.

"Share another?" he asked her.

She consented, though she didn't much want to.

On the walk from the restaurant to Stephansplatz, Duncan's steps weaved a little, his arm hung around her shoulder, weighty. On the train, though, under the bright lights, he seemed to sober up, chatting about the places they might visit the next day. When the train pulled into Nestroyplatz, a man entered their car: pale with pockmarked cheeks and a scar over one eyebrow. He studied her and Duncan, and she supposed he must have identified them as Americans, because he soon began singing in an exaggerated American accent.

"For all those times you stood by me. . . ."

She didn't recognize the song, which the man continued crooning, in a mocking saccharine tone. *"For all the truth that you made me see. . . ."*

"Very good, thanks." Duncan tried to stop the man, but his singing only grew more strident. "We're the next stop," Duncan whispered to Gina, so she'd know she wouldn't have to endure this too much longer, and she felt relieved. The train pulled up to the platform, the doors opened, and a moment after they were through, the man behind them exited the train as well and caught up to them, still singing.

Finally, Duncan turned to address him. "Okay, thanks, show's over."

"If you like it," said the man, "then pay for it."

"So this is a shakedown, huh?" Duncan was still trying to be friendly, but a new toughness showed in his posture.

"It won't be costing much to help support a local singer."

Gina could smell the alcohol on the man's breath. "Go ahead," she urged Duncan, hoping to resolve this quickly.

Duncan reached for his wallet and offered the man a bill. "You have a good night, then."

Duncan took Gina's hand and turned to go. They stepped outside, under the darkening sky, and hurried away from the station, in the direction of their hotel, leaving behind the relative crowds for a deserted square. Gina hadn't dared to look behind and so hadn't realized, not until she felt Duncan's hand yanked from her grip, that the man had come racing toward them. He toppled Duncan and dropped him to the ground.

He was reaching for Duncan's pocket, for his passport and wallet, straddling Duncan, who was squirming beneath him. Alongside, Gina stood frozen, afraid to leave Duncan to get help, yet feeling useless for doing nothing.

She began shouting. "Robbery! Police! *Polizei!*" The man turned to look at her and screamed at her to shut up, offering Duncan just the chance he needed to buck the man off of him. On his feet, Duncan followed up with a hard kick to the man's stomach. Gina jumped back, shocked to see such fierceness in Duncan, in whom she'd never witnessed the least violence. While the man remained doubled over, Duncan kicked him again, this time on the side, knocking him down. He went to kick him a third time, but Gina pulled him back.

"Stop, stop, please. Let's just go."

Duncan stood, panting and patting himself down to be certain he'd lost nothing. He began backing away, afraid to turn and take his eyes off of the man. He walked that way, backward, until the crosswalk, and then he and Gina broke into a jog, dashing across the street, down the block, and into the lobby of their hotel.

"We need to lock the doors," Gina informed the man at the desk, the same clerk who'd checked them in the night before.

"What's happened, madam?"

"A man attacked my husband and we ran."

"Good God!" The clerk nervously hurried from behind the desk and turned a key in the front door. "I don't believe this is my city now. How awful. Are you hurt?"

"We're just shaken," she replied, while Duncan stood silent all the while, still panting, looking at the door.

"But you did see him?" the clerk asked, peering out also. "You can give a description to police?"

"No police," said Duncan gruffly, speaking up at last.

"If you're uncomfortable," said the clerk, "I can speak to the police for you."

"I said no."

The clerk looked up at him, startled by his roughness. Gina was taken aback too and recalled the way Duncan had kicked that man, and kicked again—with such mad determination, as if he were fighting not over a wallet, but for his very survival. What was it, this new desperation?

"You don't think we should at least report it?" Gina asked him gently.

"There's no point to it. Police won't get anywhere. That thief's long gone by now." Duncan exhaled, clearly mustering calm and trying to sound reasonable. "And on the off chance they do catch him and choose to try him, then we get held here or called back to Vienna from wherever we are, and spend what should have been our vacation in an Austrian courtroom, watching some lowlife get put in jail for five days. No, Gina. Not after everything we've done to get here." His tone softened and he wrapped an arm around her. "I'd rather that guy took my wallet than be robbed of this time with you."

43

Standing against him, she could feel his body heat and smell his sweat and the odor of this other man, which made her uneasy.

"What's the matter?" Duncan asked her, nervous.

"You smell like that thief."

"I'll go clean up," Duncan suggested, and started walking toward the elevator. "We'll revisit this tomorrow," he called over his shoulder to the clerk, who looked unhappy with the outcome but wasn't capable of contradicting the wishes of a guest. Together Gina and Duncan entered the elevator and rode up to their room.

Inside, Duncan yanked off his shirt and then went to take a shower. She waited for him to finish, still absorbing the shock of the evening, still unable to calm down. The image that had come to her earlier that evening returned: the woman lowering a wineglass. This time Gina saw her face: pale, with full lips and large, wide-set eyes.

Who could this woman be? What could this mean? Why, Gina wondered, was she so on edge? She had no rational basis for thinking Duncan had ever been unfaithful. She hadn't caught him in a lie, or in possession of secret pictures or letters, or sneaking off to make a private call. Or had she? Thinking back upon that last day in the Walensee, she remembered how he'd spoken softly to the person on the phone. His mother, he'd claimed, but the tone wasn't one he used with his mother. *I hope you know I never meant to hurt you.* No, no, that was a tone he might have used with Gina, with a lover.

When Duncan stepped out, clean, warm, wrapped in a towel, he came over and began to kiss her. She could feel that he was seeking relief from the incident, a way to overcome the strangeness between them, and yet, for her, that sense of strangeness did not pass.

"Duncan." She put her palms against his chest, holding him off.

He murmured inaudibly, still kissing her neck.

"That call you made, in the guesthouse at the Walensee, was that to Marina?"

He stopped kissing and looked up at her, surprised. "What? What are you asking me?"

"Before we left Lake Walen, you made a call. I heard you speaking."

"It was to my mother, like I said. Why would you doubt that?"

"I don't know. That couple today . . ."

"Today was unsettling. I got shaken up too." Gentle again, he took her in his arms and pulled her down onto the bed. He no longer kissed her, but simply held her, in a way she knew was meant to comfort her, but which made her feel too that he was trying to control her.

"I think maybe we need to just lie together and relax, okay? It will all be okay. We're safe. We've got each other," he said, now stroking her hair. "Right?"

Gina slept fitfully, hovering between thinking and dreaming— every so often she would remark the clock, time passing, and Duncan dozing beside her. At around four in the morning, she sat suddenly upright, struck by a scene, a memory involving the woman she had pictured. She and Duncan were at a party inside a town house, a fancy building with a hundred people crammed inside. An argument had broken out over a line that had formed outside the bathroom.

One of the guests was knocking aggressively on the bathroom door. "There are people out here. Quit fucking!"

Gina heard voices from inside, a woman shouting and giggling.

"One sec," said a man's voice, also from behind the door.

But the man in line had no intention of waiting. The lock must have been weak or the door improperly closed, because it swung open to reveal a thin blonde pulling up her skirt. Another person, a young man, was with her. When he heard the door open, he jumped and turned. It was Duncan.

Gina had spun and walked away and Duncan had come after her. Nothing had happened, nothing sexual, he promised. The blond girl had jumped into the bathroom and pulled him in and he hadn't known what to do.

"I didn't want to offend her. She's your friend. You'd wanted me to meet her."

And this was when it hit her, what she must have known instantly at the time, but had to reconfigure now, in Vienna, a year later—the girl in the bathroom was the same girl she'd met in Vienna the summer before, the same girl she'd asked Duncan to meet hoping she might get him work, and who would go on to pay Duncan the commission that was funding their trip now: Marina Du Bellay.

Gina looked around the dim room, too agitated to sleep. She had to move to rid herself of the irritation. At times it felt as though only through movement could she find the way to how she felt, whereas while lying down her feelings became knotted and illegible to her. So she walked, first circling the room and then out in the hall alone, letting her feet and thoughts move in one direction and then in another.

Was Duncan cheating? Having an affair with an aristocrat's

daughter? He could have been taken in by her flattery—he'd always quietly craved affirmation. And Marina had believed in him, had offered to help him, pay him, this young woman with her good taste and her connections. Had he been motivated by a combination of ambition and lust, the two together too much for him to resist?

For some time she was convinced by her own story, but then she'd as effectively dismissed it as what it was: a story. Probably Duncan had only allowed himself to encourage Marina's interest a little, knowing she might be of use to him, and knowing that her interest otherwise meant nothing to him. Was this any different than the young girls from her Vienna visit who allowed the older men to pay for their shopping trips? She didn't have any proof that Duncan had cheated on her, nor did she have any past experience leading her to think he would.

She returned to bed but found herself unable to lie still. After a time she was up again, pacing the room. He'd never made her doubt his loyalty to her. She knew she shouldn't be suspicious, but then again, she wasn't herself. Why not put her mind at ease, if she could?

She stepped up to the suitcase and opened the zippered pocket where Duncan kept his work folder. There was an understanding between them that she wouldn't look inside, wouldn't pry into what Duncan was writing, but await the time when he was ready to present it. Duncan's sensitivities even trained her to avert her eyes when he opened that folder. Yet, tonight, driven by this phantom sense of betrayal that wouldn't leave her, that was precisely what she chose to do.

She took a last look at Duncan, peacefully sleeping, before she carried the folder into the bathroom. There were pockets on each side. The left pocket was filled with sheet music, some of the pages blank, and a few with notation. Inside the right pocket were other documents Duncan had deemed important during travel—medical records, hospital bills—nothing inappropriate, so that for a moment she felt ashamed of what she'd done. She shut the folder and lifted it to return it to the other room, but as she did, something slipped out from between the sheets of music. An envelope. She picked it up from the floor and recognized the address, in her writing: *Frank Reinhold, 112 Sandoval Street, Santa Fe, New Mexico.*

The letter from Lake Walen. Might Duncan have simply forgotten to send it? Though she was almost sure she recalled seeing it on Ms. Arner's desk before they left the guesthouse. Perhaps there was some reasonable explanation for his holding on to it, and still the doubts this letter raised prompted her to continue searching. The next item she found was also nestled in the far back, behind the composition sheets. A postcard addressed to her closest friend, Violet, now living in Prague.

Violet Sharpe, care of the National Marionette Theater, Prague.

The card was dated, she noticed, the same day as her accident. She must have meant to send it then. She sat down at the edge of the tub, feeling dizzy.

According to Duncan, she and Violet had argued, experienced a rift, so that Gina had determined not to see her on this trip. The postcard, meanwhile, started off with a friendly announcement of her visit.

Dear Violet,

Good news. I'm planning to make the trip to Prague after next week!

Can't wait to see you. It feels like ages since we've met, so much happened after you left New York. That whole world collapsed for me. The worst is behind me, as you know, and I've been happier lately, and will be even happier to see you. I'm so excited to see what your life in Prague is like. Changes are a blessing—and so are those good friends we hold on to through them all.

Love,
Gina

Reading the note dismayed her further—not only was there no indication of any argument like Duncan had mentioned, but Duncan's description of the last year as uneventful seemed to be a lie as well. According to this note, her world in New York had *collapsed.*

She sat still, unsure what to do next, whether to awaken Duncan and demand answers to her many questions, or to put these things away and wait until her thoughts had time to settle and she could reach a steady judgment.

Why would Duncan choose to pretend she and Violet were at odds, why would he wish to keep her from her friend? She could only summon one explanation for it: he wished to prevent a visit with Violet because he had genuine cause to fear a meeting, because—Gina could only imagine—Violet knew something of their past that Duncan was frightened would come out.

What could he have done? How awful could it be?

She wanted to forget it all, put the folder back and return to loving Duncan the simple way she had before. The idea of not loving him, of not believing that he was truthful to her, was so unsteadying that the postcard fell from her shaking hands.

It was only then that Gina noticed the picture on the other side. The postcard was from her father's gallery, and the image was one she'd seen before, her vision: a photograph of her back as she stood before a portrait of Duncan and herself. Duncan's image was only half visible in the postcard because it was obscured by a figure, a man, tall, slim, blond, standing to Gina's right. He was standing so close their shoulders nearly brushed, and he was turning to her as if to whisper something in her ear.

She breathed. She gathered herself and went, wrapped in a sweater, wobbly-legged, to the hotel lobby. She'd brought the postcard with her to consult the return address where they'd been staying in Berlin: *Hotel de Rome, Behrenstrasse 37.*

The clerk sat at his desk in front of a miniature TV. A drama was playing: *The X-Files* in German. The clerk was absorbed by the show and startled by her sudden entrance. He hurried to lower the volume.

"Sorry to bother you," Gina said, "but I'd like to make a call. My husband is sleeping and I don't want to disturb him."

"You wish to call police, then?" the clerk asked her, hopeful.

"Not the police, no. I need to make a call to a hotel."

The man seemed disappointed, but obligingly pulled out a phone from behind the counter. With the clerk's help, she dialed information first and had him request, in German, the number. A woman picked up promptly. Gina spoke with her, explaining she'd been a guest at the hotel some weeks ago.

"Very good, Ms. Reinhold, and what can I do for you?"

She wasn't entirely sure herself what she was expecting, and yet a premonition drove her to inquire whether someone might have been trying to reach her. "I left abruptly and I'm wondering if maybe you have any messages for me?"

"Let me check, madam."

The woman placed her on hold, with music playing in the background, and the desk clerk slowly, after what he deemed an appropriate time, drifted back into his chair and resumed watching his program, with the volume low.

"Ms. Reinhold?"

"Yes, yes, I'm here."

"Sorry to have kept you, but, in fact, there is a message for you."

Her heart was beating fast; she closed her eyes before whatever words came next.

"It's from a Graham Bonafair. He says to please get in touch with him as soon as possible, wherever you might be. It's very important, he says, that he reach you."

Graham Bonafair. The name was familiar, and yet she couldn't place it.

"He's left a number for you, here in Berlin. If you have a pen, Ms. Reinhold, I'll give that to you now."

Her hand was trembling so much she struggled to write. She considered whether she might dial the number now. No, she'd settle herself first. Back in her room, she placed the paper with Graham's number in her purse, then returned to the bathroom to clean up the folder she'd left, in her impatience, lying on the floor. With everything straightened, back in its place, she lay down in bed beside Duncan.

For hours she lay awake, tormented by her doubts, watching him quietly breathing beside her. She'd resolved to spend her life with this man, she thought, believing there was no one with whom she shared a deeper understanding. Her Duncan. Possessed by her, known by her. Only now, in their dark room, he seemed all shadows, hidden. How much of the truth was he concealing? For how long? Was this Duncan who lay before her the man she believed him to be?

Four

Duncan // Toms River, New Haven

1971–92

          His mother's moods were the weather of Duncan's childhood, the sky under which he'd moved. When she was better, he'd be able to forget about her a little, exist for days almost guiltless and free—hanging out after school with friends, walking home slowly with the neighbor's pretty daughter. But then, abruptly, without warning, his mother's fear would erupt and he'd come through the front door to find her crying, held by his frowning father, her pretty milk-white face grown contorted as she sobbed, *"How could you run off like that? How could you leave me to worry?"*

    "I'm sorry, Mommy, I'll stay right here. Please don't cry."

    Even at a young age he'd felt his inherent badness, overwhelmed to see his mother in such pain, and to know he'd caused it—so selfishly—in order to snatch some trivial pleasure. He'd feel thoroughly demonic and, for the weeks that followed, he'd strive to make it up to her, to do the things she wanted from him—listen to classical music with her or help her around the house. As he grew older, he began to recognize the extremity of his mother's demands, and how deeply he and his father were enslaved to them.

This insight might have relieved him, but at the same time he came to understand her history, and the horror of it made it impossible to blame her for anything she did. His mother's childhood in France had been a nightmare: for several years she'd wondered if her parents were alive or dead, if she would ever see them, if one day one of the kids in her town who knew she was a Jew would tell the Germans and she'd be picked up and killed. After the war, when she was reunited with her family, only half remained. Her father had died of pneumonia while in hiding, and her brother, sent to live with another family, had run away and had never been found. So Duncan's mother had come with his grandmother to the States, and, fifteen years later, married Duncan's father, the meek son of Polish immigrants who'd been crushed by the Depression.

Together, Duncan's parents had opened up a stationery store and set up a home in Toms River, New Jersey, that on the surface seemed as secure as any other. But inside, Duncan's home was different: darker and less hopeful. Fine for others to believe life was a playground, fine for them to go riding skateboards into town, or make out with girls behind the movie theater, but Duncan had to stay within his mother's sights.

Thus, he turned his energies to piano. His mother played well, and purchasing a piano for their home had been one of her few indulgences. From his perch at the bench, his eyes would wander from sheet music to the window and beyond, where other kids swatted badminton racquets or splashed around in inflatable pools.

He'd discovered music in much the way he supposed other lonely children had before him—to express all the feelings and curiosities he couldn't give voice to any other way. His mother seized on his interest and ability, and gave him lessons herself. Around the time he turned thirteen, though, his skill exceeded hers and she decided to spend the little extra cash they had on a piano teacher who came to the house two times a week. Her name was Lillian and she was pretty and kind and a little shy, with glasses and dark hair cut into bangs and a soft, singsong voice.

Duncan quickly came to adore her and not to mind so much the hours he was kept at home to practice. All week he'd prepare for when they met, hoping not only to amaze her with his playing, but to find other ways to impress this rare, beautiful interloper. He listened to all the classical music he could get his hands on and in the library found music criticism, which he could paraphrase to sound insightful. He also began to invent pieces of his own, modifications on those Lillian gave him to practice. None of these was especially original, but his first attempts astonished Lillian more than he'd thought possible.

"Duncan, that's beautiful," she'd said, her small, pale hand on her chest. "Can you play it for me again?"

Of course he would! There were no words he craved hearing as much as that she'd liked something he'd done and wanted more. As he played, he couldn't keep himself from smiling, or peeking over to see her close her eyes, or lean her head back, exposing her pale, perfect neck. It felt like magic to be able to elicit such responses from a grown and lovely woman. As if he'd stopped being a shy thirteen-year-old, someone beneath her interest, and become the master of her feelings. Powerful. A man.

He began to fixate on a future where he'd be a successful composer, admired by his peers, adored by some delicate, romantic woman like his teacher. Soon, nothing else interested him as much as sitting home and writing music. No type of frivolous play with neighborhood boys and girls compared to having Lillian declare that he was special, in possession of a gift—something that his mother, too anxious to admit to any goodness, never did.

If only that gift had stayed their secret, he and Lillian could have continued that way for much longer, but eventually she got the notion that Duncan needed more than she could give him, and felt compelled to tell his mother her opinion. She believed Duncan to be a musical prodigy who, with the right instruction and support, had a chance of becoming a very talented composer.

"And have you told him this?" his mother asked, Duncan listening in from the next room. "Have you given him these ideas about himself?"

"I've tried to encourage him, if that's what you mean."

"You weren't hired to do that," said his mother, in the stern tone that made her Alsatian accent even more pronounced.

Duncan realized that he'd made a terrible mistake in not preventing Lillian from speaking with his mother. He was immediately angry at himself for failing to predict her reaction. Lillian couldn't have guessed—why would she assume that any mother wouldn't be overjoyed at the thought of her child being a prodigy? She didn't know what sort of woman Esther Lowy was. Playing music was a hobby in his mother's mind, part of becoming a cultivated person, but it shouldn't be permitted to interfere with schoolwork or plans for a legitimate career. Neither she nor Duncan's father had been able to attend college, and even by the modest standards of most Toms River residents, they lived frugally. Any savings they amassed was put in an account for Duncan's college education. Like many immigrant parents in America, his mother maintained the view that she was denying herself luxury so that Duncan would be able to afford it later. In turn, her expectation for him was that he'd eventually pursue a secure and lucrative field like finance or law, to repay their sacrifices. Music—the piano—was a distraction, a fantasy of his artistic greatness that only threatened to divert him.

Still, Lillian hoped to convince her, and soon the women stepped out from the kitchen and Duncan was asked to perform the pieces he'd composed.

His fingers stiffened as he played, as if his mother's judgment penetrated skin and joints. The melodies he'd been so proud of when Lillian heard them now sounded like lifeless imitations. One piece was simply a variation on the main theme from Schubert's Unfinished Symphony, another sounded like the second movement of Mendelssohn's First Cello Sonata, and a third was a modified étude by Chopin.

"He has an ear, all right," his mother began, "and some technical dexterity. But I don't see any evidence of much musical imagination. Nothing like the genius you're leading him to think he has."

He was devastated. Anger sounded in him like a song. He wanted to summon his defiance right then and there, to say in forceful sound what his mother's fragility prevented him from ever expressing in words. He heard the beginning of the piece already, haunted, full of the gloom his mother cast upon him, moving between frustration and sadness—only then did he recognize how much his musical idea recalled a melody in Prokofiev's "Alexander Nevsky," and he felt more furious still. Could it be that his mother was right? That all he could do was ape the masters and fool a young woman into thinking he was capable of more?

Lillian never came back to the house after that.

Duncan's mother didn't abandon lessons altogether, but she replaced this gentle woman who believed in him with a bitter older man who cringed beside him at the smallest fault in his playing. Duncan resented his new teacher and dared to risk, for the first time, feeling resentment toward his mother. Bad enough that she'd isolated him from his classmates and made him an oddity, stuck at home alone; then she'd taken away the one person who'd lifted him out of his loneliness and made him believe in his talent. No matter the motives his mother might give—that she was only concerned with what was best for him, for his future success—he now saw her efforts at protecting him for what they truly were: a deliberate campaign to trap him with her in her misery. A change took root in him. He began to cultivate a private freedom, to keep his motives secret, to dream of a life separate from his mother's that he would hide from her. Silently, through his seeming obedience and diligence, he began to work toward his escape.

Duncan's admission to Yale—on scholarship, after achieving the high marks that came easily to him, with nothing much else to do at home but study—meant he'd earned his way out of the Lowy house. He'd managed to achieve a place his mother believed would set him on the respected path she wished for him. For her, his acceptance implied security; for Duncan, it meant freedom. The future was wide open to him now.

Duncan had been thrilled to be at Yale from the day he'd stepped onto the campus. Every detail suggested an adventure: the wide, bright lawns and dim, echoing halls, the majestic Gothic buildings and the rougher streets of the city beyond. He wasn't the least bothered by the reports his mother delivered about New Haven's crime rate, nor by the roaches he discovered in his dorm room. He wasn't even bothered by his standoffish roommate, Blake Flournoy.

On first glance, Blake seemed like just the sort of spoiled prep school jerk that would end up playing pranks on Duncan, making him feel nervous and hopeless and destined to a despair as certain as the primrose path would be for blessed Blake, who'd arrived after him and still managed to claim the better top bunk.

"On your toes, buddy," Blake instructed, piling his clothes inside the larger bureau. "You're not living with your mommy anymore."

Blake was patronizing and aggressive and smug. Duncan saw this right away, but with time, he discovered other qualities in his roommate that eventually endeared Blake to him. Blake was loose with boundaries; he took, but gave generously too: he lent Duncan his clothes, and paid for his drinks when they went out, knowing that Duncan was in the work-study program. He also readily made up excuses to Duncan's mother, reducing her control over her son in ways Duncan was eager to discover.

Blake's glibness about the truth came as a relief to Duncan— there was great relief to be had in giving up on being good and pleasing people, and, for the first time, through Blake, Duncan was acquainted with some of the more selfish and darker sides he hadn't yet acknowledged in himself.

He had much to learn from Blake.

Alongside his roommate, Duncan discovered, finally, how to get what he wanted, especially from women. On the weekends, after they'd slept late and then Blake had beaten him at squash,

Blake would take Duncan out for dinner and drinks at Yorkside Pizza, or else at local dives that didn't card, and Blake would go up to any girl he wanted to and pull her from her chair to dance. On weekday evenings, with Blake as wingman, Duncan would have his chance at the girls, practicing on the piano in the college common rooms—for the express purpose of attracting female interest. His experience with Lillian had taught him that at least a certain kind of girl might be drawn in by his talent, and anyway, this was the only trick he had. So he and Blake would arrive around dinnertime, when dozens of coeds were coming and going from the dining hall, and Blake would call them over to notice the sweet-faced boy who played so nicely.

"The maestro here's named Duncan," Blake would say when a girl settled in to listen. "I have to make the introductions because he's a bit shy."

Duncan had been furious with Blake the first time he had said this, but after getting over his embarrassment and observing how the girl made an effort to draw him out, he soon saw the value in Blake's method. To his surprise, his being shy and sensitive counted in his favor with a fair number of girls—so many, in fact, that it soon became a problem. At first he was so flattered by the interest he was getting and so afraid of disappointing anyone that he went out with every girl who asked him. Some of these weren't too pleased to learn about the others—feelings were hurt, and, out of guilt, Duncan committed himself to a string of girls he didn't especially like. Finally, by the spring of his freshman year, he swore to himself he wouldn't get involved with anyone he wasn't head over heels for. He stopped playing piano in the common rooms and began to practice, privately, on a piano in one of the campus performance spaces. Then, one April evening, he heard music coming from a room down the hall. Inside, a girl was dancing on the stage.

She was facing the wall as she moved, her bronze curls swaying behind her. He watched her for a while before she turned and looked up, and he was suddenly aware that he hadn't spoken or moved away, but had just stood there, maybe twenty feet from her, watching. One stage light was on, but the rest of the room was dark—could she even see him?—and she looked so completely caught up in what she was doing, in a trance. As she began to dance again, she let out a small laugh—it might have been at him, or maybe at herself, at her own pleasure. But he found himself overcome with the desire to hear her laugh again.

He began rehearsing with practiced dedication, mostly out of the hope that he might cross paths with the girl again. When she didn't come, he'd stay and practice, secretly waiting, finding himself idly experimenting for hours. One evening, a melody took shape, and soon he'd come up with most of a sonata, a single-movement work rich with melancholy yearning, but punctuated with a lighter theme that he'd come to think of as the girl's laughter. He quickly jotted down the score, and waited a few days before he dared replay it.

When he did, his hope was confirmed: for the first time in his life, he'd written an original and rousing piece of music.

Summer break arrived soon after and, despite reminders from his mother that he was at school for a practical degree, he signed up for his first composition class upon returning in the fall. He spent time perfecting the sonata, and presented it as his midterm assignment, impressing his instructor so greatly that he suggested Duncan offer a recital. In November, Duncan performed his composition in Woolsey Hall, a space so grand he was lucky to see a third of it filled. Secretly he hoped the girl might be among the listeners, but he could hardly believe his luck when, after the show, as he was met by admiration and outstretched hands, the girl strolled past him with her bronze, wavy hair swept over her shoulder. Up close, she was shorter than he'd realized, more petite. She wore a white peasant dress, not the sort of clothing that most of the girls on campus wore. Her name, he'd learned from Blake, was Gina Reinhold.

She was a dance major, Blake told him with obvious contempt. Duncan could guess his thinking: what serious person would waste a Yale education performing pirouettes? Duncan didn't dare tell him, then, how his experience performing and hopes of meeting Gina were already tempting him to spend more time on his music. Soon he was spreading the word around that he'd be interested in composing for dancers. Not long after, he received a call from a student choreographer who was arranging a show; he immediately agreed to come to a rehearsal. Nervous, hopeful, Duncan arrived at the rehearsal space the next evening, and onstage among the many dancers, there she was, Gina Reinhold.

Gina was toward the front, possibly because she was smaller than the other dancers, but also, he was sure, because the choreographer had recognized she was the most commanding. The piece, the choreographer had told him, was meant to capture the struggle for human connection. At this point, the dancers were improvising, moving in and out of sync, engaged in cautious, stilted reaching, but Duncan kept his eyes on Gina, who was different, winding among the other bodies, sending one and then another dancer into a series of elated whirls across the stage.

Her energy riveted Duncan. He had the sensation, watching her, that everything he longed for in himself—conviction, liberation, transcendence—was here distilled within a five-foot-two-inch frame.

He wanted to amaze her, and so spent the next days trying to come up with a gorgeous and profound piece of music. But nothing he wrote seemed any good. He began to panic at the prospect of failing; he'd acted impulsively to get closer to this girl he admired, and had agreed to do something he couldn't. The next morning, he came by rehearsal early to meet with the choreographer and discuss his change of heart. When he arrived, though, the choreographer was running late, and the only person waiting was the person he most feared to see: Gina.

He must have looked ready to bolt, because right away she asked him what was wrong.

"I just came to say that I can't do this. Do this show. Can you relay that for me?"

"Well," she said, frankly, "first, I'd like to know why do you think you can't?"

He was surprised by her question, hadn't expected he'd need to confess his limits to her. "I . . . I can't force myself to do it. Melodies just come to me sometimes. It's not anything I can control."

He'd expected her to drop the matter, but Gina seemed to be as bold offstage as on.

"So when those melodies do come to you, how does it usually happen?"

He explained himself, his way of starting with another person's work, experimenting with deviations, building up from there. One exception sprang to mind, but he was too embarrassed to acknowledge that much to her then: the piece he'd written about her had been different. The idea had come to him all on its own.

"Have you ever worked with another person before? Another musician or a dancer?"

"No," he admitted, "never."

She went on to describe the way the pianist at her dance school in Santa Fe had worked. She would watch the dancers perform a sequence several times and then come up with music to accompany their movements. "Should we try that?"

He agreed to try, dubious as he was, because he couldn't imagine denying her. She bounded up to the stage and he sat down at the piano to watch her dance. Without the other dancers present he imagined she'd be hampered, but she launched in unreservedly, her form contracted into loneliness, then surging outward, searching. For his sake, she exaggerated the sentiment in every move, so that he could better grasp the tone, and he let his fingers run to keep up along the keys. A song began emerging.

After a moment, Gina stopped him. "That's pretty there, but maybe too pretty? I'm feeling the movement is more uncertain, even strained."

"Oh, okay. I see that. I'll try that then." He added more ambiguity in the form of suspended and diminished chords and quickly decided that yes, Gina was right. He continued until, a few moments later, Gina stopped him again.

"Here, though, the tone shifts. There's less ambivalence, more daring."

"Maybe this way." He tried a bolder, major-key passage.

"More tender, dreamier."

He slowed, taking in her words. Until now he'd been struck

by Gina from afar, by the intensity that she projected, but here, working with her, he began to get a feel for what sort of spirit animated her. Gina's instincts were so sharp, her confidence in them so total, that every phrase and motion to come from her seemed singularly persuasive. Her vitality hit him in a way that made him feel she was more real to him than he was to himself.

He proceeded to follow all her suggestions, and it startled him to find, in the end, when he played the piece over, incorporating her changes, that it was far better than he'd even imagined.

You're brilliant, he felt like telling her—the pressure of this private admission, this revelation, was so great his heart began to thump. He could feel himself blushing at this thought that gripped him: that Gina elevated him, brought him closer to the best that he might be. Something miraculous had taken place, and he didn't know how to convey it or what to do with all the energy stirred up in him, and so he played the piece for her again, this time with more fluency, and more quickly. Gina kept up, inventing new moves that matched still better with his notes. When they were finished, she was panting, and he was too, and both of them, not sure what else to do, began to laugh.

From that day on, he knew he had to find some way to get Gina in his life.

He had three weeks of daily rehearsals during which he might grow closer to her—though this setup didn't lend itself to privacy. He began to linger by the piano after rehearsals, while she changed into her regular clothes, and he'd pretend to take notes so that he could time his exit with hers. If she knew what he was doing, she spared him the embarrassment of letting on; either way, in his determination he found he didn't care. After a few

nights of this charade, he saw her holding the door for him as they left, so they might walk onward together.

Gina was friendly to him, and, though he was shy around her, she easily filled the quiet as they walked down the campus streets.

"I've been wondering when you started playing. To be that good, I'm guessing young."

"Oh, five or six. I don't remember exactly. I always tinkered a little. There was a piano in the house—my mother played— and there wasn't a hell of a lot else to do at home." He was bungling things already, he thought, as if describing a childhood that was painfully dull could make him seem interesting. He quickly turned the focus onto her. "But I'm more interested in your story than my own."

As they strolled slowly across the Old Campus quad, she told him about herself, how she'd grown up in Santa Fe, the only child of two artists. "Not famous or anything, but my dad lives for it, paints every day."

"And your mom?"

"She had a stroke when I was nine."

He didn't know yet what this meant—had her mother lived or died?—and he was too afraid to ask. He was too afraid to ask her also how this event might be connected to her dancing, and to her intensity onstage—but he'd had an intuition, an image that came to him of a child Gina dancing while her mother sat stiff, as if that overabundance in her came from absorbing all the liveliness her mother couldn't express.

He'd felt such tenderness for her then. His whole body seemed to tingle in the cold.

"I'm very sorry. For your mother and for you."

Gina looked at him, taking this in. Her eyes were wide; probably she was surprised, herself, at letting a virtual stranger come so close, so fast, to what must have been such private pain.

"Thank you," she said, her voice ragged with emotion. "I'm sorry also, for my mother. But for me, I don't know, there was something that her accident taught me. It forced me to wake up and realize, there's no guarantee of a tomorrow, and no such thing as a safe choice." She slowed her pace as if contemplating the gravity of this thought. "You can lose it all in a minute. So why wait? Why compromise? If you want something, you grab it!"

"Right! Absolutely!" And yet those hands that wished so much to grab her remained buried in his pockets, pressed in so deeply he might tear the seams. She was right: if he wanted her, he ought to do something about it.

The more they talked, the more he realized just how well she knew herself and her future already. By her sophomore year in college, she'd figured out what sort of life she wished to lead. After graduation she meant to move to New York and join one of the experimental dance companies downtown. She planned to dance until the age of twenty-five, then have a child, take off a year, and resume dancing for as long as she was able. "Hopefully until I'm forty."

"And after that?" he asked her, teasing. "Don't you have the rest worked out yet?"

"Oh, I don't tend to think past forty. Who knows if I'll even make it beyond that?"

She said it lightly, without fear or self-pity, or even much awareness of how strange a sentiment this was. He began to think it over, to piece together the few details he'd collected so far of this lovely young woman. Her mother had suffered a stroke when

Gina was just nine. Maybe forty was the age she'd been, and maybe Gina envisioned her life unfolding the same way. Perhaps this explained the urgency he'd sensed in Gina; her determination to live presently, recklessly even, issued from her fear that her time here would be brief.

He looked at her again, vibrant and cheerful, any sadness in her kept far from the surface, where he had no right to touch it. Silently, he took hold of her hand.

Gina wrapped her fingers around his but said nothing. Brightly, lightening the tone, she filled the silence he'd let linger, lost in his thoughts.

"And what are *your* plans, then?"

"You mean for my life? I don't think I've got it worked out like you." He was too ashamed to tell her that his notions of life after college were quite practical and dull. He'd get a job in finance to pay off his loans. "I'm not sure yet what I'll do. But I'll have debts to pay off to begin with. And I know my parents are hoping Wall Street or law."

By now, Gina and Duncan were standing at the entrance to Pierson, her college, at the end of the path, beneath the redbrick tower. He wondered if she might say good night and go in, but Gina stood there instead, facing Duncan, her breath forming clouds in the air that seemed to linger magically.

"Don't they recognize your talent in music?"

"I mean, sure, somewhat, but music isn't a career to them. There's pleasure and there's work. They see those as two very different things."

"And do you?"

"I don't know, myself, but I can understand where they're

coming from. They've struggled financially and want more for me, that's all."

"But what sort of more?" she pressed, becoming agitated. "Don't you think what they want for you is to be happy?"

"Hell no. Happiness would just make a mess of things," he joked.

"You don't believe that!" She'd challenged him, and he'd grinned wider, because no, in Gina's presence, he didn't believe it. With her he felt that happiness was the only thing that mattered, and that it meant always having her near.

"Of course you won't actually give up your music in the end," she told him brashly.

"And why won't I?" he asked her.

"I won't let you."

He laughed, thrilled by her behaving as if his fate mattered to her.

"You remind me of my father," she went on to say, and Duncan, taken aback, couldn't decide if this was a good thing or the very worst.

"Until he met my mother," she went on, "he didn't imagine that he'd ever pursue art. He was meant to go into the family business. But my mother wouldn't let him. She told him that she had no interest in being with somebody who wasn't true to himself."

Talk of true selves, such intense romanticism—this would have struck Duncan as false or off-putting in anyone else. He'd been raised to be a skeptic—the worst could always happen, and most likely would—but Gina made him feel like this was precisely the reason to take risks.

"The only point in living is to follow your passion," she concluded.

He wanted to do just that, wanted to take the big risk, which was to tell her how he felt about her. He thought about it constantly in the next days: during breaks in rehearsal, or when he waited for her, as he soon did openly, outside the changing room. But every time he was about to get up the nerve, his heart would pound and he'd start sweating, until, at its worst, he'd need to take a jog around the theater so that she'd think this was the reason his face had turned red.

On the third-to-last night before the show opened, he made up his mind to admit his feelings once and for all. Each block they traversed on the way back, he'd order himself to make his move before the curb, but by the time they reached her dorm at Pierson he still hadn't done it. He must have looked so miserable standing there that she'd taken pity on him and suggested that she walk him to his dorm at Calhoun instead. They'd nearly made it there when he felt her hand on his shoulder, and then the other on his cheek. She turned his face to hers and he saw, in the second before his eyes closed, her lips rising to meet his.

They kissed so long his toes started to go numb, though he hadn't noticed this until she finally pulled away and said goodbye to him near the entrance to his dorm. He went bounding, giddy, up the dorm hall stairs. He couldn't feel his fingers, his feet were throbbing, and the blood was pulsing in his head so much he felt he might explode.

Gina Reinhold wanted him! It was the single most amazing fact of his young life. Every difficulty he'd ever faced, every lonely moment hadn't been suffered in vain any longer. All that emptiness he'd filled with music was preparation for the day when he'd meet Gina. All those disappointing events were put in place to lead to this point when he'd find Gina and fall in love and his real life would begin.

He and Gina were inseparable the next weeks. In the beginning, they took turns sleeping in one another's rooms, but soon they stopped going to his because Blake began complaining.

"You never made a fuss with other girls," Duncan pointed out, but Blake wasn't up for discussing the difference. Of course they both knew there was a difference between Duncan merely sleeping with a girl and getting carried away, the way he was with Gina.

"I've had crushes before, sure, but I've never had anyone get inside my head like this," Duncan made the mistake of confessing to Blake one afternoon. "It's like I wasn't fully awake before Gina. She's done something amazing to me."

"She's pussy-whipped you," Blake replied. "It's really not that complicated. Take a break, hook up with someone else. You'll be cured."

But Duncan had no interest in anyone else and no desire to be cured. Instead, he craved access to more of her, and became drawn to anything that interested her: an exhibit she wished to see at the art gallery, a lecture series that compelled her, a new novel she'd been reading. There was hardly a free moment when he wasn't engaged in exploring with her some new passion they could share.

"What's Gina got you up to now?" Blake would say when he and Duncan crossed paths, more and more briefly. Blake's hostility toward their relationship surprised him. Could Blake be jealous? Over time, Duncan began to have an inkling as to what his friend's envy might be about—Blake had lost his sidekick and had his place as Duncan's role model usurped. Before Gina, Blake had been the one to free Duncan from his inhibitions, the person to help him become braver and more alive.

Or perhaps there was more to it than that. As time went on, Blake's distrust of Gina deepened and he began making accusations against her, citing facts about Gina he'd uncovered from a girl he'd begun seeing too, a girl who, not coincidentally, thought Duncan, happened to come from Gina's hometown.

"In school, you know, she had a reputation as a liar," Blake announced to Duncan one afternoon. "It was so bad, the school shrink had to see her."

"For God's sake, her mother had a stroke. She went through hell. What would you expect?"

"You'll find any reason to excuse her."

"And you'll find any reason to condemn her," Duncan told him. "Whatever's behind this"—he didn't have the courage to speculate—"whatever's got you acting so crazy, I don't want you insulting my girlfriend."

"I think you do need it," Blake retorted. "You refuse to see what she's about—"

"Stop," Duncan had ordered firmly, and proceeded to set out the policy that would allow his friendship with Blake to survive. "You don't have to like Gina. You don't have to hang out with her. Think what you want about her, but if you want to spend time with me, if you want this friendship to continue, Blake, I don't want to hear it."

"Your choice," Blake agreed, "but I'm only trying to protect you."

Protect him from what? Despite himself, he began to wonder

if his love for Gina—and by now he was certain it was love—was in some way throwing him off course.

Even if she was innocent of blame, it remained true that since meeting Gina he'd been neglecting most everything but her. As winter turned to spring, he scarcely made it to any class outside of his musical studies. After a year-end meeting with his advisor, who warned him he was in danger of losing his scholarship, Duncan admitted his trouble to Gina.

"I don't know what's been happening with me. I can't get myself to give a damn about my classes, or about anything except being with you."

They were lying in her bed after sex in the later afternoon, Duncan still in the pleasure-fog he fell into with her. The sun was bright, the sheets damp with their sweat. Gina was flushed along her cheeks and chest, adorable that way. The pressure of desire turned into a different sort of love in such moments, one that didn't seek an easy resolution, and was more overwhelming for that fact. He didn't know how to have her more than he already had, and yet that wasn't enough.

"I'm sorry if I've let that happen," she began, but Duncan quickly assured her that none of this was her fault.

"I think it's just the fact that feeling strongly for you, it's made me see more sharply what I don't care about. So much of what I've been doing is stuff I don't really want to do."

"So what do you want to do?" she asked him, propping herself up sideways on her pillow. Her pleasure at what he was saying showed in her face, encouraging him to go yet further.

"I love music and I love you," he said, that phrase still new and wild on his lips. "The rest is nothing to me, really. That's the truth."

She began kissing him then, kissing him and kissing him until they both fell backward in the bed, until he had to pin her down just to contain the excitement in him.

For the first time in his life, Duncan resolved to live more according to his desires. Though he kept his economics major to appease his mother—and his scholarship funders—by senior year he was singularly enthralled by composition. In his spare time, he joined Gina in fifteen campus productions. Soon, the pair of them had become a phenomenon, a super-couple bound for stardom. It began to seem inevitable, simply assumed, that after graduation they would move to New York together, he pursuing music, she dancing. And yet his mother's practical voice lingered in his mind.

"At some point you'll need to make clear to your family what it is *you* want," Gina pressed him, unable to grasp how it was that Duncan could keep his parents so much in the dark about the parts of his life that mattered most—his art and her. By then, they still hadn't met Gina, nor did Duncan bring her up in conversation again after his mother—much like Blake—referred to her as a *distraction*. In some ways, he envied Gina's inability to grasp the rigidity of his own parents; of course he could hardly expect that she would understand, as a girl whose father approved of her every move and from whom she hid nothing. It had always disturbed him, and frankly made him envious, to come home and find Gina on the phone with her father, with disturbing regularity, recounting the day's events just like she would with him, or, worse, turning to her father with her frustrations over him. "If Duncan can't stand up for what he loves, how strong can that love be?" he'd overheard her say once.

He'd confronted her about it, finally. "If you complain to your dad about me, you'll only succeed in turning him against me. Is that what you want?"

"At least my father knows that you exist," she'd retorted, letting her hurt be known.

And so, two weeks later, on a rainy May Sunday, he and Gina made the trip by train to Toms River. He was giving Gina the family introduction that she wished for, though he wasn't at all sure that it was smart. He feared that being faced with his parents, with their modest achievements and immense anxieties, would only make Gina less admiring of him. The parts of him that were hesitant or pessimistic, the parts that were uneasy accepting pleasure, believing in his entitlement to happiness, all these would come out more strongly once she'd seen their source. His immediate concern, though, was that Gina would say something to outrage his mother or his mother would say something to outrage Gina. They both held such strong and opposing positions, he was afraid the tension between them that he'd so far carried inside him would become external, real, and disastrous.

They arrived at his modest, cheerless family home at noon, in time for lunch. His mother brought out plates of lettuce, bread, and tuna salad, and for a time, while they ate, they were all on their best behavior. Duncan's mother asked the mostly polite questions she might direct at any of her son's friends. Still, even during this exchange, his mother found three occasions to observe that Reinhold was a German name.

"I never thought of my father as German," Gina said the first time. The second time she explained: "He's American, a mix."

The third time, Duncan's mother made the remark to him instead. "It must be Rheingold, originally, like the opera, right, Duncan?"

"I don't know, Mom. I wouldn't know." Though of course it hadn't really been a question. Clearly his girlfriend shared the same name as the Wagner opera, Wagner being the one composer Duncan had always been forbidden from playing in the house. And now his mother meant to convey a similar message about Gina—*This girl does not belong here*—which Gina had naturally sensed.

How ashamed he felt of his mother's tribalism, how offended for Gina's sake. Yet Gina was unfazed. She'd kept her wits no matter how his mother tried to provoke her—asking after her political opinions: Had she followed the violence in Germany, the attacks on immigrants? Did she maintain the same stupid optimism about reunification as president Bush?

"I'm in favor of freedom, generally," Gina replied, "for those in East Germany, and those in New Jersey too."

She'd smiled at Duncan then, a gesture of complicity, and he understood that now was the time to do what he must do: here, with Gina in his corner, let his parents know that he would not be going on to law school or pursuing a career in finance either.

"Gina's a dancer," Duncan explained, coming around to his admission slowly. "She's a very talented one, enough to be professional. After graduation, she'll be moving to New York."

"That sounds exciting," said his mother, though she hardly said it with enthusiasm. "It's quite a struggle, though, isn't it? Life in the arts. Better if you have a partner engaged in something solid, I'd think."

"That hadn't occurred to me," said Gina calmly.

"Well, then I hope your family has money," his mother pressed, to Duncan's mortification.

"Esther," Duncan's father cautioned from where he sat, on

the other side of the room, reading the paper. Gina looked over at him, though Duncan's mother took no notice and simply went on.

"The phrase 'starving artist' exists for a reason."

"My family has some money, yes," Gina replied, simply, "and I don't deny that gives me a certain freedom. But that freedom can be Duncan's too. He's an extraordinary talent. I know that parents can't always see what others do, but others do see it, Mrs. Lowy. I certainly see it, and intend to do what I can to encourage him. I'd like to help him."

"Help him?" His mother's expression turned grave. "And why would you need this woman's help, Duncan?"

"I don't. I mean, we support each other, that's all. In the things we want to do." Here it was, he must say it, though it was bound to break his mother's heart. "I've been thinking, not that I'll necessarily rule out finance as a career forever, but I'd like to spend my first year out of school trying my hand at composing. See if I can make a career of that."

His mother's face was pale. He studied her: her hair, which she refused to dye, had turned prematurely white, her worry lines etched deeply between her brows. She was as marked by life and as hardened by it as Gina was unblemished and elastic.

He couldn't help but feel pity for his mother then, and some remorse for what he'd done. He understood how fearfully she clung to her idea of security, what a challenge, in her own life, feeling safe had proved to be. And here he was dismissing this, her hard-earned wisdom, and all the effort that she'd made to give him the peace of mind she'd never had.

"I know you're disappointed, Mom, but I felt you deserved to know how things stand. Gina and I will be moving to New

York after graduation and I'll be trying to establish myself as a composer."

"This is her idea, I take it?" His mother was demanding an answer, and he'd become instantly flustered.

"N-no, it's not her idea. It's what makes sense for me, what fits me. She's just come to help me see it. We've come to this together."

"No, no." His mother shook her head. "I don't believe this is what you want."

He could feel his anger rise, his frustration driving him to snap at her for one of the first times in his life: "What the hell would you know about what I ever wanted?"

After lashing out, he'd been frightened that his mother would crumble, but instead she'd surprised him that day. Without tears or theatrics, sitting calmly, she'd addressed him. "You're right, Duncan, you're right. It's my fault that you can't make choices for yourself and that you let this girl make them for you."

"I am choosing for myself!" He meant to be decisive, but his voice sounded childish, not at all the solid, manly tone he'd hoped to strike in front of Gina.

"If you want to rebel against me," his mother continued, "I can accept that. I'm old and fearful, I realize. But I will say this: I'm not a fool, and there are some things I do see." She turned her gaze almost imperceptibly to Gina, then back to her son. "She comes from privilege, and from people who've let her live inside a dream. If you give in to what she wants, you'll just end up in a dream with her, cut off from your true potential and what you might become. I can tell you right now what will happen. You'll go traipsing after her, and she'll lead you nowhere. One day you'll look up and realize you're lost."

He might have been shaken by this if he hadn't looked over at Gina and seen her then, so small and yet so huge, brimming with confidence, eyes flashing and cheeks ruddy, like something from a propaganda poster, an image of health and vitality and hope.

Seeing her then, he felt as if her daring had infused him, compelling him to throw himself into adulthood without any guarantee of safety. He would be reckless and single-minded; he would go after what he wanted, no matter if he or others suffered for it. All that mattered was to keep Gina proud and to keep her by his side. Whatever hardships they might face, he was ready to accept, because she was the one who'd saved him from a cautious and meager existence, who'd taught him, finally, at the brink of first adulthood, what it meant to be alive.

"So then I'll be lost," he said, looking his mother straight in the eyes. "And if I'm lost with Gina, I'll be lost happily."

Five

If Duncan's childhood was shaped by isolation and restriction, Gina's had been shaped by plenitude and loss. She'd grown up wealthy, in relaxed and sun-filled Santa Fe. Her fondest childhood memories were of dancing out on the back porch of her family home, where her parents would play records, and Gina would sway and twirl between the chairs and plants and flowers, under a vined trellis and a giant paper lantern, which she could jump up high and touch, her own graspable moon.

Music always seemed to play in that house, emanating from whichever room her mother was in, usually her sculpture studio, where Gina would come while her mother worked and dance beside her, watching herself in the gilt-framed mirror that stood on the floor, seeing herself growing until her head no longer fit under the frame.

She must have been around six when that happened, which was also the year that her mother began driving her to ballet classes five afternoons a week. Gina didn't recall ever deciding to be a dancer; in a household where both parents were artists, it was assumed everyone should have a creative passion. Only once she was older did she come to understand how unusual this was, how most other parents were occupied with jobs they held in order to survive.

Gina had grown up in a romantic universe, maintained by family money. Just before the Great Depression, her maternal grandfather had received the second state-issued oil and gas lease, allowing him to drill in southeastern Mexico in the Permian Basin. Within a generation, her mother's family had amassed a fortune. Her father's family was more modest, but they'd risen from laborers to business owners, running a small local shipping company that Gina's father was expected to inherit. His own artistic ambitions had been kept hidden from his family until Gina's mother had encouraged him to break away and become the painter she believed he was meant to be. Success had never seemed an issue—neither of Gina's parents, though talented, ever sold much work. They gave their art away, to the many friends who gathered in the years when Gina's mother was still fit to host them, when it seemed all the world's troubles were left at the threshold of their home.

That idyll had survived until Gina was nine.

She'd been in the fourth grade and attending a small private school where her mother worked as the art teacher. Every morning, they drove to school together, and though she'd made a fuss about not getting to ride with her friends on the school bus, the truth was Gina enjoyed the morning drives with her mother— sitting up in the front seat, with music playing on the stereo, Janis Joplin or Patti Smith, and her mother tapping the wheel, bracelets jangling. They didn't talk much—her mother had a mistrust of language, or a preference for quiet enjoyment. It was only later that Gina learned, from her father, that her mother was dyslexic and had been considered stupid by her family, in response to which she'd rebelled, running away from home five different times. She was the family hellion, apparently, though that side of her was hard to see in the mother Gina knew, who was devoted and warm, full of energy and appreciation for the beauty around her. When her mother wasn't working, she'd take Gina down to Abiquiu Lake or on long hikes; she was always the first one to dive into the water, always the first to crest a mountain peak. It was easy for Gina to admire her mother and long to be like her. She saw her mom as indomitable, until, suddenly, she wasn't.

One morning, Gina lay in bed listening to the sound of her mother in the shower. Every morning, after her alarm rang, she'd laze around in bed a while longer, knowing that she had until her mother shut off the water to get up, and then would have to rush to be on time. This morning, something was strange. Gina had woken, and then dozed, and then woken again to realize she was late. She'd called out to her mom and had gotten no answer. Finally, she crept toward the bathroom, where the water was still running.

The curtain rod was down. Blood was pooling in the shower. Her mother lay in the tub, unresponsive, with a gash along the left side of her head. Gina stood there shouting until her father came and called an ambulance. She'd been so terrified, so guilty—how long had her mom been lying there? At the hospital they learned that the fall had been preceded by a stroke, a severe one. There was nothing anyone could have done to prevent the damage, and nothing to be done to repair it either. What sort of damage? How would Mom be now? she'd asked her father. He hadn't had an answer for her. He'd only sat beside her crying, until she realized there would be no simple answers, or simple comforts, after this.

Following her mother's accident, the music stopped, the house grew silent. Words felt inconsequential—there wasn't anything to say or do to change the pain that weighed on her and her dad so heavily it blunted everything, made all else seem unreal.

Her mother continued to live at home, looked after by Gina and her father and by a nurse who came several times a week to check her vitals and perform tests of her progress—what little she ever made. Her mother's once-graceful movements were now stiff, her speech halting and basic. For the most part, she sat in her room, emerging only for the slow walks she took each day with Gina's father. Gina was uneasy around her, and found her mother's presence too painful a reminder of the woman who was gone. Now her mother never hugged Gina or kissed her, and it wasn't clear what emotion, if any, she could feel. Gina came to think it was a blessing if her mother didn't feel things; she'd have gladly chosen to feel less as well.

Eventually, Gina returned to classes, now dropped off by her father, who drove her to school seeking, in any way he could, to occupy her mother's place. And yet, as much as he was there, he couldn't possibly rescue her from the grayness she'd sunk into.

The only respite she could find was in the stories she told herself—of her mom's miraculous recovery, or of moving to some more exciting city, or of men appearing to whisk her off on some adventure. At points Gina's fantasies were so intense, it seemed she was confused between them and the life she was living. A neighbor's daughter, seventeen years old, had gotten pregnant, and soon ten-year-old Gina became concerned that she was pregnant too. When she mentioned this notion to her classmate, a teacher overheard and she was taken to speak with the school psychologist.

Her father came in for the meeting, which consisted of two parts. During the first, Gina sat alone with the psychologist, who had thick gray hair and a deeply dimpled smile. The woman asked her questions about the story that she'd told. Did she understand how a woman became pregnant? She had some idea: through being with a man. Had she been with a man herself? She hadn't, but she'd thought about it, she admitted, and wondered if in this case it was enough. And had she started ovulating? She had not. The woman assured Gina she was fine, had done nothing wrong, and then asked her to step into the hallway while Gina's father entered for a brief discussion, which Gina caught bits of through the thin door.

"She's always been dramatic," her father was saying, "but I'm worried she might be losing her grip on reality."

"My sense is that she doesn't really believe she's pregnant," said the woman, "but that this fantasy is playing a role for her, providing comfort. Maybe it's the idea of having a baby that would make the family a triangle again, and whole. Or maybe she wants to imagine she would mother this child to make up for the mothering she isn't getting."

After the meeting, Gina could feel her father's worry over her, and quickly decided to abandon the fantasy that had so gripped her. "Dad, I'm not crazy, okay? Sometimes pretending things makes me feel better."

"Of course you're not crazy. I know that. It's the loneliness, this awful loneliness without her." He reached out to take her hand and squeezed it, hard, in comfort and in need. "I feel it too."

Following their conversation, her father took an emergency

leave from his university position. Gina, he'd decided, required his exclusive attention.

"I think what we both need to get through this is one another. As long as we can trust in that, we'll be all right."

From that day on, her father had redoubled his involvement with her, to the point where others, she knew, might find their closeness strange. He'd seen to it that he was always home when she returned from school, always available for anything she needed—shopping trips and volunteering at the school, help with homework or conversations about puberty or boys. As she grew older, and her friends began dating, she failed to show interest in anyone. No one ever lived up to the figures in her imaginings, and finally she decided that her father was the only actual gallant man she knew. He'd adored his wife, had written her poems and painted her portrait over and over, with infinite care and fascination. When she grew debilitated, he maintained his devotion, looked after her and took her on those long walks each afternoon. Gina had asked him, through the years, why he didn't try to meet another woman, maybe marry again, and he would tell her that he'd had the two most extraordinary loves already in his life, with the family he had. Nothing else interested him.

Gina had given up her dancing for the past year, feeling guilty, perhaps, for exhibiting the vitality in her that her mother had lost—but now she came to feel this was precisely what she needed: an extraordinary love in her life. When she danced she had no thoughts, no memory, no wishes, no regrets. There was nothing to her but parts moving through space and the music that led her. She threw herself into dance like others might into religion. From ballet, she switched to modern, which was more improvisational, and better allowed her to become absorbed in what she was doing. Her dance school encouraged her to perform in small parts professionally, and by senior year she planned to attend art school and concentrate in dance. Instead, her college counselor persuaded her to apply to several liberal arts colleges as well. Her grades were good and there were several schools that had dance majors, including Yale. That spring, moved by her personal story and her success as a performer, the admissions committee offered her a place.

"New Haven is pretty far, though," her father pointed out, and there were other, closer schools. He stopped short of admitting how the distance would pain him, but she understood he found it hard to let her go. She felt awful about leaving—or, more precisely, guilty over the fact that she felt propelled to leave. All these years she'd never fully acknowledged her craving to be freed from her home and from the atmosphere of loss that hung in every room.

How exhilarating to arrive at Yale in the fall, where everything seemed grand and romantic in a way that spoke to the fantastical in her. She loved walking among the college courtyards, with their fragrant rosebushes and dreamy stone walkways hidden behind walls. She loved the dorm rooms with their dark wood and arched windows, the high-ceilinged dining halls with their raucous noise, and the sense she carried in them of having escaped Santa Fe and her small-minded peers to find herself among an exciting and worldly group of future friends. Within her freshman dorm lived a British aristocrat—an earl or duke of some sort—a daughter of an Indian diplomat, a son of a French politician, and a daughter of an Italian TV star. She befriended a few of them, but they proved less compelling than she'd hoped, and then she became involved with a young man, a guitar player, whose playing impressed her, until she realized nothing else about him did. She had to wait until sophomore year to meet the people who would really engage her, starting with a girl who was to become her best friend and set her on the path she'd follow years after their acquaintance: Violet Sharpe.

Violet was two years ahead of Gina in school, already a senior and the head of the college dramatic association. Everybody in the arts knew Violet: she was impossible to miss, a loping six-foot-tall Chinese girl with hair shaved on one side and the remainder dyed white-blond. Violet's face was also riveting, with thick, straight brows; full lips; and wide-set eyes with bold green streaks of shadow on the lids. Violet was the adopted daughter of two prominent figures in the world of New York theater; she'd therefore come onto campus with an automatic authority about the performance scene, and with the tacit promise of future connections—all of which caused those around her to seek her favor: the best actors turned down roles in other shows to work with her. The best crews attached themselves to her productions.

Gina knew of Violet, of course, even though their creative cliques only overlapped slightly—but sophomore year she'd noticed Violet coming to dance performances and showing up after rehearsals. The lure was a freckled brunette named Bette, whom Violet would continue to date on and off long after college. That October, Gina and Bette were in a show together, arranged by a student choreographer. The set designer had devised a system with screens lit from behind, which would make the dancers appear as silhouettes. The arrangement had worked during rehearsal, but during the second performance, one of the screens was kicked a little and brought too close to the hot lights.

The screens were apparently made of a very thin, dry paper and sprayed with flammable glue, so that in seconds the paper began to smoke and then curl into flames. The audience gasped and several of the dancers ran off. Gina had the presence of mind to return with the fire extinguisher—and then continued dancing. No intrusion from reality could sever her connection to her art. The audience sat bound by her singular force, lured back into the illusion, as one by one other dancers crept back in around her.

The next time Violet arrived at dance class to meet Bette, she drew Gina into their conversation.

"That was quite a performance last week," Violet remarked, tugging Gina's sleeve.

Gina shrugged, her smile knowing, even flirtatious. "What's a little fire to get in the way of a show?"

Violet was studying her, those green-painted eyes fixed. "I'd always thought you seemed a bit too normal, honestly, but I was wrong. I see it in you now. You've got some real crazy in you." Violet had grinned at her, revealing large teeth with a gap in the center, the sort of oddity her parents had known, in their circles, it would be best not to correct.

Gina supposed she might have been offended; there was a time when being called crazy would have frightened her, but now, with Violet, she felt relieved, accepted, seen. She'd known she contained the extremity that Violet named, but she'd never, until Violet put it that way, considered it any sort of gift.

"We're going to New York this weekend," Violet remarked with an air of casualness. "If you want to come."

"Love to," Gina told her, feeling the urge to leave behind the sheltered world of the campus and go exploring. "Though I don't have anywhere to stay."

Violet assured her that she had a place Gina would be free to use. "Anytime, really." The invitation carried the promise, already, of future adventures.

In the city, Violet took Gina to a dance performance downtown. The theater was at First Avenue and Ninth Street, a plain auditorium with columns obstructing the view. The outside was redbrick, institutional—it didn't look like a theater at all. In fact, she learned, the building was an abandoned public school.

The show she'd seen that night had confused and then astonished her. It seemed to break with every expectation she hadn't realized until then she'd been bound by. The dancers had looked so mismatched, tall and short, gangly and thick—each in distinct costumes that might have been their real clothes. At times they stopped dancing and sat and even talked to one another, or to the audience—dancers had voices!—and there were steps within the performance that might have been mistakes, and which Gina realized were intended to look that way, to break confidence in the dancers, to rouse in the audience a doubt, which would then be mocked by some act of virtuosity. The whole notion of a dancer, of what a dancer was, had been thrown up in the air that night, and Gina felt at once unsteadied and amazed.

"That was incredible," she'd effused to Violet after the show, though Violet was less impressed. It would take Gina longer to understand the history of such work, how much had been borrowed from other, greater figures in the dance world, but none of that altered the wonder she'd experienced that night when she was too young and unschooled to form a more measured reaction. Measured reactions could come later—wonder was what she needed then.

"It was incredible anyway," she insisted, persuading Violet

too in her enthusiasm, grabbing the girl's arm. "I want to dance that way someday."

"I'm sure you'll do whatever you want to," said Violet, impressed with Gina's determination, and infected by her reverie. "I can see you in a few years, gently bending the whole world to your wishes."

Gina laughed, both gleefully and guiltily, sensing Bette's discomfort with what was happening between them, Gina's effect on Violet. A change was taking place, a magnetic sort of friendship quickly binding these two young women together.

From the performance, Violet whisked Gina and Bette off to a party, somewhere west. A single small lamp underneath the drinks table served to light the whole space, so that at the edges of the room people disappeared into darkness. Every now and then Violet would come clutching Gina's arm to introduce her to a choreographer or to announce that Laurie Anderson had just been through. Is that Eric Bogosian? Oh my God, is that Grace Jones? In the dark it was nearly impossible to make out faces with any certainty, and everybody in the room had the look of someone famous, an aura of consequence about them. Even the people who were ugly were gorgeous.

If Violet's intent had been to hook Gina on the scene, she had succeeded. By the end of the night, Gina believed that there was simply nowhere else for a dancer like her to be than in New York, working wherever these people worked, living in a loft like the one Violet's fathers lived in, with exposed beams and brick and light streaming in through white curtains in the morning.

Gina had seen her future clearly, how the next decade should look. The only part she hadn't filled in yet was Duncan.

It was possibly sheer chance that, the week after she'd joined

Violet in New York, Gina was invited by a student choreographer to see a composition by a fellow sophomore. She'd found the music lovely, and was also taken with the boy onstage: shy, handsome, serious—someone whom she'd somehow never seen before. Though, hadn't she seen him? It had been briefly, the previous spring, in the rehearsal room where she'd stopped to try out an idea. As she'd danced, she'd caught him watching her, this stranger, and now here he was again, half a year later, no longer hidden in the dark, but in the spotlight, center stage.

She'd had an instinct about Duncan. She couldn't have said quite what it came down to, but some curiosity in her had been aroused—enough to persuade her choreographer friend to enlist Duncan to compose for a dance performance he was mounting. Duncan had agreed, but on the first day he was to join in the rehearsal, he lost his nerve and came in early to relay his apologies. Only Gina was around.

"I can't do this, I've never done anything like this," he'd admitted shyly.

Of course he could! She felt she knew this, that the young man she'd seen performing his extraordinary piece had far more talent in him than he acknowledged, or was even aware of in himself. In his sudden apprehension, she spotted something new in Duncan, a critical voice that interfered with his being the great musician she'd been so taken by before.

"There's no harm in trying at least, is there? I mean, maybe I can help."

She wasn't sure, once she'd said it, exactly how she might do that, but she sensed that what Duncan required was encouragement, and she felt, stirring in her, some desire to spur him on. And so she invented a story about a composer who wrote music while watching dancers dance—she hadn't really known one, but it seemed plausible enough.

She'd danced for him that morning, a solo performance with an air of dangerous intimacy. Maybe it was the strange nervousness arising in her—she liked this boy, wanted *him* to like *her*, and his opinion therefore mattered—or maybe it was the parallel fear she sensed in Duncan, the risk that he was taking in playing for her. As Duncan played, he seemed to grow more confident, and she became surprised by how the notes he chose fit to whatever she was doing. At first, it was imperfect—she found it necessary to adjust her movement, or suggest an adjustment to him, but soon it all seemed automatic and instinctual, the way his melody traced her movements, supported her and held her. She'd been startled by it, uncertain what it meant, this wordless resonance between them, but afterward, she couldn't get the experience out of her head. Dancing had been her escape, but a lonely one— before Duncan.

Most every night for the next weeks, Duncan would wait for her after rehearsals, pretending, at first, he was busy with his work, and then abandoning the pretense. He was nervous with her, his hands thrust inside his pockets as they walked, as if expressing the wish of his whole being to hide. But why? Could he be so blind to everything remarkable in him? He seemed not to realize that he was handsome, for instance, his dark hair pulled back from his thoughtful, lovely face, those red lips he'd sink his teeth into when he was thinking hard. Nor did he recognize his own talent, just how rare a gift he had, to be able to draw beauty out of thin air.

When he played music there was this boyish effortlessness about him, so different from the seriousness with which he spoke.

As they walked and talked, long pauses would open up while he considered his opinions and searched for what he meant to say, until, sometimes, she'd chirpily fill them. She was clearly more brash, but she could see that Duncan didn't mind this. In fact, it seemed to relieve him when she chimed in while he was laboring to answer some question, like what he meant to do with his life— a question she'd brought up without realizing it would send him into a tailspin. He considered all the factors—his parents' wishes, his sense of obligation, his notion of what was respectable—until she'd easily gushed her opinion: "The only point in living is to follow your passion."

"Tell me what you really think," he'd replied, laughing, and she could feel that he was grateful to her for speaking up for his desire, for briefly eclipsing the many stifling voices in his head.

If he felt lightened by her, perhaps he could have the same effect on her. She found herself relaxed with him from the start, and only more so as time went on. He was so enamored of her boldness, she felt bolder still. It became easy to tell him things she hadn't allowed herself to admit to anyone—not even Violet—like her urgent wish to have a child. Violet, who considered domesticity imprisonment, would have cringed to learn that Gina had been fantasizing about pregnancy since she was a girl. Catching sight of a mother and child together she'd feel an ache, or sometimes, just on her own and without cause, she'd envision scenes that she'd shared with her mother, but recast. She'd take her little girl swimming and let the small body cling to hers. She'd teach her how to swim and dance, and all those small, sweet childhood skills, how to tie her shoelaces, recite the alphabet, skip rope.

She hadn't let Duncan know what was behind her wish, had only mentioned motherhood, and her own mother, in passing, but it seemed to her that Duncan caught on to the sentiment behind it. After she'd told him, he'd grown thoughtful, and reached out to take her hand.

After that one touch, he hadn't dared touch her again, so it had been up to her to take hold of him one night outside his dorm, and stand on her toes to kiss him. It was the sort of kiss she'd hoped for, receptive, connected, like the way they were when she was dancing while he played. He held her tightly in the cold, the pair of them shivering after a time, from the cold and the import of what was happening.

Her daring seemed to kindle, slowly, the same within him. Sensible Duncan became more romantic, impulsive. He began showing up at her door with surprise invitations—to performances on campus and movies in town, anything she happened to mention she was curious about, his style of dating being much more quaint than that of other boys on campus, who simply showed up in girls' rooms for an evening of fun. He even made an effort to fit in with Gina's friends, though Violet made clear her suspicion of him from the start. An economics major, friends with a guy like Blake Flournoy, who represented every chauvinistic, conservative materialist Violet had set herself aggressively against—"How can you want a guy like that? He's not even an artist."

"He is," Gina insisted. "He's a brilliant one. He's just finding himself still. And he's changing."

Two weekends later, Duncan confirmed this hope in her when he arrived at her door with an invitation to a piano performance.

"The woman performing was my teacher when I was younger. Lillian. She was the first person to think I had talent, so my mother fired her, of course." He smiled at this, gloomily, then grew earnest again. "In a way she reminds me of you, or set me on a path to you, inspiring me."

"We'll go, of course," Gina told him, pleased by all the ways Duncan was embracing his musical self, loosening up his rigid devotion to his classwork, and by all the ways she was affecting him to do this. Now here was another woman who had encouraged him, long before her, and likely aroused his fantasies too. The small twinge of envy Gina felt was more than matched by her curiosity.

They took the train into Manhattan Saturday, and ended up in a small room at a library where the concert was being held. The teacher was older than she'd seemed from Duncan's descriptions, with streaks of gray in her hair and glasses that hid a pair of warm and pretty eyes. When they met after the show, Lillian hugged Duncan with such obvious affection that Gina might have been jealous, if she hadn't felt so sharply how Duncan cared for her, and how lucky this other woman thought her for that reason.

"He's an extraordinary person, this one," Lillian said, beaming, and Gina was sure that it was true, sure from how shyly grateful he seemed around them both, and for how sweetly he ended up playing, over coffees after, with Lillian's little daughter, a girl of five who hung over Duncan, enchanted.

That night, since it had gotten too late to take the train, Lillian invited Duncan and Gina to stay at her cramped Chinatown apartment. Lying curled up together on a futon, Duncan admitted something to Gina that he'd been embarrassed, before, to say. "That first piece I performed at Woolsey Hall, I wrote it for you."

Gina turned to look at him, incredulous. "But you didn't even know me yet."

"I'd seen you, though. And when I thought of you, that song

just came. I thought if I told you that, you might think I was crazy."

"You are crazy," she said, laughing, not letting on how much this thrilled her. How delighted she was to know that Duncan, with his reasoned and balanced arguments in each direction, his pragmatic future plans, Duncan, whom she feared might be a bit too sensible for her, had some madness in him too. Of course they each had to be a little crazy to fall so passionately for each other. Without passion, there could be no art and no love either, and they were going to build their lives on both. They were going to forge a love story that would be bigger and braver than either of them could ever dream up apart.

Six

Duncan // Vienna

June 1996

D*uncan woke* to knocking on the door. In his half sleep he called out, "Who is it? Who's there?"

"*Polizei,*" the voice replied.

He thought he must be dreaming, that this had to be a nightmare, a fabrication of his unconscious, images and ideas he'd somehow imbibed from his mother. Guilt and persecution, authorities with hard German accents shouting, and he in bed with lovely Gina, which was itself a sort of crime.

"Allo? Police!" the voice called from outside. "Please open the door!"

Duncan stood, shaking, seeking a way out. Their hotel room was on the top floor, and he wasn't about to go crawling through the windows anyway, with Gina standing near, looking at him worriedly, wondering what could be wrong—why the police would be knocking on their door and he would be standing with an expression of such guilt and fright.

He took the few steps to the door and paused, exhaling and

breathing in again, accepting his fate. Here it was, the moment that he'd imagined must come at some point, in some hotel or other. That he should meet such an end seemed a fitting punishment for having been greedy over his happiness. His conscience had such a hold on his perception then that it didn't occur to him to look for other explanations for what was happening, more plausible or more mundane, until he heard Gina's voice behind him. "The police. The hotel clerk must have called about the mugging."

He had to refocus his attention. The incident with the drunk from the train. Might that be all this was about?

He opened the room door and two officers strolled in, one a tall woman with a beaked nose, the other a bald man with a red moustache.

"Duncan Lowy, is it?"

"Yes, that's right." He was trying to stay calm, though it gave him a jolt to realize this officer knew who he was. The man looked at him, skeptically, it seemed. "We're sorry to be barging in on you. But we were told you were the victims of a crime last night."

"That's right," Gina replied, behind him. She'd risen to her feet, dressed in just a shirt.

The male officer averted his eyes. "We've come too early, I apologize, but we hoped to speak with you before you headed out. Maybe take a few minutes to dress, miss?"

A few minutes, Duncan thought, that might give him the time he needed to craft his responses in advance, to ready himself for whatever eventuality he might face next. The officer's English was remarkably good, as if the department had gone out of its way to send the officer most equipped to deal with Americans. And to send two officers all this way, and have them banging on a hotel door—it made no sense to go so far simply to apprehend an incompetent street thug.

The officer tapped on Duncan's shoulder and urged him to step out into the hall. Apparently he found Duncan's shirt and sweats a perfectly adequate outfit in which to continue with their interview.

"Again, apologies for catching you this way," the officer began, "but tourists like yourself, you come and go, which is why a criminal will choose to pick on you the way he has. We've had a number of such crimes reported in the area, and it's been awfully hard to get information before the victims have left. Of course, I understand it's the last thing you wish to be bothered with on your vacation."

"It's the right thing to do, though. I'm glad you've come." Duncan smiled, though inwardly he was positively furious with himself. If this really were the reason the officers had come, he'd been a fool to let it happen. He ought to have handled things better, to have made clear to Gina he didn't want the crime reported, and before that meddling clerk heard what had happened. "We should have called you ourselves, I know, but I admit that I was worked up last night."

"You're better now, then?" The man pulled a small notepad and pen from his back pocket. "Able to write up a statement?"

"Yes. I think so."

"Good. If you'd just give me your passport so I could copy down your information meanwhile."

"It's back in the room."

"I'll need you to get it, then, it's standard," the officer replied, which seemed plausible enough, and yet, as Duncan crossed back into the room to retrieve his passport, he found his thoughts drifting to more dangerous scenarios. The clerk had tipped off the police to his staying here, and they had discovered who he was and what he'd done.

Inside the room, he looked over at Gina, who was dressed now and speaking with the female officer. It seemed to him that Gina avoided meeting his gaze.

"Very good, sir," said the officer, once Duncan had returned with his passport and handed it over. The officer copied down the information and then offered Duncan the notepad. "Please write down anything you can recall of the event, every detail, especially of the assailant."

Duncan scribbled a few sentences, not wishing to be especially helpful. He had no desire to see these officers apprehend the man in question and drag this matter out. "I'm afraid I've forgotten so much. The shock of it all maybe. And to be honest, I'd had a few beers. And the beers here are twice the size they are back home."

"Do what you can," the officer replied curtly, and then went inside to confer with his partner. When the officer returned a moment later, he was examining their passports.

"I see the two of you came over to Europe separately? You and your wife?"

"Yes, um, yes." He hadn't thought the officer would take notice of that, though it wasn't too hard to account for, really. "I had to start our trip a little later." He lowered his voice, aware that Gina likely couldn't remember they'd come to Europe separately. "I had some work to finish up back home. Is that relevant in any way?"

"Only in case you are ever called in to testify. The Viennese authorities will need to be able to reach the both of you. So I did wonder if you'll be traveling together."

The End of Getting Lost

"As long as I don't piss my wife off, right?" He was trying to make light, though the prospect of Viennese officers keeping tabs on their movements alarmed him. He cleared his throat. "We'll be traveling together. Yes."

"Very good. And if the two of you could be in touch with our department when you settle in next, we'd like to have a record of where you are, so we can reach you if need be."

"Do you really want to be apprised of our every move?"

"Is that a problem?" The man's expression became stern. "I realize it's an inconvenience to you, but we do take criminal activity seriously, sir. That man attacked you. I can't imagine you'd want the same to happen to the next tourist who comes to town."

"No, no, of course not." It wasn't as if there was a way for this officer or anyone to enforce the requirement, or to know, if Duncan did offer the name of a certain hotel in a certain city, whether he was telling the truth or not. The smart approach would be to smile and agree to everything asked of him, then lie later on. "My wife and I like to be spontaneous, is all. But I don't see why that precludes my telling you where we do land."

He handed the officer the notebook with the statement he'd written up, feeling that, hoping that, their interview was over.

"Good, sir," said the man, and apologized again for bursting in upon them. "I hope it didn't give you any sort of scare."

"Well, it's a pretty effective wake-up call."

At last the officer smiled, and Duncan began to feel relieved. Cheerily, he stepped back into the hotel room, where Gina and the female officer had also evidently finished speaking. The woman tucked her notepad into her breast pocket and shook hands first with Gina, then with Duncan. The group moved over to the door, where the male officer withdrew a card and handed it to Duncan.

"When you do choose to make your next move, this is the number to call."

"Actually," Gina put in, "I think we'll leave Vienna today."

Leave today? They hadn't spoken of leaving; on the contrary, they'd discussed several destinations in Vienna they were intending to see. Suddenly, Duncan didn't know where Gina was coming from. They were moving out of sync. He turned uneasily to look at her, but she again avoided meeting his eyes. She continued to address the officers.

"We're off to Prague. I've a friend there we planned to visit."

"You have this friend's address?" the female officer inquired.

"We have a place she can be reached. Her name is Violet Sharpe, and she gets her mail through the National Marionette Theater, 1 Zatecka Street."

She knows the address, Duncan suddenly realized with dread. When and how had Gina come across it and decided on her plan?

At last the officers stepped out and Duncan closed the door behind them. He felt a nervous urge to laugh, to discharge the energy he'd been holding in, but Gina's face was grave.

"Something wrong?" he asked her, his thoughts returning to the tension of the night before. She'd had so many questions about Marina—had even managed to guess correctly that she was the person whom he'd phoned from the hotel by Lake Walen.

He stepped forward now, seeing Gina back away, and then the paranoid thought came that perhaps while he'd been led off into the hall, the other officer had been speaking to Gina about the real matter at hand. "Did that woman say something to upset you?"

"What could she have said?"

"I have no idea, I'm just asking. But suddenly you're insisting on going to Prague, announcing Violet's address. Which you couldn't even remember yesterday."

He was fishing, seeing if she might give herself away—had she been looking through his papers? Though he'd thought it wise to hang on to Violet's address, in case circumstance required that he reach her, he should have copied the information down, in hidden form, elsewhere. How careless he'd been to keep that postcard with their things.

"Memory's funny that way, isn't it?" She was staring off at the wall, still with that fixed and humorless expression.

"Gina, what's this about?" He was trying to contain the panic mounting in him. "You're acting strangely."

"*I* am?"

"Yes. And I wish you'd just open up to me. Tell me whatever's on your mind." She was still facing the wall when he came forward to touch her. As he did, she turned and looked directly up at him, so that, he later imagined, she could catch his spontaneous reaction to her question, one that shook him far more than the police had.

"Who the hell is Graham Bonafair?"

*   *   *

It was in early April, just a few months before he departed for Europe, that Duncan was home alone preparing dinner when he heard the front door buzzer. "Who is it?"

"Graham Bonafair," said the voice through the crackle.

"Do I know you?"

"Not directly," the stranger answered, "but we know someone in common. Gina Reinhold."

Duncan buzzed the man inside and stepped from the kitchen

to the door. He took a look around his living room, self-conscious suddenly, aware that he was being visited by a person—a *man*—who knew Gina, and who might report back to her what he'd observed. Since Gina had left, he'd done nothing to remove the evidence of her former presence. The postcards from their performances, the photographs of them together: these still hung on the walls. He felt a pang of shame and sadness too, thinking of the past seven months, how paralyzed he'd been. He'd written no new music, had abandoned his commission from Marina and sought no others. The house was filthy; he rarely cleaned. What did it matter? And then cleaning would involve putting away the things that Gina had left here, it would involve admitting that this was no longer her home, that she was gone. He wasn't ready to admit this, and he had a premonition that this visitor was here to press the point.

The front doorbell rang and Duncan answered, coming face-to-face with the young man out in his hall. Graham was tall and lean, his build similar to Duncan's own. He was good looking, if in a generic, bleached-out sort of way. His hair was longish, blond. He wore corduroy pants, torn at the knees but not cheap, and a linen shirt. Duncan noticed then the necklace Graham was wearing, braided leather with a turquoise stone. "Did you come up from Santa Fe?" Duncan ventured.

"That's right!" Graham offered a big, white-toothed grin. "How did you know?"

He had an open way about him, Duncan thought, the sort of openness that came from an untroubled life.

Duncan only smiled, and gestured toward the sofa for Graham to have a seat. "You and Gina, you're related? Or old family friends, is that it?"

"Sort of. My granddad was a big investor with her granddad.

But really my connection is through her dad," Graham explained. "I'm a painter. I studied with him for years. He's an amazing guy."

So Graham was Mr. Reinhold's pupil, properly admiring and obsequious. No wonder he and Gina's father got along. "And how long have you known Gina?"

"About six months. We met a few weeks after she left . . . um, New York." Graham looked away awkwardly and appeared to spot one of the photos of Duncan and Gina on the wall. He frowned before he caught himself, and Duncan sensed the reason. He could feel his mood rapidly souring, wasn't sure he wished to know anything more about this man's relationship with Gina.

"So what brings you, then?" he asked a little curtly.

"I know it's awkward, my coming by like this," Graham said, sitting forward in his seat. "Maybe I should have called instead, but I wanted this meeting to be in person."

"That's fine, you've found me."

"Okay, right. I'll get to it, in that case." Graham leaned over to pick up a bag he'd carried in with him. There were papers in it, printed, stapled. He handed them over to Duncan. "I met with a lawyer myself, to save you the hassle and the fees."

"These are divorce papers." The sight of the documents shocked him. They'd been married so briefly, he and Gina, it was a fact he'd only begun to accept when, suddenly, they were together no longer. And yet on paper, legally, he was bound to Gina still. He went searching through the pages for Gina's signature, the mark of her approval, but he found none. "Gina hasn't signed?"

"Well, I was waiting to ask her. I mean, I knew if I showed her the papers she'd wonder why I was doing this. I'd tip my hand. I'm hoping to propose, this June."

"After knowing her six months?" He was overstepping, sure, Duncan knew that, but here was this man he'd never met announcing his plan to marry Duncan's wife—it seemed to him he was entitled to be impolite.

"I realize we can't marry for a while. There's the matter of the divorce and all that. But I wanted Gina to be aware of my intentions and how serious I am."

Offering these statements to the man who'd occupied most of Gina's past—it would be cruel if it weren't a product of Graham's guilelessness. Gina couldn't possibly be satisfied by someone so naïve, Duncan thought, however well-meaning he might be.

"You're a direct sort of person, aren't you?" said Duncan.

"I guess I am." Graham appeared to rethink this. "You feel I've been too blunt with you."

"It's not an indictment. It's good to be up front."

"Well, you know. The truth was going to reach you anyway. And this seemed the more respectful thing to do, talking to you directly. I don't see why we can't be amicable. Gina never made out like you were a bad guy."

"Oh? What did she say about me, then?"

"Excuse me?"

He could see that he was making Graham uncomfortable, but to hell with it. Let him be uncomfortable. This was Duncan's chance to get some answers, after six months of uncertainty, six months during which Gina had refused to speak with him, or explain her behavior to him. She'd left him in such a state of bafflement, he couldn't bear it. Now, finally, he might understand Gina's decision to abandon him and their life together—for what? For this bland and callow stranger seated across from him now?

"I'm asking what she told you about me. About what happened. Why we split. She must have said something."

"She, um, she didn't get too detailed. There was another woman, I guess. A friend of hers."

"You mean Marina."

"She said something went on between the two of you."

"Nothing went on between us."

"Look, I, um. I'm only reporting what she told me."

"Right, sure you are." Duncan smiled to hide his irritation. He was feeling his old anger arising at the unfairness of it all, and at the uselessness of trying to convince this man of his innocence. It was a conversation he ought to have been allowed to have six months before instead, with Gina.

Looking uneasy, Graham started to fumble with his bag. "Anyhow, the papers. Why don't we get on to that, then, so I'll be out of your hair. Just a few spots for you to sign."

But Duncan wasn't letting the matter go that easily. "And what are her plans now, if I can ask? Now that she's with you?"

"Her plans?" Graham lowered the papers and exhaled. He didn't wish to answer, that was clear, but there was a favor that he wanted, and so he must have felt obliged to indulge Duncan's curiosity a while longer. "We were talking about her joining a dance studio in Albuquerque."

"Albuquerque. And you don't think that will feel like a step down, after New York?"

"Maybe that's not the worst thing. New York can wear a person out."

"Not a person like Gina. She loved this city."

"Maybe her feelings have changed."

"Maybe she wants to think they have."

"Well, you're not there with her to say one way or the other, are you?"

He could see Graham growing unnerved, offended by the implication that he knew Gina less well than Duncan. But so what if he was offended? It was the truth, wasn't it? Wouldn't Gina—his wild, marvelous Gina—be bored out of her mind living in New Mexico, with a man like this? Duncan sat there, facing his rival, determined to insist on the reality of the woman that he'd loved. "No, I'm not there with her now, but for the past six years, I have been. I think I know Gina a little."

Graham paused, as if perhaps realizing Duncan was correct, and then offered a simple "Anyway," with a sigh. "If you wouldn't mind signing the papers. That's what I came here for."

Graham handed the pages to him once again, and this time Duncan accepted them. "All right, then, I'll look these over and get back to you. How's that?"

Graham didn't appear pleased. "Don't you want to sign them now?"

"I don't sign anything without running it by my lawyer." He had no lawyer, but it had seemed the thing to say—that was what people did in such cases, consulted lawyers. The excuse would buy him time.

"I'm not sure why you'd need a lawyer, unless this is about money. Her father might be willing to arrange something for you. A little support to carry you over."

"I don't want money, for God's sake," he snapped at Graham, not meaning to, but this was really more than he could take. Had Mr. Reinhold made him out to be that desperate?

Graham hurried to apologize. "Right, I'm sure. It wasn't my intention to imply—"

"Not to worry." Duncan rose and put out his hand jovially, thinking it would be best to end the meeting now, while the mood was mostly cordial and he was coming out on top. He was feeling that he'd held his own, considering—not only because he hadn't done the thing Graham wanted, but because he felt he'd glimpsed the insecurity of the man's position with Gina. Graham had performed this errand on his own, which meant it wasn't necessarily something that Gina herself wanted—or at least it might not be.

Early the next week, Graham called to ask if Duncan had met with his lawyer yet. Duncan told him that he hadn't, and when Graham called again, he said the papers must have been misplaced. Graham offered to send another copy. For several more weeks Duncan evaded him, claiming he was still waiting on his lawyer, until Graham threatened to show up at his house again. He was leaving for Europe in two weeks with Gina, where he hoped to propose and have the paperwork finished beforehand.

"Where in Europe?" Duncan asked, explaining that he had a few meetings there himself. In fact, his good friend Blake had moved to London, he explained, and he'd be visiting Blake to interview for a job at his London ad firm. "For their music department, you know. My friend's been asking me to do it for some time."

"Too bad, we'll be in Germany," Graham replied.

"Ah, well, if my lawyer doesn't get to this before you leave, I'll come over to Germany and deliver the papers."

"Why would you do that?" Even Graham had begun to grow suspicious. "That's a lot of trouble."

"Well, I've caused you a lot of trouble, haven't I? It seems the least that I can do."

A week later, when Graham announced that he was leaving for Berlin, he'd given Duncan the name of his hotel: "Hotel de Rome. Near Potsdamer Platz."

Duncan, meanwhile, gave Graham the name of a hotel in London. In fact he had no intention of visiting London and no hotel reservation, but he assumed, and had been right to assume, that Graham wouldn't bother to check. It made him feel guilty to be lying in this way, but he told himself he wasn't duping Graham entirely, that he would give the man what he wanted and sign the papers, finally, if it turned out that this was what Gina wanted too.

But first he'd have to learn: *was* this what Gina wanted?

He devised a plan. To start, he'd told Graham that his path of travel would only take him through Frankfurt for a connecting flight, and not Berlin—could Graham meet him there instead? Graham consented, though his tone over the phone suggested an increasing amount of irritation over an otherwise simple transaction. Not that Graham's mood was Duncan's big concern when Duncan arrived in Berlin just as he calculated Graham must be leaving, and took a cab straight to the hotel. He was thinking only about Gina, worried she might have traveled with Graham and might now be in the wrong city; but Duncan relied on what he saw in Graham as a predisposition to be overly sentimental—he wouldn't ruin the surprise of the engagement by telling Gina that divorce papers were what awaited them in an excursion to Frankfurt. What excuse he gave to Gina for his quick solo jaunt hardly mattered to Duncan; all that mattered was that she trusted Graham enough to stay behind.

Arriving at the hotel in Berlin, Duncan asked after Graham at the front desk, just to make sure that the man had really gone.

"Mr. Bonafair set off this morning."

"Oh, that's a shame. A last-minute meeting, I guess. He said that he might have one."

"Are you a friend of his?"

"Of his and Gina Reinhold's. We went to college together. I assume that she left with him?"

"I don't know, sir. If you'd like to give a name, I'll call up to her room."

"Thank you, yes." He'd given the man a name, not his own—instead he'd mentioned the choreographer that had enlisted him to compose for his first show—the classmate who'd brought Gina and him together.

The desk clerk lowered the receiver. "Ms. Reinhold says she'll be right down."

He'd waited, pacing the lobby, and then forced himself to take a seat in a large leather chair, facing the elevator bay. At last an elevator opened and Gina stepped out, with an expectant look. She'd cut her hair shorter, and with the curls less weighed down, they were more girlish, her face more youthful, as if time had moved backward. She breezed through, glowing, awaiting a surprise, an old friend, ready to laugh and throw her arms around someone familiar in this very strange part of the world, having just been left alone in an unfamiliar city by her lover. And then she saw Duncan and stopped smiling. She stopped altogether, stopped right in her tracks and simply stared, her arms crossing slowly over her chest.

"What are you doing here?" she said as he approached.

"I'm sorry to catch you like this. I had to talk to you."

"*Catch me* like this? How did you find me? Who told you I was here?"

"Graham told me. He reached out to me a few weeks ago."

"Reached out to you why? Does he know you're here now?"

"No, no, that part he doesn't know. But like I said, Gina, I had to talk to you."

This discussion had all taken place in the romantic hotel lobby, between marble columns and velvet sofas, amid a cast of European characters that made it all feel that much more cinematic and unreal. He'd felt a bit ridiculous, making these grand statements, which didn't seem at all to suit him, but Gina they did suit. Another woman might have been embarrassed by the high drama, but he knew that, more than anything, Gina loved a bold gesture, and so he hoped that what he'd done might be judged favorably by her.

"Just hear me out," he told her. "Graham came to me, asking me to sign some divorce papers. He planned . . . Well, he wouldn't want me saying."

"I assume he wouldn't want you doing any of this."

Gina's sharpness threw him off. She seemed so angry that he'd come. Why should she hate to see him when seeing her aroused in him only longing and regret? "Look, I know it's selfish of me, but I had to tell you how I felt—how I *feel.*"

The meaning of all of this was dawning on Gina. "You sent him off on this Frankfurt trip."

"I had to, I—"

"For divorce papers. And why would he keep this a secret? Oh God, he's going to propose, isn't he?"

The way that she said this, not eagerly, but with a note of embarrassment even, gave Duncan the confidence to continue.

"Yes, he's going to propose. So he came to ask me to sign the papers and I didn't want to do it. I don't want to be divorced.

Maybe the marriage was a mistake in a certain sense—it was too soon, we were unsteady, and I think we both scared ourselves. But even if we were afraid of what it meant to be together, that doesn't mean we didn't want it. I know what I want. I still want you."

He awaited her reaction, tears, fists, something, but instead, Gina turned and walked away to reception, said something to the man behind the counter, and then stepped out through the revolving doors. Duncan was unsure what to do, whether to wait or run after her. In retrospect he should have run, but at the time he'd been confused and stunned still by their meeting. After a moment, he went up to the man at reception and asked what the young woman had told him.

"That she's gone out and you shouldn't bother waiting."

Still he waited. Useless as it might be, he was too miserable to do anything other than sit slumped in a chair and reflect on all the ways that he'd gone wrong. Hours went by—long enough that it occurred to him Graham could be on his way back from Frankfurt already, furious, even more furious to learn from Gina, who might call, that Duncan had accosted her. After another hour, he began to wonder whether Gina had assumed he'd go on waiting and never intended to return. Could she be so determined to avoid him that she would check in somewhere else, maybe have her luggage delivered after her? Twice he approached the staff behind the desk to ask if any messages had come from Gina Reinhold, but they assured him that none had.

After several hours spent pretending to read the paper or walking in circles outside, Duncan began to feel that he was crazy. He must be, to have come all this way to tell Gina something she didn't care to hear. She didn't wish to give him another chance.

She'd found a different man to love, and this man, unlike him, hadn't given her any cause to feel he would let her down.

Despairing, he stood, about to leave, when he saw one of the receptionists coming toward him.

"You're the one who's been waiting for Gina Reinhold, yes?"

"Yes, right. Did you hear from her?"

"Not from her. But from the hospital. Ms. Reinhold has had an accident."

He'd rushed to the hospital by taxi—it was a lucky thing, really, that he'd been notified at all. Gina had been carrying her hotel key, and whoever found her had phoned the hotel with the room number and told them to notify anybody staying with her. The receptionist had asked Duncan if he knew how Ms. Reinhold's partner might be reached.

"She told me he's out of the country. Until he's back, I can look after her."

At the hospital, a building on Luisenstrasse, the desk clerk informed Duncan that no one except family members could get information on Gina's condition or speak with her doctor. Duncan announced, truthfully, that he was Gina's husband. Shortly after, Gina's doctor stepped out to explain that she had fallen at a construction site on Potsdamer Platz and had suffered a concussion and intracranial swelling. She'd been unconscious for several hours and had woken about half an hour before, disoriented and unable to say where she was or how she'd come to be there.

"It's impossible at this stage to determine how temporary the damage to her mental functioning might be. I tell you this so that you won't be alarmed when you do see her. It's likely she won't even recognize you."

He felt as if the ground were dropping out beneath him—was

she gone, the Gina he'd known? Was he to blame? Possibly she wouldn't have taken that walk had he not appeared, or she wouldn't have been in such an agitated state after seeing him and she might not have lost her balance. In his selfish inability to let her go, he'd destroyed her, the most wonderful woman he'd ever known.

He entered the room, hardly able to bring himself to look at her, though when he did, he was relieved to find that she didn't even appear injured. There was a bandage around her head, but her face was unchanged, lovely still, and the expression she wore was remarkably focused, calm, and kind.

"You poor thing," she said to him, which had surprised him utterly, her sympathy for him, at such a moment.

He'd gasped a little, and felt a warm tear roll down his cheek.

"Oh, don't cry," she said, "I'm fine, baby, I'm fine."

He'd looked up at her, startled by the warmth in her face. He hadn't seen a look like that in so long, not since she'd left for Vienna the summer before, the summer that had ended them. Until he'd seen it, he hadn't felt so acutely how much he'd longed for exactly this.

"I'm just a bit confused," she told him. "They tell me I'm in Berlin."

"You are. We're in Berlin."

"Have we taken a trip? Our honeymoon?"

He stared at her, trying to make sense of what she was saying. Did she believe they'd come to this place together, that they were a couple still? Could she have forgotten the past year, his mistakes, all those stupid events that had come between them?

The sense of unsteadiness was overwhelming—she believed that they were starting their shared life. She had no notion that this possibility had been destroyed. He stepped forward and took a seat at the edge of her bed. He thought what he must tell her next to stop this—she was confused. She'd long ago stopped wanting to be with him.

But how could he tell her that when he could see now, in her eyes, how she did want him? Gina was brimming with emotion— the terror of her experience had woken her to what mattered, and pushed her to say things she wouldn't otherwise have dared.

"I want to start our life, to move forward, to have a child. Let's make a child on this trip, our child. Let's do that, please!"

He searched her face, that lovely mouth open a little, expectant, the half-closed eyes that begged him to join her in forgetting. He moved closer so that he could smell her sweet, familiar breath, and before he could form any words of objection, before he could collect himself enough to point out her misunderstanding, she leaned in toward him, reached for his face, and, like a figure from his dreams, drew him to her for a kiss.

He'd known he couldn't keep Gina in Berlin, and not, certainly, at a Berlin hospital. Graham wouldn't be gone long. By now he certainly would have realized he'd been stood up. Perhaps he'd guessed the reason, perhaps not, but regardless, he'd likely call the hotel to leave a message there for Gina, and also, very likely, when he did, he'd be informed of her injury and would catch the first flight back. It would all happen very quickly, and Gina's doctors were telling Duncan that they wished to keep her for more tests and observation. What might be done? He didn't know the workings of this country, had no connections here, hardly spoke the language. He'd realized that he needed help, and considered where to turn.

There was one nurse who'd distinguished herself in just those first hours. Her name was Greta and she was older, knowing, an East German. To ingratiate herself with him, a privileged American, she'd begun to offer favors: she might get Gina better bedding or an extra pillow, she might bring her some nicer food from a restaurant. Here was a woman, Duncan quickly sensed, who'd made her way through deprivation and had learned a thing or two about survival. He'd chosen to take a chance and told her—not the whole truth, he wouldn't dare do that—but as much as was needed to communicate his wishes. "I wondered if you could advise me what to do if I needed to get my wife quickly and quietly out of Berlin."

Knowing better than to ask questions, the nurse suggested he identify another clinic in another region and give a reason for her transfer. He might say Gina had a familiar doctor there, or friends or family in the area who wanted to be able to see her.

The next few hours were frantic. First, he'd enlisted Greta's help in finding a small clinic in Switzerland that seemed suitable. Then he went back to Gina's hotel and informed the receptionist that Gina would be needing her things at the hospital. The receptionist allowed him to go up to her room and pack, and Duncan had thrown everything inside the suitcase and hurried out. After, on the ride back to the hospital, he went through Gina's belongings and removed anything that might put an end to the illusion: a fresh postcard to Violet she hadn't yet sent; Gina's address book, which contained information for the new contacts she'd made in Santa Fe—colleagues at her dance studio, friends she'd made through and with Graham. He'd had to throw away her journal too, inside of which he'd found plenty of accounts of her new life. He'd felt guilty reading over her private entries, but he told himself that if he found something in her writing to persuade him what he was doing was clearly wrong, that she was happier with Graham than she'd been with him, then he would dispense with his deception.

Instead, he came upon a passage that gave him just the hope he needed to go on.

Each morning I wake up with him in Santa Fe it feels like I'm in the wrong place. It shouldn't be birds that I hear from my window, but the honking of Manhattan streets. It shouldn't be Graham reaching to stroke my hair, it should be Duncan kissing my sleeping mouth. When will it change? When will this life feel like my life?

After reading this, he knew he had to act. He must get Gina out of Berlin before Graham found her, but to do this required money. The clinics were expensive, travel was expensive, and he couldn't afford either. So he'd done the thing he'd never planned on doing. He called Marina Du Bellay.

"Duncan Lowy?" She'd been surprised to hear from him. They hadn't spoken in six months, not since he'd left the project she'd commissioned. That conversation had been brief: he'd let her know he couldn't see her or be involved with her in any way after what had happened, and yet she still insisted upon paying him at least a part of what she'd promised.

He'd refused her money, not wishing to exploit her guilt— and now here he was, forced to do precisely that.

"Hi, Marina, I'm, um, I'm sorry to call out of the blue."

"You okay? You sound agitated . . . is something wrong?"

He wasn't sure what to say; he didn't want Marina knowing

too much, just that he was in Berlin and in need of money he couldn't hide. "I'm in a bit of a jam, I guess. Otherwise I wouldn't trouble you." He had to pace the room, so tense was he that day, and overcome by the familiar and now painful cadence of Marina's voice.

"I'm glad you've called. I've felt so badly about you and Gina."

And here, he sensed, was the point to work from, the way to ask for the favor he needed.

"Actually, this is about us, Gina and I. She finally seems maybe ready to forgive me. I'd like to take her on a trip, a fresh start, that sort of thing. But trips cost money, and, well, I never did feel right accepting what you'd offered before. . . ."

"Ah, I see." Marina sighed. "I understand."

Duncan had sensed, perhaps, some small hurt he'd caused her, which aroused his regret. But he felt he had no choice, no other way of going forward. Marina promised she would wire thirty thousand dollars to a Zurich bank.

From the hospital, he and Gina took a taxi to Potsdamer Platz Bahnhof and boarded a train bound for Zurich. He'd been nervous all the way, envisioning police or checkpoint guards pulling him aside with questions, but in fact, no one approached them or even asked to see their passports. It had dawned on Duncan, as they made the passage, that for the first time in history, a visitor to Europe might move seamlessly from one nation to another, might slip unseen among twenty countries. The plot that was taking shape—to escape with Gina, crazy as it was—might also be possible.

In Zurich, Duncan breathed more easily. The culture of

anonymity that defined Swiss banks seemed to be shared by hospitals too. He'd let the head of the clinic know that privacy was a great matter to them, implying that Gina was someone of note back home. Thanks to Gina's status, as a budding starlet or heiress or whatever they imagined, she was a Swiss Jane Doe on the books. No one in Berlin knew where Gina was—he'd deliberately left the name of a different clinic with Gina's doctor there. Even if Graham were to call around to clinics in the surrounding countries, it was unlikely he'd find this rather obscure one, and once they'd left the clinic, he and Gina would be harder to find still. A detective might check the larger European hotels, but no one had the resources to keep up with the smaller guesthouses. It would be better to stick to quieter areas, regardless, for a time, in case Graham had brought his story to the press as well as to police.

In the next days, Duncan took care of smaller business. He located a jeweler and stopped in to buy two secondhand wedding bands. He'd held on to his own band, but hadn't thought to bring it with him, and he hadn't the first idea where Gina's might have been. At the store, he'd found two that looked much like the pair they'd picked together, but when he'd given hers to Gina that day, he'd been distressed to find it was too loose. After this, he arranged for an answering service to deliver his messages, in case Gina thought to check the machine they'd once shared. He was beginning to believe he had succeeded in his escape, especially since the papers he checked had nothing about Gina's disappearance. It seemed his malfeasance wasn't of interest to anyone. Only then, that night out dining in the Walensee, that pink-cheeked man at the corner table had recognized Gina.

"Sorry for staring," the man had said when Duncan went to

speak with him while Gina was in the bathroom, "but the lady you're with looks just like the girl from the Berlin papers." So her story—the accident, the disappearance, or both—hadn't gone unnoticed. In fact, it had gotten coverage significant enough to reach Switzerland. Still worse, her picture had been included with whatever was written.

He could imagine the sort of story it could be: Graham had offered up some vacation shot of her, lovely and smiling, and the tabloids had gone mad for it. *Romantic Holiday Hijacked!* the headline would read, and then below, they'd describe a young tourist who'd lost her memory and been abducted, unknowingly, by an obsessed estranged husband.

"What girl in the papers?" Duncan had asked the man, attempting innocence, heart pounding.

"There was a girl who had an accident and lost her memory. When her fiancé returned she'd been hurried off by another man."

"That's a lot of effort to make to avoid marriage," Duncan said good-heartedly, and to his great relief the man had laughed.

"You've got a point there," the man said.

"I hope my wife doesn't find marriage to me so awful."

"I'm sure not!" The stranger laughed again and apologized for staring earlier. "Obviously I mistook your wife. I'm sorry if I bothered her."

"No, no, not at all. I'll share the story with her, she'll find it funny."

Duncan shook hands with the stranger and then walked away to join Gina, all the while concealing his panic.

Gina's story was out. Anyone, any stranger at any other time, might recognize her. If he allowed himself to stop and think about the risks, really think, he'd not be able to continue. He had no long-term strategy, no inkling of how this deception could end happily for anyone, but for the time being he was focused on the here and now, on whatever machinations were required to keep from getting caught. His goal was just to make it last a little longer—the love Gina seemed to bear toward him, the bottomless devotion he felt then toward her.

To do this he'd have to manage Gina's correspondence. Her father, Violet, Graham . . . any contact with these people would easily cast suspicion on him, if not expose his ruse entirely. He'd luckily managed to convince Gina that calling home might upset her father, but he still must intervene with the letter she'd planned on sending. Instead of the actual letter, he'd given Ms. Arner an empty, misaddressed envelope, and he'd held on to the original in case he should need to write another one in Gina's hand, on her behalf.

Later, on his first night in Vienna, after hearing Mr. Reinhold's message, Duncan had decided it was time to write a letter to set him at ease. After he'd returned from his phone calls, he read Gina's letter over, gathering clues about the style she employed with her father:

Dear Dad,

I'm writing to you from the countryside not too far from Zurich where Duncan and I have been resting up after Berlin. Berlin was thrilling and exhausting. I'm sure you'd be inspired by it. Everywhere the past is being smashed and rebuilt. Imagine a whole city intent on erasing history. . . .

Duncan had to smile, reading this—Gina, who had no memory of Berlin, was lying too! True, she was doing it for the best of reasons, to spare her father worry over her injuries, but she wasn't just adjusting the truth a bit, she was *embracing* the lie. So much of her letter was false that he was able to keep most of it, excluding just the references to his being with her. From this beginning, which he wrote out again, he added two more paragraphs in her excited, rounded script.

> *I've been wracking my brain over how much of this to tell you,*
> *since we're apart and you might worry. Though I promise you,*
> *you have no reason to. I'm fine, really better than fine. I think*
> *you probably need to hear that from me, especially since Graham*
> *might come to you—might have come to you already—and give*
> *you a different impression. I can imagine what sort of speculation*
> *Graham might have engaged in, and probably triggered in you*
> *too. So I want you to hear the story from me.*

After this, Duncan had described more or less accurately what had happened in Berlin, that Graham had gone off for a meeting, that she'd taken a walk and been injured:

> *I'm sure it must be very scary to hear that—and Graham might*
> *have suggested that I've only left him because I'm not myself. But*
> *I am myself, Dad, I really am. That accident gave me a shock.*
> *I woke up, like a stranger to my life, and suddenly it seemed so*
> *clear—I've been living in a way that doesn't fit me. One thing*
> *that I felt, with some sadness, but also relief, because I'd caught*
> *myself in time: I don't want to be married to Graham Bonafair.*

*He's a good person, I know that, and he loves me, and maybe I
even love him a little. But not enough. Not the way I want to love
the person that I marry. As for Duncan . . .*

He left off there, thinking over what precisely would be the
thing to say about himself. He might, for instance, choose to tell
Gina's father that the two of them were reunited and traveling
together, but he worried that to do it now might add to Graham's
alarm. "You see," Graham would say, "she's clearly not in her
right mind if she ran back to Duncan so quickly." Whereas if
Gina were to travel on her own for a few weeks, and then decide
to give Duncan another shot, well, who could find fault with her,
really, for that?

*I'm well aware that Duncan's hurt me in the past. But this
accident has made me feel that I need to give myself some time to
sort through my emotions. I've decided to travel for a while on my
own now. I might go to Rome or Paris or Budapest—I'll write to
you again or call once I'm more settled, but, for now, I want you
to know that things are good with me and you don't need to be
concerned.*

*Meanwhile, I hope you're staying cool in the Santa Fe
summer. Wear a hat—maybe I'll pick one up for you, something
stylish from Paris or Rome. Miss you, Daddy, and love you.*

*Your girl,
Gina*

When he was through, and having thought it over at some
length, the letter seemed to him the right one to send. Certainly

it offered a more plausible explanation for those events Graham might have outlined to Gina's father already. Was there really any question which account was the more likely? That Gina had chosen to go off to contemplate her future, taking time to consider Graham's proposal, or that she'd been kidnapped by Duncan, kept in a state of permanent illusion? This story sounded so outrageous that, if he hadn't been living that wild reality daily, he wouldn't have believed it himself.

The letter had come out so well—even the penmanship matched Gina's—that Duncan imagined he would be writing again. For this reason, he'd held on to Violet's postcard, too, in case he should see a motive to write to Violet as he had Gina's father. It hadn't occurred to him what a great risk he was taking by keeping these items with him, how one day Gina might stumble across them and he'd face a moment like he was facing now.

*   *   *

Standing before him, in their Vienna hotel room, unsettled yet determined, Gina was describing the events of the last night that had led her to ask after Graham Bonafair.

"I couldn't sleep and I'd thought I'd write a letter, so I'd gone to look for paper. I couldn't find the stationery, but I know you keep some in your folder, so I thought I'd take a sheet. I'd only picked it up when a postcard fell out, with Violet's address and a return address from the Hotel de Rome. You hadn't mentioned that we'd stayed there, so I called them, out of curiosity, and they told me I had a message waiting. From someone named Graham Bonafair."

He stood there, hearing all this, sweat broken out over his lip. He was an instant from confessing the truth, which he was sure she must have discovered already. If she'd gotten this far, then nothing would keep her from speaking with Graham, who would tell her the whole story. And even if they hadn't spoken, Gina must have deduced the truth on her own. He took a breath and studied her more closely, her brow knit and eyes wide. There was confusion in her face, fear and hope, and, he sensed, some tenderness.

She doesn't know, he thought. He might survive this still.

"Graham's a friend of your father's. A former student. A painter from Santa Fe." He was impressed by how matter-of-factly he offered up this information.

Gina too seemed somewhat disarmed by his neat explanation. "And why is a friend of my father's calling me?"

"Gina," he said gently, gaining time, "I can see whatever you're thinking right now isn't good. I guess you're wondering if I hid that postcard on purpose. And you must be thinking that if I did, that means I'm hiding other things from you."

"You never sent my father's letter," she fired at him. "I found that in the folder too."

"All right, yes. I can explain all of that. I intended to—I wasn't planning to keep you in the dark forever, but you'd suffered a trauma, and I didn't want to overwhelm you right away." He took a step from her, arms crossed, contemplating. He must think quickly. "So, to start with Violet. You're right I kept her address from you for a time—though I only held on to it because I knew we'd make the visit at some point, when you were ready. But Violet's a loose cannon, and if we were to visit her, I couldn't know what she might say."

"Say about what?"

He took her hand, leading her over to the bed—giving the

impression he meant to proceed with care, though really he required the extra seconds to formulate his answer. "It hasn't been an easy year for you, and after your accident, more disorientation wasn't what you needed."

"Well, I can handle it now," she insisted, though worried wrinkles appeared across her forehead. "Whatever happened, I want you to tell me."

He sighed. "There was an argument."

"The one with Violet?"

"No, I just said that to protect you. The rift was with your father."

"My father?"

"You weren't speaking, which was why I couldn't have you calling him or sending him letters. Or seeing Violet either, for that matter, since she's not one to keep her mouth shut."

Gina was peering at him sideways, incredulous. "But what could my father have done that was so terrible?"

"I didn't say it was terrible. He's human, he's got his own selfishness too." What had begun as a lie told out of expedience was becoming, Duncan realized, a small act of revenge. There was a time he'd begged Gina's father to help soften Gina's anger against him, to move her to forgive his failings, but the man had only turned him away.

"Tell me what happened, Duncan," she asked, growing impatient.

"I really hate making you relive this, but all right. You'd gone down to Santa Fe to visit him and he was trying to persuade you to stay. To get out of New York for a while. You know how he's always pushing for more time with you, and he was eager to have you to himself, away from me."

"So there was an issue with *you*, then?" The suspicious look was back again.

"No, no. I mean, he's not my greatest fan, you know this, but your fight had nothing to do with me." Gina seemed so ready to blame him. He must not give her any grounds to do so. "While you were staying there I had a call from the artistic director at PS 122. He wanted you to produce a piece for their spring festival and I tried to get the message to you, but your father chose not to relay it. You'd have had to come back to New York, and he didn't want you leaving."

He watched her take this in, knowing how meaningful that invitation would be, and knowing how much conviction the story possessed because it was mostly true. PS 122 was the venue she'd first visited with Violet back in school; the performance she'd seen there had inspired her fantasy of moving to New York. To stage her own work there would be to fulfill one of her dreams.

"So what happened?" Her voice was tentative now, smaller, childlike.

"What happened was the spot was given to someone else." He nodded and exhaled, as if he were finally letting go of all his secrets. "You were so hurt and angry after. There was a fight about it, with your dad. You didn't tell me details, just that you'd realized he was interfering in your life in ways that were not healthy and that you needed to get distance from him. That was part of the motive behind this trip, to get away. We both knew the situation would be less painful if you were distracted, and your dad wouldn't be able to get ahold of you. Though naturally he would try. I can only assume that's why this Graham Bonafair person was calling. To persuade you to get back in touch with your father."

"This is crazy. Some stranger phoning because my father won't."

"That's how bad it got between you."

Gina spun about the room, moving restlessly, as she always did when something upended her understanding.

"You can call the theater to confirm this if you need to. The artistic director will remember."

Gina heard this and slowed down. It must have occurred to her that he wouldn't lie about a detail that could be so easily checked. Moreover, even if Gina hadn't objected to her father's efforts to control her, she'd begun to recognize them, over time.

"No," said Gina, speaking more calmly. "I believe you."

"Gina, I'm sorry." He *was* feeling sorry then, for so many things. "I'm sorry I didn't tell you sooner. I hated to lie, but with all you were facing, to make you doubt your connection to your father seemed too cruel." He meant this, he really did, and so the words came across with conviction—which was really the most awful part about it all. It *was* cruel to make Gina doubt her father in the midst of all the uncertainty she faced, and yet this was precisely what he was doing now.

For several minutes after hearing what he'd told her, Gina sat quietly at the edge of the bed, and he assumed her thoughts and mood had finally settled. But then, rather suddenly, she moved to the hotel dresser and began tossing their clothes into the suitcase.

"You're packing?" He tried not to sound nervous, though this action could mean different things: that she meant to leave Vienna or Europe altogether—or that she meant to leave *him*. Had she not believed him?

"Like I told the officers," she replied simply, "I'd like to get moving today."

"To Prague, then?"

"Unless you have some objection. Now that I do know the truth," she went on, "there's nothing to fear from my meeting Violet, is there?"

She turned then, with a strange smile on her lips, and in that instant he knew that his success in convincing her—if in fact he had convinced her—would be short-lived. Prague would be the end for him. If Gina managed to find Violet, their meeting would allow her to test every lie he'd told her until now. And Violet, who'd never liked him, would be only too happy to reveal his hoax. He'd barely survived Vienna—Astrid Du Bellay, the mugger, the police—still the police might come back for him, and yet he'd have preferred staying where they were to traveling to Prague. As it was, he was only trading in one set of dangers for another that was worse.

Seven

Gina // Prague

June 1996

They left for Prague from the Westbahnhof station. Tired from her sleepless night, Gina curled up in her seat and managed to doze for nearly all of the four-hour ride. Her exhaustion was so deep she wondered if more might be behind it—the shocks of the past day, Duncan's lies and the explanation that he'd given, her estrangement from her father. She would call her father, she'd decided, the first moment she found herself alone—so as not to clue Duncan in on her doubts about his story.

Now and again, while she dozed, when the tracks would squeak or someone would walk past her and stir her from her sleep, she would open her eyes and observe Duncan, staring out the window in the seat across from hers, handsome, caring Duncan, whom she'd loved and trusted more than anyone for years, and whom, it panicked her to think, she wasn't sure she should trust still.

They arrived at Hlavni Nadrazi station around one, and Gina suggested they head straight to the National Marionette

Theater, to see if anybody there could provide them with Violet's address.

"Before we go searching the city, we should at least drop off our bags."

Duncan's point was sensible enough, though this meant they'd need to locate a hotel and book a room. He took an especially long time calling around from the station before Gina finally insisted on a spot—a small guesthouse on Kaprova Street, just south of the Old Town and walking distance from the Marionette Theater.

They took a taxi the short drive from the train station, through charming streets that were more crooked and individual than Vienna's, the buildings smaller, uneven, brightly painted in different pastel shades. After they dropped their things, Duncan proposed a short detour to the river on the way to the theater, and since this would only delay them slightly, Gina agreed. They proceeded north, to the pathway on the right bank of the Vltava River. The walkway was planted with trees and there were benches where one could sit and look out over the iron fence to the left bank of the city, at the neat white buildings with orange roofs, green trees spread throughout.

After walking for some time, Duncan proposed they sit and enjoy the view. They were near the Charles Bridge, and in view of Prague Castle, which was situated across the river, on a hill. Duncan read aloud from the guidebook about the castle, but Gina wasn't listening. The briny smell of the river was making her feel ill and she was eager to get on to Violet's. She stood, impatient, and pressed Duncan to go on.

The National Marionette Theater was only a short distance, in the Old Town of Prague, just below the Jewish Quarter. The theater itself was housed in a rather modern building on Zatecka

Street—the only hint this was a theater was the large puppet perched above the wooden entrance. Inside, a cluster of young people were chatting and smoking in the corner, and an old man with a beard was seated at a desk, behind stacks of books. All around him puppets hung slack at the ends of their strings, staring at whatever visitor should step up to the desk. Gina asked the man if he might know how to find Violet Sharpe.

"Violetta, the American, you mean?"

The man called out to the group of young people in the corner, and one of them, a man in a black turtleneck, gestured for Gina and Duncan to follow. They stepped out onto the street and went around the corner to a café, a simple space crowded with tables and ugly vinyl booths. The air was choked with cigarette smoke and a smell of grease so strong Gina feared she might throw up. She was in a hurry to get out, but the young man proceeded slowly, stopping to chat with his many acquaintances. The patrons were mostly in their twenties, a mix of nationalities, but seemingly at the same stage in life—between being students and adults, caught in limbo, she imagined, in a city that was caught in limbo too, stuck in a reckless moment between the solid past and the soon-to-be-defined future.

The young man stopped in front of a table at the back of the café and spoke in Czech to the five people seated there. One of them, a young woman, stood and introduced herself as Buella.

She was very tall, with freckled, pale skin and eyes an almost burning yellow brown—stunning, in that lizard-like way of certain Eastern European beauties, a model of impenetrable perfection. Unthinkingly, Gina glanced at Duncan, who quickly looked away from the stranger. She'd never felt awkward in Duncan's presence with pretty women in the past, but the events of the last day had upset her faith. As she more clearly began to realize, she still had misgivings about Duncan and Marina Du Bellay. Violet, hopefully, could tell her what had transpired.

"We're here to visit Violet Sharpe," Gina informed the pretty stranger.

The girl nodded and paused to light a cigarette. "The car is outside. I can take you."

They drove together in the very old, small car while the girl smoked in the front with the window down, the wind blowing the smoke back in Duncan and Gina's faces. They were driving to the Zizkov district, Buella explained, as they entered an area populated with cheaper, simpler buildings covered in graffiti. Between some of the buildings were open lots where homeless people had put up shanties. In the distance stood a very tall and narrow tower, white with a red-and-white-striped tip. It looked so much like a spaceship that Gina asked Buella to tell her what it was.

"The TV tower," Buella answered. "Under communism, people called it the ugliest building in Prague. But now it's different. Now the city is made beautiful for tourists and we begin to love the ugly parts."

Naturally Violet, Gina thought, would be drawn to the ugly parts of Prague, where the disgruntled and dispossessed were bound to be, those who didn't simply embrace the West and its smug improvements. In the ugly parts, where there would be unrest, there would also be the impulse to make art. It was a brave thing her friend had done, she felt, leaving the comforts of New York, where Violet had always been accepted, to seek her own place in the unsettled and unknown. She found it beautiful and also vertiginous, and marveled to think that Violet had made this move, leaving behind a place where she'd belonged much more than Gina could imagine ever belonging anywhere. In that instant, Gina experienced a slight tremor herself—a sense of her own disorientation, her distance from her home, geographical and emotional—caused by her doubts about her father, and about Duncan too.

The car turned onto a block of six-story buildings in light greens, pinks, and yellows. Violet's was a fading shade of peach. Buella rang the buzzer, and after a long pause, the door opened. A girl answered and at first Gina took her for a stranger, but then the woman spoke to her familiarly in perfect English.

"Gina! I had no idea you were coming today!"

The voice she knew—rasping, high. "Bette, my God!" She hugged her old classmate, surprised that Bette was still with Violet and embarrassed that she hadn't recognized her. Bette's curly hair was shorter, a thick, dark mane around her face, and she was plumper than she'd been before.

"Duncan." Bette looked him over, clearly taken aback. "A lot of surprises today."

Duncan stood, rocking on his heels, hands in his pockets, smile tense. "Sorry to drop in suddenly midday. I'm assuming Violet must be out?"

"She's at our performance space, a few blocks south. But she usually comes back home for lunch around two or three, so your timing's perfect. I was just finishing cooking."

Buella returned to the car and the others proceeded up two flights of stairs and into the apartment, furnished with cheap, old-fashioned items: a worn sofa, a threadbare rug, pillows piled on the ground. Gina was sure that if she were to sink into one, it would release a plume of dust. She headed for a sliding door across the room, which opened up onto a balcony. She needed some fresh air.

"You can wait outside if you like." Bette pulled the door open wide and gestured to the four chairs gathered around a rain-wrecked table.

The balcony floor was made of tiles, many of which were chipped or loose. The guardrail was missing for about five feet at the end of the balcony closest to the street—though Gina assumed that even where the rail stood, it offered at best an illusion of security. Below the balcony was a patch of ground overrun with weeds, and a pile of rotten boards that must once have formed a walkway or a fence. When Gina turned to peer over the edge, she felt her heart beat faster.

"It's not much now," Bette said, gesturing to the open lot below. "But Violet has plans to make the whole building a residence for artists."

"She owns the entire building?" Gina asked, impressed.

"This and the theater space, yeah. Where Violet is now."

"Maybe we should call her and let her know we're here," Gina proposed.

Bette smiled wistfully. "Oh, now you're reminding me of home. We don't much do phone calls in Prague. I mean, hardly anyone that we know has a working line. It takes six months to get a phone installed, and that's assuming you're lucky. Nothing to do but wait, I'm afraid. But if you're hungry, we can at least start eating. I'm sure with some bread and rice we can stretch things out to four."

In fact Gina was ravenous, hungry in a gnawing way that seemed strange to her—as if she'd just run miles.

Bette entered the kitchen and returned again after a few

minutes carrying two platters of food, one piled with dumplings, the other with potato pancakes.

They'd only begun setting out the dishes when there was a noise in the next room and Violet came strolling in. Her hair was different—cut jaggedly and then dyed orange—but otherwise she was eternally the same: tall, bold-faced, and smiling. At the sight of Gina she tipped her head back and grinned, revealing her large, gapped teeth. She crossed the room in two grand strides and pulled Gina in for a powerful hug. "I don't believe it. No way. Gina Reinhold. The one and only."

When Violet finally released her, Gina saw her look over at Duncan—once and then again, clearly startled and far from pleased to see him there.

"I realize we came unexpectedly," he offered. "I hope we aren't putting you out."

"A visit from Gina could never put me out." Again Violet cast an assessing glance in Duncan's direction, while Gina sat, perplexed. Then, after an awkward pause, she pulled up a chair alongside Gina, and suggested to Bette that she bring out some cold drinks. "There's beer in the fridge," she said, and, turning to Gina, added: "People don't know that some of the world's best beers are from here."

When the drinks were brought and poured, Violet offered a toast. "To old friends and fresh horizons."

Bottles clinked around the table, and Violet's words seemed to echo in Gina's head. It was uncanny, really, meeting familiar people in an unfamiliar place. She'd been feeling so unsteadied by her accident, by the past that she had lost, that everyone and everything seemed to be floating, unmoored, like objects in a dreamscape.

Violet was watching her; she seemed to be guessing at her thoughts. "It's a strange meeting, isn't it, all of us here? I can't seem to make sense of it myself."

"Well, I think it's remarkable, really, what you've done. Starting from scratch somewhere with no connections. It takes enormous courage."

Violet closed her eyes, a gesture between modesty and the savoring of a prize morsel. "Either courage or just stupidity."

Across the table, Duncan gave a nod.

Violet noticed this and turned to look at him, eyes narrowed. "And what brings you here, Duncan? I can't say I expected our meeting again."

There was a beat, a tense silence, before Duncan replied. "A lot has happened since you and Gina were last in touch, I think. And, well, I should tell you. She had an accident not long ago. She's still recovering, so we're trying to take it easy."

"What sort of accident?" Violet turned to Gina now, abruptly.

"I had a bad fall in Berlin. There was some swelling in my brain."

"Oh no," exclaimed Bette. "Are you okay?"

"Fine. Some memory issues still, but fine." She didn't mention the dizziness she was feeling then. She'd had only a few sips of beer, but drinking in the heat of the afternoon and on an empty stomach had not been a good idea.

"She's doing well," Duncan confirmed. "We're just easing back into things, you know. It seemed like a good idea for her to be surrounded by old friends."

"Just how much have you forgotten?" Violet asked Gina, ignoring Duncan and leaning in, thick brows furrowed.

"Hard to say. It's getting better, though."

"Thankfully," Duncan added. "But I'm sure Gina doesn't want to just talk about her injury. Bette says you're opening a theater."

"Well, yes." Violet couldn't help but show excitement at the chance to talk about her project. "It wasn't something I'd planned to do, but the arts here are in jeopardy. The cost of property is skyrocketing, foreign investment is flooding in, so other forces need to assert themselves also. The city is so charming, people will to try to claim it, and you want it to be the people who genuinely get it and not, you know, *the guys who just want to take advantage.*"

There was a tone of challenge in Violet's statement, Gina observed, though she couldn't say quite what it was about, whether what was at play between Duncan and her friend was any more than the old antipathy.

Violet had been at odds with Duncan from the very beginning. Gina supposed that they were very different people, really. Violet had grown up with parents in the arts and had always operated as an insider and connector of people. Duncan, meanwhile, was by nature an outsider. That hadn't mattered much in college, but in New York people relied on contacts from music schools, which Duncan didn't have, nor was he capable of cozying up to those who could help him—like Violet, or even, though he'd finally, shamefully accepted her commission, Marina Du Bellay. There was just some stubborn part of him that refused to compromise or ingratiate himself, which Violet took as arrogance. More than once she'd let Gina know her view: that Duncan was rigid, dour, and selfish, and sure to hold her back.

In any case, if Duncan picked up on Violet's hostility today, he didn't let it show. Smiling, he congratulated her on her projects.

"It all sounds very impressive, what you're doing here. I'd love to see the theater."

"Yes," Gina chimed in, "I'd love to see it too."

"Actually, you can see the building from here." Excited by their interest, despite whatever other reservations she had, Violet rose from her chair and went to stand at the balcony's edge, a hand perched on the precarious rail. "It's in the direction of the TV tower, there on the right. With the yellow roof."

Gina came to join her, peering out over the city at the bright rooftops and spires, and the odd futuristic tower they'd seen as they drove in. A tile wobbled underfoot, and she made the mistake of looking down over the railing at the ground below. Suddenly her vision swirled and was flooded with light, and she had the sense that she might faint. She stepped back quickly and grabbed onto a chair for support.

"Are you all right?" Duncan asked her, on his feet now, holding her arm.

"Tired, I guess. Maybe the beer."

"Did you drink the water here?" Bette put in. "I was sick as a dog my first week."

"You look pale," Violet observed, coming closer to her. She took hold of Gina's hand. "Come inside for a minute. I've got a thermometer somewhere." Duncan began to follow, but Violet told him to stay put. "You all finish eating. I've got her."

"I'll be fine," Gina said, though she had a momentary fear that she might not be fine, that these symptoms might be connected to the light-headedness and nausea she'd felt after the accident. She hadn't had such symptoms in almost two weeks, and her memories were beginning to feel less foggy, but still the fear gripped her. The issue could be neurological; this was a residue of childhood, her dread, back to a time when every headache and dizzy spell made her jump to the word *stroke*.

Violet entered the bathroom first, where she rummaged through an old cabinet with a cracked mirror. After a minute, Violet was cursing. "I swear we had one."

"Never mind. I don't think I have a fever."

"Something's wrong with you," said Violet, "I can see it."

Yes, Gina knew this to be true, even if she couldn't say what it was. The sensations were familiar, eerily so.

"I think I should just lie down for a few minutes," she told Violet, who led her into her bedroom, which was stuffy like the rest of the apartment, with musty, heavy furniture, lace curtains, a floral rug. Candles stood on the bedside table, alongside an odd little sculpture of an enormous woman, which Gina stared at while she breathed in deeply. She was trying to focus on the room, on where she was, but images began crowding her thoughts: She was in a room that seemed to spin around her. There were mirrors on the velvet walls, and hanging lamps. People were laughing, hardly noticing when she stood from the table and walked out. One man followed her, the Frenchman she'd met in Vienna. He'd asked if she was feeling well: *You look like you might faint.*

She felt the same way now, thoughts coming to her as in a fever. She jerked upright at the impression that the sheets around her must be bloody. She searched the floral pattern, but there was, of course, no blood.

"What's going on?" Violet was sitting on the bed beside her, watching her, concerned.

"I . . . I don't know. Probably it's the water, like Bette said."

"It's not just that," Violet said, lowering her voice. "I mean all of it, your showing up like this, with *Duncan*. Is it the accident? Just how much have you forgotten?"

"I don't know."

"Our talks last fall? The time you called me crying?"

"About my father?"

"No, not your father. You really don't remember?"

"How's my girl doing?" Duncan's voice startled her. Gina hadn't seen him enter the room.

Violet turned to face him, impatient, even hostile. "We're managing fine, thanks."

Duncan ignored this and came to sit ahead of Violet on the bed. He put his hand to Gina's forehead. "Maybe I should get you back to the hotel."

"We're not done talking," said Violet.

"That can wait, can't it? Probably it should wait, if Gina's not well." Duncan peered down at her, studying her as she studied him too, the thinly veiled anxiety behind his show of care. "I think maybe she needs a doctor," Duncan concluded.

"If she needs a doctor, I'll call a doctor," Violet countered.

"I think I'll be all right," Gina spoke at last, addressing Duncan now. "I'm fine, just need to rest a bit. I'll join you out there soon."

Violet heaved a sigh as Duncan stepped out of the room without shutting the door behind him. He walked away, and through the opening Gina could see him moving hesitantly toward the balcony.

"You said I'd called you crying," she resumed in a whisper, trying again to concentrate on Violet. Violet began to answer, but Gina hardly heard her, for in that instant, a very strange thing occurred. At first, she imagined it was another illusion, a product of her illness. Duncan was there, across the room, on the balcony, and then he wasn't.

She'd never been so frightened in all her life. The only event she could compare it to was that awful day, when she was nine, when she'd found her mother fallen in the shower. A terrifying moment, but then she'd only heard the crash and come in after, whereas this time she'd turned to look at Duncan and caught sight of him at the precise instant he'd leaned back on that perilous balcony in a spot where there was no guardrail to hold him.

She'd seen his body tip backward into the air, and, disbelieving, she'd seen it sink out of her sight, soundlessly, arms out as if wishing to be caught in a saving embrace.

Eight

His body hit the ground with such a powerful jolt it felt like the breath was sucked out of his lungs. He felt nothing but a buzzing numbness; he heard nothing but ringing in his ears. When he slowly opened his eyes he saw blue sky above, and then Gina's panicked face above his own. She was speaking to him, asking him if he was okay. Her voice came out muffled. His was a gasp.

"Gina."

"You can see me? Hear me?"

"Yes."

Her hand was trembling as she reached for his. "Are you in pain?"

"I don't know. What happened?"

"Ask him if he can move," said Violet, standing out of view, some feet away.

"No, don't!" Gina ordered him, pinning down his arms. More calmly, she explained: "I think the rule is to lie still until the paramedics come."

"Is that right?" Bette's voice now, Duncan realized, coming from somewhere near. He was afraid to turn his neck to see.

"Somebody needs to call an ambulance!" Gina shouted, looking up to where the other girls must be standing. "Please call whatever 911 is here, tell them what's happened!"

Duncan was dimly aware then of a discussion taking place around him. The ringing in his ears was growing dimmer, and he could make out phrases, even those spoken in a hushed voice, at some distance. "The hospitals in this city . . . who can say when or even if . . . but we know someone . . . a real doctor, absolutely. . . ."

"All right, then, get him," said Gina, and came again to crouch by Duncan and take his hand in hers. He was squeezing her palm, holding on for dear life. He felt her grip against his, squeezing back. *He had her.* And so, he told himself, even if bones were broken, even if the damage was worse, what he'd done was worth it.

"Duncan, eh?" A stranger was kneeling above him now, with his thinning black hair pulled into a ponytail.

"Duncan, yeah," he croaked.

"My name's Terry," said the man, in a thick Australian accent. "I'm the next-door neighbor but I'm also a doctor, right? And I'm gonna give you a little look-see, eh?"

The man leaned down next to him and peered into his eyes. He then wagged his fingers back and forth in front of Duncan's face, and asked permission to check under his shirt. "This hurt you, mate? When I press here?"

Duncan writhed away. The pain was searing.

Terry slapped his knees and stood, addressing Gina. "Your friend's bloody lucky he landed somewhere soft." Turning back to Duncan, he explained. "You've got some bad bruising in one spot on the side there. Possibly a fractured rib, but there's really not much to do about that except stop falling off of buildings."

"Thanks," said Duncan weakly.

"Pick up a thermometer," the man resumed, facing Gina, "and if his temp goes above thirty-nine, or if you notice some red or yellow in his eyes, you get him to a hospital. Other than that, get your hands on some good painkillers and he should be all right. So, anyone got a ciggy?"

The Australian went to get a smoke from Bette, and Gina came to tell Duncan that Buella would pick them up by car. When Buella arrived, Duncan tried sitting up. A shooting pain in his chest made him cringe, but other than that, he seemed to be all right. He rubbed the back of his head to be sure there was no blood.

Soon Gina and the Australian were helping Duncan into the back seat. Gina sat beside him, telling Buella to take them to a hospital.

"No hospital," Duncan insisted. If he were admitted, he'd be stuck there, a sitting duck, while Violet would be free to tell Gina everything, to uncover his ruse and call Graham or Gina's father, or else notify the police to come pick him up. "You heard Violet's opinion of the local hospitals. And that doctor says I should be fine."

Gina eyed him, concerned. "You could have a concussion, internal injuries."

"If anything goes wrong, we'll go then." He didn't wait for Gina to agree, but sat achingly forward to give Buella the address of their hotel.

As Buella started the engine, Violet and Bette stood looking on, Violet frowning, obviously frustrated by all that she still wished to say. Meanwhile, the Australian doctor leaned down to Duncan's open window to offer some final advice.

"Don't forget to stop at the pharmacy first, pick up the strongest painkillers they have." He reached in to clap Duncan on the shoulder. "And don't be stinting, mate, because that's gonna bloody hurt heaps later on, eh?"

When Duncan awoke his mouth was dry, the sheets were wet, and his entire body ached so much he was terrified to move. He'd fallen asleep before nightfall, as soon as he and Gina got back from the pharmacy to their room, when the pills he'd taken had kicked in. He'd taken three times the recommended dose, and that was of the strongest formula he could buy without prescription. Still, by now the medicine must have worn off. Gasping as he did, he turned in bed to see Gina beside him, sleeping. The pills, he recalled, were in the bathroom. Digging his teeth into his bottom lip, he swung his legs down to the floor and sat up in bed. After catching his breath, he readied himself for the next jolt of pain, got to his feet, and tottered to the bathroom to collapse against the sink.

He studied himself in the bathroom mirror. There was a bruise along his left side, turned a deep purple. He was grimacing and he imagined that his jaw might be locking. Could it be tetanus? Had he ever had a tetanus shot? What if there had been rusted nails among the dirt and rubble where he'd fallen? Was tetanus fatal? Was he putting his life at risk by failing to care for himself properly? He swallowed two more pills with bottled water and stripped off his sweaty clothes—stiffly, painfully—dropping them on the floor. He felt like an old rusted nail himself. Wrapped in a towel, he sat down on the toilet seat to wait for the pills to take effect.

His thoughts were racing, circling over the madness of the last days, the sheer insanity of this thing that he'd done—throwing himself off of a building. It *was* an act of insanity, and yet he'd been so rational in his thinking just before. He'd seen no other way to stop Violet in that moment, other than throwing Violet herself over the balcony. She was going to tell Gina everything and his blissful time with her would be over. What, then, was there to hold onto, what more really was there to lose? He'd looked down at the ground below, the weeds and threadbare shrubs. Then he'd come to stand in the place without any railing, closed his eyes, and leaned back, as if to brace himself against the rail he knew would not be there. He'd felt his body pitch backward, a sickening thrust in his stomach as he fell, his foot scraping the balcony's edge. Falling, he'd told himself not to be stiff, to let gravity deposit him however it might—if he were lucky, at the feet of the woman whose love he would risk his life to keep.

The pain had subsided a little but he couldn't stop shaking; his mouth was so parched he felt like he'd swallowed sand. He ought to get himself some water—he'd gone through the only bottle he and Gina had picked up, so he'd check the lobby. He slipped out of the hotel room, dressed in a robe, unable to stop shivering as he staggered to the stairwell, taking a full ten minutes to make it down three flights of stairs.

As he neared the lobby landing at the bottom of the steps, he heard a voice, a young man's voice, distressed, speaking English.

"Let me call up, please."

"I'm sorry, sir," said another voice, softer, official. "The phones don't work in all the rooms. And anyway, we can't allow our guests to be disturbed in the night. Not unless it's an emergency."

"It *is* an emergency. You're harboring a criminal, you under-stand? If I have to I'll come back with someone from the embassy."

He knew this voice. He'd imagined words like these, a scene like this—so much so that he had to wonder if it might be a fe-verish hallucination. He had to have a look, as risky as it was to step into view where he might also be seen. He tiptoed silently and peered around a pillar and into the main lobby. There the man was, looking much the same as he had when Duncan had met him: linen shirt, shaggy blond hair, but with a newly strained and weary expression on his handsome face. Graham Bonafair had found them.

Duncan returned to his room in a panic—how stupid he'd been to give Buella the address of their hotel! He ought to have con-sidered the danger, the likelihood that Graham had reached out to Violet, or that she, grown suspicious, would reach out herself. He'd led Graham right to their door. Now he must think of a way out. Perhaps he ought to wake Gina, make an issue of his injuries and insist on going to a hospital. Though the risk was that Gra-ham would intercept them, and even if not, he'd probably come looking for them at hospitals next. There had to be a solution, but Duncan couldn't come up with one. As he took a seat on the bed, his mind felt thick from medication and from sheer exhaustion. His body seemed weighted, sucked against the mattress. At some point he gave in and lay down, intending to rest only briefly, clear his head—instead, he fell into a sleep deep.

He awoke to morning light; the sun was coming in hotly around the shades. The sheets around him were dry; his fever must have passed. He stretched and felt some aches, and sharper pains in his chest. When he turned over, slowly, he realized that

Gina wasn't in her place in bed beside him. He stood up with a throbbing jolt. What if, in the few hours when he'd foolishly allowed himself to sleep, Graham had found his way to Gina?

"Gina!" he called to her, and then, when there was no answer, he hobbled to the bathroom: she wasn't inside. When he returned to the bed, he saw, on his bedside table, a small note written on hotel stationery.

Didn't want to wake you so I've gone out walking. Back soon.
You rest.

He took a deep breath. Maybe she'd simply gone out for a stroll. Still, it seemed odd, her leaving him alone in his condition, and dangerous besides, her out and about when Graham was looking for her. What if he'd waited for her in the lobby all evening? In his agitation, Duncan crumpled up the note, and some of the ink came off on his hand. The ink was wet, which meant Gina had just left. He might still catch her. Grabbing the room key and pushing his feet into his shoes, he hurried, wincing, to the lobby. There was an unfamiliar woman at the front desk. Duncan asked her whether she'd seen his wife, a young auburn-haired woman, leave that morning.

"My shift only just started. But I think there was a woman leaving as I came."

"And was she with a man, by chance? About my age? Tall, light-haired?"

"I don't believe so," said the woman, to Duncan's great relief. "Were you expecting a visitor?"

"Yes, I think he may have come by, possibly he left a message. Room nineteen."

"There is something, yes." The woman produced an envelope from the row of cubbyholes behind the desk. The envelope was unsealed: Duncan pulled the paper from it, expecting to see Graham's name at the bottom. But the signature was Violet's.

Dear Gina,

I need to speak with you in private, as soon as possible. I wish I'd been able to say more when I saw you, but I've only realized what's happened since I've spoken to your father. He explained everything to me, and I need to explain it to you too.

If you can get away alone and meet me at one by the hotel entrance, I'll be waiting. You'll need to find a way to meet me without Duncan around. You'll understand why when I see you.

Violet

The situation was even worse than he'd thought. Now Graham and Violet, and possibly the police as well, were trying to reach Gina. He must get to Gina first, must use what he knew of her to anticipate her movements. She might have returned to the banks of the Vltava River, maybe even continued over the Charles Bridge, but she'd been that way already, and what she hadn't seen was the Old Town, Staré Mesto, which was just five minutes north of their hotel. He returned to the room to load up on painkillers before setting off again, along Zatecka Street. Each step pained him, but he hurried as much as he was able, soon stumbling into what had to be the Jewish Quarter, since he counted five synagogues on his walk through the cramped streets. The most prominent building among these was the Old

New Synagogue: an awkward construction with yellowed plaster walls and an oddly proportioned triangular brick roof, the whole effect like a child's imitation of an elegant church.

The strange building attracted him, and he stepped in, briefly diverted. There were several older people at the front of the chapel, heads bent, under shawls, praying. In all his life he'd never prayed, not even in those moments of silence in the temple as a child, not even on the holiest of days, Yom Kippur, when he joined the congregation in the ritual of beating their breasts as he counted off the many sins that he, at the tender age of eight or ten, should admit to committing. As a boy, it had troubled him that he couldn't summon any of the emotions he knew to be proper, not contrition, not humility, not faith in a greater being in whom his action would inspire pity. He'd come to feel wretched for his failure to feel guilty, as a result of which his mother took him to be guilty in the right ways and would comfort him and hug him. He'd accepted her embraces, so in a sense he'd lied even in this moment of confession, and had been convinced by this of his depravity.

Something must be wrong with him, he'd thought, and now had the thought that he'd been right. This thing he'd done to Gina, this way that he'd misled her and terrified the people who cared for her—it was more than a crime. It was a sin. He wished to feel remorse, to feel that if Gina were discovered by Graham or Violet ahead of him, so be it. Why else was he drawn to this temple, if not so that he might confront his error and accept the punishment of losing Gina forever? He ought to feel this and to pray for forgiveness, but if he were to pray, he knew, he would only ask that she be brought back to him.

Without quite believing he was doing such a thing, he brought his hands together and lowered his head to the fingertips. It felt good to him to have his head bowed, to accept his weakness in the face of what forces were upon him, to admit that he loved Gina, would always love Gina, and would endure whatever mad adventure and whatever loss or pain loving her might bring upon him. His love was stronger than his will—he couldn't, no matter how he might wish to, stop adoring Gina for her courage and her beauty and her vivid pure desires. He couldn't find a way to think of life without her as any sort of life at all. He might seem to have Gina as his victim, held by the illusion he'd created, but he knew that, finally, she was the one who had and always would have control over him. He yielded to her power, to becoming a subject of her love. This was his form of devotion.

He offered these thoughts up to whatever forces might be listening, and then he opened his eyes again and turned to pass among the worshippers and back outside, into the light.

The time was approaching half past noon when Duncan found his way from the Old Town and began his slow and dreadful walk back toward the hotel. His back was so stiff it was like glue had seeped in under his skin, and shooting pains assaulted him at every step.

He reached the entrance to the hotel at ten to one, ten minutes before Violet had vowed to meet Gina, though, assuming Gina hadn't read the letter, she had no notion of this, and might be wandering still, or might already have returned to the room. He went into the lobby to check with the woman behind the desk, but she insisted his wife hadn't returned. Through the window, as he stood there, he noticed Violet waiting across the street—a foot taller than most, her hair as orange as a traffic cone, she was thankfully easy to spot. As he looked on, she checked her watch and started off toward the hotel. His heart thudded. If he stayed in the lobby, Violet would see him. If he stepped out, Violet would see him. If he went up to his room, Violet might come up after him.

He hesitated, then turned to the clerk: "If a young woman comes asking for Gina, please send her upstairs to our room."

Taking the room key, he headed for the stairwell. At the second floor he exited and waited the amount of time it would take, in his imagination, for Violet to ask for assistance, then climb the three flights to their floor. He waited until he believed she'd reached the top, then reentered the stairwell and started down. A minute off and he'd have met her on the stairs, but he had not. He hurried out onto the street and, almost exactly as he did, he noticed Gina walking toward their hotel. So she had read Violet's letter, Duncan assumed, until, to his surprise, he saw her stop several doors over from the hotel and enter a storefront. He hurried after her. The business she'd wandered into was a travel agency.

"Duncan!" She spotted him across the room and came over, concerned. "I thought you'd be resting. Are you strong enough to be out like this?"

"I'm better, much better." He stepped up to her and kissed her and she kissed him back, as if all were well, though on closer inspection, he wasn't sure. Her cheeks were blotchy and her eyes were red and overbright.

"Have you been crying?"

She turned away and shook her head, making him wonder if the worst had happened—she'd read Violet's letter or come across her and discovered the truth. But then she drew up against him, pulling his arm around her.

"I'm sorry I went off like that. I didn't want you to see me so upset but I had to let it out, all the emotion from yesterday. It was terrifying. I thought you were dead."

She buried her face into his neck and he held her, until he became aware of people watching, the employees of the agency. Three of them sat around waiting, decked out in yellow uniforms.

"Can I help you with something, then?" asked one employee.

"Yes, thank you." Gina seemed to recall herself and let go of Duncan, heading over to the desk. Duncan followed behind her, uncertain what had brought her to this place.

"I was just walking by and saw the advertisement for the Palio up in the window. Do you by chance sell tickets?"

"The Palio?" Duncan turned to Gina as the woman behind the desk searched her computer.

"It's a medieval horse race in Siena," Gina explained. "I overheard a couple talking about it this morning and it's one of those things people come from all over the world to see. The race is tomorrow and I thought if we left Prague today, we might make it. Assuming, obviously, the idea appeals to you and you feel well enough to do it."

He studied her, searching her eager face. Yes, of course it appealed to him. There was nothing he wanted more than to get the hell out of Prague, and as fast as possible. The plan was perfect. So perfect, he couldn't quite believe it.

"But I assumed you'd want more time in Prague?"

"Maybe afterward we can return, visit Violet again. But yesterday was too much. I feel I need to get out of here, find some distraction."

"Absolutely. Yes." He felt so immensely grateful he could hardly contain his glee. Thanks to Gina's whims, he wouldn't need to come up with some new story to justify a sudden move.

Until this moment, when escaping together was actually beginning to seem possible, he hadn't let himself admit how dire things had become. With Graham and Violet looking for them, there was really nowhere in this small city where he could plausibly keep himself and Gina hidden.

The woman behind the desk returned, having spoken with the tourist bureau in Siena. "I can book you passage, but the tickets for the race are only sold inside the city. Hotels too are all booked—officially. Though I'm told unofficially is something different."

"Very good," said Duncan. A city in chaos where all the arrangements were done on the sly—this seemed precisely the sort of place where he and Gina might escape discovery. "And if we were to head to Siena now, what would be the fastest way?"

The woman consulted her computer and announced there was a train to Vienna, then Rome through Chiusi to Siena, leaving in a little more than an hour.

"We haven't packed." Duncan turned to Gina. "We'd need to rush."

Gina appeared undaunted. "I'll order a car while you throw our things into the suitcases and bring them down."

"Yes, good!" How he adored her then, for her adventurous spirit and determination, for all those qualities in her that led to her unwitting cooperation. He kissed her hard on the mouth before heading out the door, where he spotted Violet at the café across the street, smoking a cigarette. He ducked back inside, considering how he might arrange the next few moves. His great fear was that Gina would come outside to the car and be spotted by Violet.

Heading back to the desk, he suggested Gina call a cab from

there, since probably the agent could arrange a better price than they'd get on their own. Then, while she was distracted with the call, he asked another agent for a piece of paper and a pen. He scribbled a note, then headed back outside in search of a messenger. He spotted an older man with a dog, holding up a sign offering tours of the old city.

"Do you speak English?" Duncan asked him.

"Few words."

"You see the girl over there, with the orange hair?"

"Yes, I see her."

"Could you give her this?"

He handed the note and some bills to the man, who showed more interest in the money than the message. Even if he were to read the note, Duncan didn't think he'd detect anything wrong: *Don't want to run into Duncan. Can you meet me three blocks north of the hotel? On the northeast corner. I'll be there. Gina.*

The next ten minutes proceeded like clockwork. From a distance, Duncan watched Violet turn and walk in the direction his note instructed her to go; then he got the key from the hotel front desk, bounded up to his room, and tossed his and Gina's things into a suitcase. All the while, below, the desk clerk prepared their bill. Duncan paid quickly, and by the time he emerged onto the street again, really too weak and stiff to carry a single bag, let alone two, he was so high on adrenaline that he felt briefly invincible. The car was waiting, an unobtrusive tan sedan. Gina saw him and got in as the bags were shoved into the trunk. He climbed in beside her, onto the cool leather seat. The car was new, with a smell that made him think happily of motion.

"To the Palio!" Gina exclaimed. "The race begins. And they're off!"

As the car pulled out, Duncan turned to gaze at her, her pretty face giddy and grinning, recalling earlier days, when they were first launching their young lives. So much had since gone wrong, so much to dim that wild, eager smile, yet here it was before him, fresh, as if no time had passed.

Nine

Gina // New York

1993–94

These were the unforgettable days. Gina felt that way even eighteen months after graduation, waking up each morning in the bed she shared with Duncan five feet in the air. Their studio walk-up contained a bunk bed, to provide some living space below, and she supposed a part of her attraction to the place was the reminder it offered of the dorm rooms of their first years together. Duncan might have preferred a more mature arrangement, but she enjoyed the playfulness of their studio, as if she and Duncan were children engaged in a game of house, acting the part of adults, finding amusement where true adults encountered obligation and routine.

Sitting up in bed, with only a foot between her and the ceiling, she could see Duncan in the kitchenette, drinking coffee while packing songbooks and composition paper into his bag.

"You're leaving already?" The clock on the wall beside her read only half past seven.

"Did I wake you? You sleep more." Duncan came over to kiss

her. When he stood at his full height, his head rose just above the barriers at the mattress edge.

She ran her fingers through the hair at the nape of his neck. "Or you could come back to bed."

"Don't tempt me," he said, smiling around their kiss. "I really should go. I think I might have an idea for something."

"Do you?" She hoped she hadn't sounded too surprised, but it had been a while since Duncan had spoken of any new musical ideas. These days, he was too tired for inspiration—or that was the excuse he offered—and given that he was working multiple jobs, she could hardly blame him.

"Go, then. Go. That's great."

He grinned at her, clearly roused by her encouragement. He grabbed his bag and paused again, to kiss her a last time on his way out. "See you in a bit."

She watched him leave, the door shutting as the neighbor's dog, on cue, began barking behind him. When they'd signed the lease on their apartment, which they'd thought an improvement on their rat-infested first one, they hadn't known about the dog. The neighbor must have been out with him—possibly the landlord had seen to it she was—so it was only after they'd moved in that they'd realized there would be constant barking through the day.

"You can't work like this," Gina had announced early on, though Duncan wouldn't admit this right away.

"Maybe I'll go deaf like Beethoven."

"Let's see if we can find a happier solution."

The solution they'd finally arrived at, after earplugs and a noise machine, was that Duncan would work at Blake's apartment over in NoHo, which was free during the day while Blake worked up on Madison Avenue. She supposed it disappointed her a little that Duncan wasn't inspired to creativity by the home they shared; she knew he'd agreed to the apartment because she loved it, and she was grateful to him for wanting to give her the sort of life she'd wished to have. And giving her the life she'd wished for, he insisted, brought him joy.

Hers was precisely the sort of New York neighborhood she'd imagined living in for years—downstairs from her apartment was a Laundromat that always smelled of marijuana and had posters in the windows for guitar lessons and missing cats. Next to that, on the corner, stood a diner that exuded the scent of bacon all day long. Across the way, an older couple sat up on their balcony, a small, bearded Jewish man and a Jamaican woman with a miraculous Afro, the pair peeking down and catching Gina's eye as she went by on her way to work, past the tattoo parlors, secondhand clothing stores, and book and record shops. The first internet cafés were springing up, with used furniture spilling out onto the street, occupied by young patrons and older bohemians too. Everyone looked like some sort of artist, and everywhere Gina went there were postcards advertising some new gallery or cabaret.

So much was happening around her. Experimental theaters were multiplying and there were several dance companies doing just the sort of work Gina wished to do. She'd been exceptionally lucky to have been granted introductions, through Violet, to artistic directors and choreographers at Danspace and Dance Theater Workshop and Trisha Brown. In her first round of auditions, she'd landed small parts in two companies, and by the end of her first year, she'd become a regular in a dance company that worked out of a progressive church on East Tenth Street.

She'd been thrilled with her place there: the church felt like a refuge from the bustle of the city, a quiet corner surrounded by trees and filled with young artists, some involved in dance, some with the poetry project or experimental theater troupe that also were hosted by the church. She'd performed inside the chapel, in a grand white space with high arched ceilings and balconies and stained-glass windows.

What better place was there to dance than inside a house of worship? Dance was her religion, after all. She aspired to live all her life as a dance, gracefully, in the moment, without fear of the future or ghosts of memory.

Daily rehearsals were held at a separate location, an old factory floor a few blocks east of the church. Gina arrived at nine, changed inside the dressing rooms, and then joined the other dancers to warm up. There were twelve others in her troupe, most around her age, though they seemed to her younger than she was, overwhelmed by the big city, happily and sometimes unhappily adrift, whereas she had Duncan to provide her a sense of stability.

The four-hour rehearsal went by quickly as they always did, though for the last hour she began to watch the clock. At one, when their class broke for lunch, she'd be able to see Duncan, who worked most afternoons in a studio upstairs. He'd been hired about a month before, through her, to play piano for one of the choreographers who preferred rehearsing with live music. The pay was less than he'd gotten at the temping jobs he'd had before, but the job gave him time to practice on the piano—and then the chance for them to see each other in the middle of the day.

As soon as the dancers were dismissed for lunch, Gina darted upstairs and spotted Duncan, his back to her, already at the piano. She crept up behind him to kiss his neck.

"Ladies, please, I'm taken."

"Hilarious."

"Oh shit, Gina, it's you."

Turning around, he laughed and reached to pull her onto the bench beside him. She'd have liked to kiss him again, but the dancers were entering and the instructor too, and they weren't college kids anymore. She supposed one of the pleasures in Duncan's working with her was the chance to feel again like students, meeting for a moment between classes. She liked being reminded of those simpler days—before they had rent to pay, or thousands of the country's most creative youngsters to compete with, when they were still a charmed couple bound to do great things.

Standing to go, she caught sight of Duncan's lunch up on the piano—a cheese sandwich and a banana. He didn't even have the money for the deli salad bar she was on her way to next.

"You want me to pick up something for you from the store?"

"No, I'm fine. You should probably have dinner without me too. I've got five lessons after this. Doubt I'll be home before nine."

She felt a wave of sadness on leaving, thinking of Duncan setting off from here and crossing the city back and forth, giving private lessons house to house. Sometimes when he got home he'd be so tired he could barely hold a conversation. But this, she told herself, was the reality of living in New York and working in the arts, an experience they were both glad to be sharing—though sometimes she wondered just how glad Duncan really was.

She'd have liked to make his life a little easier, to further his success, and it was partly for this reason that she planned to visit Violet that night.

From rehearsal, which ended at five, Gina took the train to

Tribeca and walked to West Street, where Violet lived in a giant open loft with six roommates, all of them male—a set designer, a DJ, a cinematographer, a painter, and two sculptors.

Outside the building, a metal ramp led to the entrance, and a freight elevator took Gina up to the tenth floor, where she stepped into the front area, reserved for the original tenant, Hector. Hector stood six foot five with a curly black beard that peeked out beneath the face shield he wore to work. When Gina entered, he was shooting flames at a hunk of metal—that was how she often found him. Violet was in her room, walled off by a Japanese screen, sitting cross-legged on the floor, chatting away over the noise with another roommate, Donovan, the cinematographer, a slender boy with a snub nose and full lips.

"The snake was harmless, I'm completely sure," Violet was telling Donovan. "At least my fathers' lawyer says that I'm completely sure. . . ." Violet left off as she spotted Gina at the entrance. "There she is, my favorite diva."

"I thought *I* was," Donovan teased, and stood from Violet's mattress. Gina gestured for him to stay, but Donovan brushed past her. "Oh, enough babbling. I've my opus waiting for me."

Donovan passed behind the screen, and Gina could hear him a ways off, getting caught up in banter with someone else. "What is that hideous smell?"

"Your opus?"

"No, seriously."

"Lucas is making vegan chili."

It was always like this at Violet's place—endless chatter, music playing, hammers pounding in the background. For the life of her, Gina couldn't fathom how Violet managed to get anything done in such conditions, how she could work or think or sleep, but she found it an admirable feature of Violet's, her enjoyment of creative bustle, the way she was enlivened by her friends.

Violet grinned to see her. "I'll get us drinks. You want some chili?"

"Thanks, I ate before."

Violet left to get the drinks and Gina pulled up the step stool that was the only thing to sit on in Violet's room besides the mattress.

"So what's the latest with the snake fiasco?" she asked Violet, who returned with the drinks, taking her seat again on the floor. Gina preferred not to launch straightaway into the subject that had led her here so for a while she was brought up to speed on the incident that had closed Violet's last show, a modern retelling of Adam and Eve, during which the live snake she'd employed had escaped into an upstairs apartment. The woman in the apartment had suffered a panic attack—or so she claimed—and afterward, the family lawyer had encouraged Violet to lie low for a bit, so she'd taken advantage of an invitation to participate in a theater conference in Prague. While there, Violet had met a group of young Serbs and Croats fleeing the Bosnian War. When she returned to New York, she carried audiotapes of their testimonies, which she meant to have played alongside a dance piece. She wanted Gina to choreograph and to perform.

"Good news on the Bosnian refugees," Violet launched in, changing the subject. "I submitted the proposal, and, get this, the Kitchen wants it as part of their Fall Festival program."

"That's fantastic!" Gina slapped the floor, joining in with Violet's excitement, hoping that this good feeling would incline her friend to generosity. "I've been thinking about the show too, working up ideas, but I have to say I'm at my best when Duncan and I collaborate together."

For a moment, the whole space grew implausibly quiet. Gina was relieved when the hammering resumed and Violet spoke up again.

"Trouble is," Violet replied at last, "I already talked with another composer."

"Whoever it is, I can promise you they won't do a better job than Duncan."

She didn't know how to ask any more directly, and yet, as helpful as Violet was to her, on this point, Gina wasn't sure her friend would yield. Violet wouldn't be eager to work with Duncan, whom she took to be inflexible. Even Gina had to admit that collaboration sometimes proved difficult for him, though he was perfectly capable of it with her. If only he had the chance to work with her again, that might give him the boost he needed.

"Look, all I'm asking is that you let him try. If you don't like what he comes up with, you go with your other person. And I'll defer happily to you."

Violet looked at her and cocked her head. "It's funny, really. Of all the people I know, crazy, loud, pushy people, I don't think any of them is harder to say no to than you."

"Thank you!" Gina almost shouted, and before Violet could possibly insist that she hadn't yet said yes, Gina rose from the step stool and tackled her friend into a hug.

Later that night, at home, Gina presented the opportunity to Duncan. They were on the battered sofa they kept under their bed, and Duncan, drained from the day, was idly flipping through TV stations.

"I don't know if you'd be interested," she began, "but Violet has this new idea for a performance piece. There's already been interest in it from the artistic director at the Kitchen. She's got the concept, but she needs choreography and music. That's where I said we could help."

"*We* could help?" Duncan lowered the volume and turned to look at her. "By us, you mean you, but you twisted her arm to include me."

"Does it matter? Won't it be fun to come up with something great together?"

He was silent, the TV lights playing on his troubled face. She sensed his pride might get the better of him, his reluctance to accept Violet's help and even hers. She climbed onto his lap, blocking the screen. "Wouldn't it make you happy, for us to have that chance again to show what we can do? I know it would make me happy."

He nodded and she kissed him excitedly, taking this for his agreement. He went along and then they had sex like that, her astride him, their eyes locked. It seemed to her a while had passed since they'd looked at one another that way, that mostly sex took place in the dark or with Duncan behind her or over her so that she couldn't see his face. That he could look at her now made her feel certain she'd done the right thing, that she'd correctly guessed he needed help from her, though he'd never have dared to ask.

The next week, following rehearsals, she and Duncan began staying behind after the others left, to take advantage of the few hours when the studio was free. In the course of several attempts, Duncan began to form a melody to match the tone of Gina's dancing—she'd come upon the idea first, to have a figure surrounded by violence, but dancing through it, half-aware. The piece Duncan composed was full of menace and chaos but then, when transposed to a new key, slowed and sweetened, became intensely romantic. A love song with the threat nestled inside.

"I think it's the best he's done," Gina boasted to Violet, when the time came to present the work to her. Despite herself, Violet was impressed, and, after she cast other dancers and brought in additional musicians, the show was as powerful as Gina had envisioned. On the first night they performed, at the start of June, the audience rose to its feet.

The following week, Violet called Gina and told her, in a voice choked with excitement, to go pick up a copy of the *New York Times*. Gina ducked down to the corner bodega and brought the paper back to the dining table, where the phone lay waiting, Violet still on the line.

"Do you see it?"

The festival had received a page in the Arts section and their show had been the main subject of the roundup: *"Gina Reinhold dances through the violence as though entranced, seemingly oblivious, yet moved by every shock. The mystery surrounding what she sees creates the tension and holds the viewer rapt."*

"You're famous now," Violet concluded, while Gina stood with the paper trembling in her hands. It was overwhelming to be recognized this way, but her own giddy pleasure was marred by her worry over Duncan: where was the mention of the music, of *his* brilliance?

"Doesn't she comment on the score?"

"Nope, I checked. And for that matter, not too much about the concept or direction. Just the choreography and dancing. You're the one they noticed." Violet went on, explaining the impact the coverage would have. "You'll get cast in better shows, invited to do all sorts of festivals."

Gina got off the phone with Violet then, unable to share in her friend's exhilaration, too preoccupied by how to handle Duncan.

This news would crush him, she felt, after all the struggles he'd been having. Though in other ways she could be brave, she lacked the capacity to say anything that would make a person whom she cared for sad. She was unable to do it with her father, whom she felt had suffered pain enough, and she was now unable to do it with Duncan, whose disappointment she only wished to quell.

She tossed the paper into the trash outside, thinking the best thing might be to allow Duncan to make the discovery himself. Once she'd decided on this approach, though, she was stuck with it, and had to endure an awkward Sunday during which Duncan moved silently around the house and she found herself unable to sit still. She was sure he'd heard the news somehow, but was pretending, as she was pretending, feeling too ashamed to admit his disappointment in himself. The next day, feeling trapped in the charade and unbearably antsy, she came back from rehearsal claiming someone mentioned that their show was lauded in the *Times*.

"*You* were lauded," Duncan corrected. He went then to get the article, which he had stashed in his bag, and she'd made out as if she were reading it for the first time. She'd read slowly, afraid to look up from the page and find Duncan grimacing, hurt. And then she felt his arms around her.

"I'm thrilled for you," he told her. "You deserved that."

"You deserved it too," she said, trying to hold him to her, but Duncan pulled away.

"Oh, well, you know, it's how it is. Can't expect to be loved by everyone."

"*I* love you," she said.

He'd looked at her then, and a quiver passed over him. "I hope so."

"Of course I do." Why on earth would he doubt that? Could he believe this event would in any way alter the bond between them?

"It's not that I'm jealous," he let her know. "Honestly, it makes me so glad to see you succeed. Even happier than if it had been me. I just worry sometimes. I'm not sure if I'm equally cut out for this, and if I'm not—"

"Of course you are! Just because a single critic doesn't see it means nothing. The audience saw it. I see it."

"And I appreciate that, I really do. But I'm just mentioning it because I know you have a certain vision of me, of us. I mean, if things didn't end up going that way—"

"They will," she said, feeling a sudden urge to shut the discussion down. "Right now you're just feeling disappointed."

"I can handle my disappointment," Duncan replied with a small sigh. "It's yours that worries me."

He didn't need to worry, she tried to reassure him, though she could feel that she'd misspoken. She ought to have told him his success didn't matter to her, that she wanted it only for the sake of his happiness, but she wasn't sure how to say this so it wouldn't convey loss of hope in him.

When, three weeks later, she was invited to Vienna to participate in the largest dance festival in Europe, she had a moment of similar dread. It seemed that her comparative success might, in fact, be driving a wedge between them. It took her several days to tell Duncan about the invitation, and when she did, she presented the trip as one that they should make together. Vienna was a center for classical music and there would be people from all over the world converging for this festival and for the Salzburg Festival that followed: composers, conductors, patrons. Going there might serve his needs too.

"What I really need now is to catch up on rent," he told her. "But you go, you should. It's a great opportunity for you."

In the weeks that preceded her departure for Vienna, though Duncan pretended they were fine, Gina could feel something had changed between them. Whereas before she'd wake to find Duncan on his way to Blake's apartment, pausing first to kiss her goodbye, now, most mornings when she awoke, Duncan was already gone. Was he actually writing music or simply choosing to avoid her? She was so distracted for most of the month, with performances at the church three nights a week, on top of daily rehearsals for the Vienna festival, that she could hardly bring it up. It seemed an act of mercy when, in the week preceding her departure, the chapel suffered an electrical problem just an hour before curtain, and the performance had to be canceled. Gina was given the night off, and she hurried home to enjoy her surprise freedom with Duncan.

When she reached her apartment, though, Duncan wasn't there. Instead, she discovered Blake, stretched out in her bed reading *GQ*.

"Gina." Blake glanced up lazily, peeking out over the rails. "You're not supposed to be here."

"I'd think that's more true of you."

Blake smirked and kicked his feet over the ladder. He'd worn his loafers in their bed. Seeing him up there in that top bunk, she was reminded of the cool treatment she'd gotten from Blake back in college, whenever she and Duncan had to stop off in his room. She'd never had any illusions that Blake liked her. Before she came along, Blake had been happily trying to remake Duncan in his image: lending him his expensive, preppy clothes; taking him on drinking binges; trying to get him to become some sort of slick womanizer.

Duncan had moved beyond all that once he'd met her, but Blake was still the same, going to clubs four nights a week in the meatpacking district, picking up bridge-and-tunnel girls who had nowhere to stay the night and were too drunk to drive back home. She supposed Blake missed Duncan—the only person Blake didn't treat as disposable. Such devotion to Duncan, from a man who seemed otherwise aloof, had made her wonder, at times, if Blake's feelings for Duncan were more than simply friendly. But whatever the motive for Blake's interest in Duncan and his choices, it was clear that Blake couldn't stand that Duncan was settled, with her no less, and had no interest in the sort of life that Blake was leading, working in advertising, schmoozing with execs, and bossing around creatives, people like her and her friends who never thought much of him, and whom he therefore treated with contempt.

"Duncan's using my place, so he said I could use his."

She didn't know Duncan to go to Blake's at this hour. "Is he writing now?"

Blake shook his head and crossed his arms over his chest. "I don't think he'd want me saying."

Of course Blake meant to arouse her worst suspicions, she knew that, and she hated to succumb to them. "Well, I can call him at your place and ask him what he's up to."

"No, no. Don't do that, you'll mess things up."

"Mess what up?"

"Look, if I tell you, can we agree this stays between us?"

She hesitated before agreeing, not sure she wanted to have to hold on to such a secret. But nor did she wish to interrupt Duncan and force the truth from him. "All right, it's between us."

"He's having dinner with his parents," Blake finally admitted.

It took her a moment to absorb the meaning in this statement, and to place it in context. Ever since they'd moved to New York, Duncan's parents hadn't been to visit once, despite being just an easy drive away. She'd raised the issue several times, wondering if Duncan meant to hide their circumstances, if he was ashamed of the life he had with her.

"It's not worth it to have my mother here," Duncan had replied. "Believe me, she'll only notice every little thing that's wrong and we'll both be irritated after. It's better not to have her, to send a message. As long as you intend to judge and reject, you don't get to be included in my life."

She'd been so proud of him for saying that, but how it stung her now to learn that he'd been lying, that in fact he *was* including his mother—but excluding her.

She looked over at Blake, who was smiling coyly, brushing a lock of smooth blond hair behind his ear. The only reason he'd admitted the truth at all was because he knew it would hurt her.

"You're pissed at him," Blake concluded. "And he obviously knew you would be. That's why he didn't want to tell you."

"If he'd *told* me, I wouldn't be pissed." She felt the urge to clarify herself, though it was Duncan, not Blake, whose understanding mattered. "I'm upset because he thinks he needs to lie."

"Oh, you can't be all that surprised," said Blake. She knew he was baiting her, but then, she was nonetheless eager for any insight into what Duncan's behavior could mean. From his closest ally, apparently, no less.

Blake stared back at her, his smugly handsome face with boyishly red cheeks, typically so unexpressive, now enlivened by emotion, by his loyalty to Duncan and his antipathy to her. "He's so desperate for your approval he can't possibly be honest." They stared at one another. "You know the guy, you know his history," Blake finally went on, after making her wait in that maddening way he had. "He's just doing what he's always done, being held captive to someone else's idea of him. How are you any different from the mother he's lying to right now?"

Of course she was different! In a thousand ways different. And yet, *was* Duncan entrapping himself in a life with her, the way he'd been entrapped by his mother at home? Was he simply reliving the old pattern, limiting his freedom so as to keep her happy, doing what she wanted of him, without considering, without beginning to know, really, what it was *he* wanted?

She'd never minded the compromises they'd been forced to make in the way that Duncan had. Yapping dogs and rats were things they'd laugh about one day when they were older and more comfortably settled. A fair amount of discomfort seemed part of the thrill of being young and bohemian in a big city, and she hoped that Duncan felt the same. Though she had to admit she wasn't sure when she'd catch a private, sullen look cross over his face now and then; was he worried that this was to be his lot forever? His parents had given him every advantage and here he was frittering away his chance at a comfortable life. Was that how Duncan felt about it? Was he simply pretending he was contented for her sake?

These questions seemed too much to ask him now. In three days she was leaving for Vienna, and she didn't want to fly off angry. It was an excuse to avoid the matter, of course she realized that, but she made use of it and chose to spend the next several days busy with packing, and, true to her promise to Blake, didn't mention that she'd ever run into him or heard from him what Duncan had been doing.

At the airport, she and Duncan exchanged awkward goodbyes. "I wish you were coming," she told him.

"Oh, I'll go when I have a reason to."

"I'm sure you will. Soon. Next time, probably."

"Right."

As the plane took off, later, she'd felt a jolt of panic. It felt dangerous to be apart from Duncan when she was already feeling distant from him. She'd have been worried over this throughout the trip, she was sure, if she hadn't been so distracted: sponsors of the festival, various interested parties with money and connections, took her and her fellow dancers out to expensive restaurants or on private tours. She'd enjoyed her time alone and hadn't missed Duncan in the ways she'd thought she would. This fact, and the guilt it inspired, made her dread calling him and feel like a liar when she offered assurances—"It really would be so much better if you were here with me." She was afraid to admit all that she was enjoying without him, concerned she'd arouse his envy or make him suspect she was as joyfully busy as she was. With so little to talk about, their conversations were flat, brief, and shadowed by the unsaid. Had this trip only brought into relief how they'd been drifting? Was the end for them nearing?

Naturally, here, circumstances intervened, as they tend to do whenever we imagine the course of things has been set. Just before the conclusion of the festival, Gina had a call from her father. Her mother had suffered a third stroke. This one, her last, was fatal.

Gina flew to Santa Fe. She could not cry, not until she was off the plane, when simply the smell of the summer air, the particular dryness of it that recalled home, loosened tears within her. Duncan had been the only one able to staunch them. He'd arrived before her and met her at the airport, while her father was forced to remain at the house with his guests.

"Gina," he said, palming her head, stroking her hair. Simply hearing her name pronounced in his voice while he held her erased the gulf she'd invented in her mind. This man knew her more deeply than anyone, knew what the loss of her mother must mean, and made her grief less lonely and immense just by his presence. She held him and cried, for her mother's vanishing from her, and from the near loss of him, which he must have feared too, and so held her more tightly still.

Those days, which never quite came into focus, seemed to consist of endless plates carried in and out, the heavy smell of flowers amassing in vases, bright sun and extraordinary heat, and a feeling of weightless emptiness, as if a hole she'd carried in her since girlhood had at last been uncovered.

That late August in Santa Fe, the pain of the present and the past converged: she became the nine-year-old she'd been, finally saying goodbye to a mother she'd mourned years before but hadn't been able to admit the loss of fully until now. No one would ever be the world for her as her mother once was—and it dawned on her, in those days, for the first time really, that the person closest to meaning this much to her was Duncan.

She'd felt her need for him more acutely than she ever had before. Her mother's death had occurred, it seemed, just to make clear at a moment when the doubts had gathered that she would never, in fact, be able to leave Duncan, that for all their struggles and for whatever their future might contain, she would remain with him, marry him, have his children, do all those things that felt imminent to her now.

From Santa Fe she and Duncan returned to New York with a sense of starting over. She never told Duncan of her discussion with Blake and set aside the doubts that had been raised. With the clout she still held following her rave review in the *Times*, she persuaded the head of Dance Theater Workshop to let her stage a piece, with Duncan as her composer. She and Duncan began work on an entirely new show, and Duncan began to write, almost immediately, with such fluency, often waking up in the morning with a musical line in his head.

A month or so after, she proposed to him—not with a ring or on one knee, but with a simple announcement, as they lay in bed before sleep, of her wish.

"I want to marry you," she said, hoping it would banish these feelings of loneliness and blackness engulfing her still.

Duncan turned on his side, tense. She placed her hand on his chest, felt his pulse.

"What do you mean? Eventually? Now?"

"Now. I want to be with you always and to make that clear right now."

"Really? Married?" He held the word, and she let him, let him get used to it and make it his. "Yes, I want to marry you," he said at last. "I want that too."

She reached for him, entangling as much of them as she could, connecting every possible inch of skin, and lay like that, feeling his body in the dark. Her grief surrounded her, but seemed held off by the happiness between them, as, unseen, the tears rolled down her cheeks.

The next morning, they'd discussed the realities that accompanied their promise. Gina didn't wish to wait, or make a fuss over the service. Her father had just emerged from planning her mother's funeral, and she didn't want to burden him with the responsibility of arranging yet another ceremony. Anyway the notion of a formal gathering felt morbid to her. "Can't we keep it simple, just between us?"

"And why not a real ceremony? I mean, this is the only time . . ."

Duncan was less certain, but she'd managed to persuade him.

"Think about it. Your mother, my father. They'll cast a pall. The day should feel like it's ours. Unspoiled."

Yes, the blunt truth was that neither of their parents would be thrilled by the fact of their union. Duncan's mother would sulk, and Gina's father was in mourning, and, though Gina often denied the fact to Duncan, each of them knew her father didn't care for him and would suffer their marriage as another loss. In his mind, Gina's ambitions aside, Duncan was the sole factor keeping Gina thousands of miles away.

So they agreed—they'd keep the wedding small, and private. They bought modest rings, applied for a license, and picked a day to visit city hall. For the celebration, they invited only twenty friends: Blake and Violet; a few of Violet's roommates, including Donovan and Hector; Gina's fellow dancers; the choreographer that Duncan worked for; even, out of a spirit of goodwill, the neighbor with the yapping dog. It had been precisely the sort of easy, raucous atmosphere that Gina needed: friends toasting them and laughing and dancing until Duncan forced them out so he could carry his new bride off to bed.

They'd slept together so many times in the last years that sex between them could hardly be expected to feel new. And yet that night it *had* felt new to Gina, like their whole lives and all their hopes were in their bed with them, creating a denser presence, more profound. In the next weeks, a sense of promise and fertility seemed to attend her and Duncan's every move.

As her mother's estate was settled, Gina learned that she'd come into a sizable inheritance, so that her and Duncan's financial struggles would soon be behind them. Shortly thereafter, the piece for Dance Theater Workshop was performed, and, as if in honor of the love they'd revived between them, Duncan's work was given favorable reviews by two critics, and artistic directors of several theaters began calling to enlist him in their shows. Suddenly the shift had happened, commissions came his way, and she and Duncan were both working consistently. Over the next months, they decorated the walls of their apartment with postcards of the many shows they'd done, some apart and some together—and she'd imagined that alongside the postcards would come pictures of the life they'd make, of them on honeymoon, of her pregnant, each of their hands cupping her belly, awed by the fullness of their future.

Ten

Duncan // New York
1995

It was the night of Violet's farewell party, and Duncan had promised to join Gina there after he'd finished his evening piano lessons. Violet's departure had come as a surprise: only two weeks earlier, she'd announced her plan to move to Prague—this just following Blake's announcement that he was taking a position at Ogilvy and Mather's office in London. Their friends' departures marked the end of an era, Duncan sensed, but though he would miss having Blake around, and was sure Gina would miss Violet still more, he had to admit he was also eager to make a break with recent history. The past year had been a tough one, with their estrangement and Gina losing her mother, but since their marriage especially, he and Gina had recovered their equilibrium and were delighting in each other again.

He arrived at Violet's in Tribeca around nine. What the building—industrial, neglected—lacked on the outside was made up for by the immense floor space within. The elevator opened onto a vast room, and, at the entrance, a giant metal sculpture shaped like a woman lay spread-eagled. Someone had placed a cup of wine on each of the breasts.

Duncan moved through the thick crowd, seeking out Gina. He spotted Violet instead. She was standing off to the side, by an exposed toilet. He wondered at Violet's exhibitionism: did she piss and crap in the open with her six roommates too? It was certainly a quirk of Violet, who had family money, to choose to live in such rough conditions, but he had to admit that boded well for her launching her new life in a country where Western comforts, including private plumbing, might not be taken for granted. Moving to Prague was brave of her, he thought, braver than he'd been willing to acknowledge Violet was before. Over the years, he'd been of the opinion that Violet, with her rich fathers and connections, made a show of being unconventional while operating free of risk. He'd resented the contempt he felt she bore him for his practical concerns, but tonight, possibly because his career was going well, finally, and perhaps because this was goodbye for now, he was feeling in the mood to put their differences aside.

He stepped up to plant a kiss on her wide and salty cheek.

"And one day," he said to Violet, "I'll tell the historians who ask me that the Prague theater renaissance actually started in West Tribeca."

"And you expect historians will often come to interview you in the future?"

"Why not? I'll be the husband of the great Gina Reinhold."

Violet smiled at this. Whatever competitive instincts he aroused in her, Gina did not. "Your better half is over there," Violet remarked, and pointed to where Gina was absorbed in conversation with a young woman whose name Duncan had forgotten. He'd seen her before, a dancer from college, a round-faced brunette with eyebrows plucked into crescent moons. Gina, thankfully, guessed at his difficulty and reintroduced the girl as Bette, Violet's ex-girlfriend.

"Actually," Bette corrected her, "we're sort of on again, Violet and me."

"Are you?" Gina covered her mouth, embarrassed. "I didn't realize, I'm sorry."

"No, don't be," Bette reassured her. "On this week, off next, that's what seems to fit with us. What I can't get is how you two are married. Permanence, that shit's insane!"

"I guess that's what we are," said Gina, and Duncan wrapped his arms around her waist, hoisting her off of the floor.

He was feeling so glad to see her in that moment, so glad to be her husband and even, just then, to be himself—young and strong and healthy, full of desire and hope. He loved this girl with her small body and huge spirit, her eager, laughing eyes. He loved her and was grateful to her, for holding fast to him when he was shaken by doubt, by that confusion and ambivalence she was so blissfully without. He was grateful to her for being steadfast when he couldn't be, for seeing to it that he stuck to composing, which he never could have done—never would have started with—if not for her. Gina was not just his better half, he thought; she'd made him ten times better alongside her.

"Actually, I think Gina and I haven't even cracked the surface of insane. I'm feeling like it's time for our next move, something crazier than marriage."

"What do you mean?" Gina asked, searching his face.

He wasn't entirely sure what he meant, but he imagined he was inspired by Blake's and Violet's setting off, that this had put him in mind of travel and adventure. They might move somewhere new, or maybe embark on some grander project. Possibly he could turn the piece he was developing into part of something larger, a full, modern ballet.

Once Bette had left, Gina told him, "What you said before, I've had a feeling like that too." She was looking up at him, her eyes glassy, and he had a frightening sense that whatever she was going to say next was something big. "The feeling has come over me lately, like this happiness should lead to something."

"To something?"

"To someone, actually. I . . . Well, you know it's something that I've always wanted, to start a family young, to have a child."

He'd tried with all his might not to reveal the tumult in him brought on by her words. A child. He'd known, in some abstract way, that this was something Gina wanted, something she'd mentioned to him now and again, but never in a way that made him feel that it was a pressing wish. It was a fantasy—and hers alone—he thought, a longing from her past that surely didn't fit in any way with the present life that they were leading.

Nor did it have anything to do with him. He hadn't given the slightest thought to parenthood and couldn't imagine himself up to the role. So much effort was going into hiding the dread that clutched him at the prospect, he wasn't able to focus at all on what to say, and stood there mute for a long moment, until Gina began to frown.

"You're not glad I brought it up."

"I'm surprised, is all . . . ," he stammered. She looked so hurt, so disappointed. He had to find some way to cheer her. "I'm not saying I don't want that. You've just caught me off guard."

"Well, right, sure." She brightened, the life returned to her face, her stiff body relaxed again. "I've been wanting to say something for a while. So maybe this was a bit shocking, but I'm glad I have. Now it's out there and we can deal with it."

"Right, that's true. Now we can."

Except that he didn't have the remotest notion how to deal with this. He'd only just begun to get his footing professionally, in the life he'd been fumbling along at until just months before. And that life, how was it suitable for a child? Both he and Gina were working day and night, trying to establish themselves. They barely had time to manage their own business, to do laundry or fix meals. They didn't even have the confidence to own a house-plant and now Gina was speaking of caring for a human being? Because of what? Because she was turning twenty-four and some childhood version of herself had formed a notion she'd be a mom by twenty-five? Could Gina be such a slave to her own girlhood fable?

Before he or Gina could say more, Violet came to join them, hugging Gina and causing Duncan to recall that this was an emotional night. He resolved to wait and see whether Gina raised the subject again. He didn't need to wait long. The very next morning, when he'd woken, Gina was up already, watching him.

"About last night, we were carried away a bit, so I just wanted to mention again what was said."

For an instant, he felt hope: Gina was going to tell him that, in the sober light of day, she knew a child was a mistake.

"I wanted to make clear this is something I've been thinking about for a long time now. Something you've always known I wanted."

"Gina, I realize it's an idea you've had, but ideas come and go."

"Not this one," she said sharply, looking stung. "If you know me at all, you have to know that this isn't some whim. I never got to have the time I was meant to with my mother. And I'm not about to let something like that happen again."

"Hold, on, hold on," he said, reaching for her, taking her into his arms. He could feel the heat of her tears against his neck as he held her like this, realizing how deeply and painfully this wish was rooted in her.

"What happened to your mom won't happen to you. You're going to live a long and great life. No pressure. No rush."

"It's not a rush." She looked up, her tone defensive. "It's just something that I really want. Why put off the things in life you know you want?"

Her lips were trembling as she spoke. She didn't just want a child, he realized now—she wanted one desperately.

"I love you more than anything, Gina, you know that," he began cautiously. "Which means that I want more than anything for you to be happy. I swear I do, but I need to be sure it's the right thing for you—and for *us*. This year has already been a whirlwind; so much has been stirred up in you. It seems to me we ought to wait, see if your feelings change."

"They won't change," she said, sullen. "You're only hoping that they will."

"Gina, please, let's at least try to understand better what's behind this."

"There's nothing to understand. It's the most natural wish in the world to want a child. If you don't want one, why don't you try to understand the fear that's behind *that*?"

Her voice was hard, her face flushed. She was angry with him, a rarity. Whatever disappointments he might have caused her in the past, she'd never blamed him for them—but this, this was different.

Gina wanted something from him and he wasn't agreeing to give it to her. After all she'd done for him, he was choosing to hold out, and though he firmly believed he should hold out, that bringing a creature into the world was not something to be done lightly, still the simple fact of Gina's displeasure, and the knowledge that in some way he'd caused it, was really more than he could bear.

He hoped, at least, he wouldn't need to bear it for too long, that Gina would calm down and that the things he'd said might slowly penetrate her thinking. The next day, though, Gina remained remote. She didn't kiss him back when he kissed her; her tone with him was clipped and she scarcely caught his eye. At last, he tried to engage her to speak with him about it.

"Can we acknowledge what's going on here?"

"Sure, it's acknowledged. I'm upset and you know perfectly well why. What do you want me to say?"

He wanted her to say that this would pass, that she would come to see things his way and no longer resent him. Of course it was his problem, he told himself, that he was unable to stand disappointing a woman whom he loved. But even if he knew this about himself, he seemed powerless to change it.

After another day spent in the gloom of Gina's displeasure, he began grasping at anything he could offer that might soften her against him.

"I think you're right to feel my fear plays a role here. Maybe it's the fear that I can't live up to the idea of what a father ought to be."

She looked up at him, encouraged. "Well, let's talk about that, then."

"I feel, to be a father, I'd need to be more stable. Responsible.

Personally and financially too. Maybe it's old-fashioned, but I'm not comfortable just relying on your family money."

"I see." Gina looked off, considering. "But if you were working on projects that were better paid, if that could start to happen for you, that might help."

"Yes, sure. That might help a lot."

This concession, he realized only in hindsight, was the beginning of the end.

He'd said it because he'd have said anything, at that moment, to keep Gina speaking to him in the gentle way she was. Still, he didn't feel like he'd been lying. By the time his career had reached a stage where he could support a family, he might really feel emboldened to do what Gina wanted. It hadn't occurred to him that any such shift could happen quickly, or that Gina, who'd always encouraged him to ignore financial considerations, would switch her position easily.

A few days later, Gina announced they'd been invited to a party that coming Friday, where she could introduce Duncan to a young woman she wanted him to meet.

"Marina Du Bellay. We spent time together in Vienna. Her mother is a French aristocrat who sits on the festival board. Marina's in New York now, making her first film. A few months back I put her in touch with Violet's roommate Donovan, the cinematographer."

"And why do you want us to meet?"

"Well, you want to take on more lucrative projects. Seems to me that a film score would be a good place to start."

"You realize most independent film pays next to nothing."

"Marina's loaded," Gina said bluntly, uncharacteristically so.

The party was held at a town house on the Upper East Side,

hosted by the producer of a documentary Donovan had been working on all winter. The house was expensively furnished, and many of the guests were older, friends of the producer and her husband. None of the people looked familiar to Duncan, but, after stopping at the bar for drinks, Gina led him over to the one guest he did know, Donovan, who stood talking to a tall, striking woman with straight blond hair tied up in a knot.

"Marina," Gina said, as the woman turned and saw her, clapping her hand to her heart as if overwhelmed by the surprise.

"Gina!"

Marina was a few years older than Gina, long and angular, shoulders a little hunched. She had a high forehead and wide-set, blurry blue eyes. Duncan wouldn't have called her pretty, not like Gina, but there was no doubt she was arresting.

"This is Duncan, my husband," Gina let her know.

"Husband, my God. Benoit will be destroyed."

Benoit. Duncan had never heard the name before, and couldn't help but wonder who he was. That whole Vienna trip remained mysterious to him—so much of it never discussed in the wake of Gina's mother's death. This name made him anxious, but he tried to put his thoughts aside.

"Will you be going back this summer?" Marina was asking Gina.

"If they invite me, I guess I might."

"Oh, they'll invite you. You were the best dancer there."

"I was not, not by any stretch."

"You were! You were amazing!" Marina was effusive, even manic. She grabbed hold of both of Gina's hands. "I want to dance with you, amazing dancer. Let's go dance."

"But no one's dancing. . .," Gina trailed off as Marina pulled her to a small, uncrowded patch between the sofas.

Duncan and Donovan stood watching the women as first Marina and then Gina began dancing to the music playing in the background, while the stiffer guests looked on. Donovan was smoking a joint, which he soon handed over to Duncan. Duncan inhaled gratefully, becoming aware of how much he required relaxation. Minutes later, as Duncan finished off his drink and eased into his high, he felt calm enough to confess to Donovan the reason he was there.

"Gina's got it in her head that Marina might hire me. For her movie. To do the score."

"Marina might, you know. She hired me almost on the spot. Goes on instinct, she says."

"And how's that working out for her?"

"Filming hasn't started yet, so hard to say." Donovan paused for a drag. "But hey, however it goes, the lady pays."

Duncan looked over at Gina and Marina, joined now in their dancing by a towering, bearded man and a woman in overalls who backed into a vase that was propped atop a shelf. At the noise of the crash, Marina grabbed Gina's arm and pulled her away, back to Donovan and Duncan.

Marina was laughing, but Gina was upset.

"I hope it wasn't worth a fortune," Gina said.

"They can afford it," Marina assured her. "Plus, the host's a bastard anyway. I know the couple. My mother had me meet them when I moved here because the wife makes films. Or pays others to make them. And her husband supports her hobby just so she won't leave him. He fucks everything, by the way."

"How do you know?" Donovan asked her.

"How do you think?" said Marina, grinning. "He fucked me."

As she broke into laughter, she fixed her eyes on Duncan. He laughed along, lightly, which seemed the safest thing to do.

Marina watched him, smiling. "You're not sure if I did it or not, are you?"

"I mean, I've just met you. Too soon to form any opinion."

Her smile widened. She was enjoying this, his nervousness, the chance to sound out his first feelings for her. She had to be aware of her effect on men. The height, the yellow hair, the wildness in her eyes, all these would garner her immediate attention. "I must have created some impression, though?"

"Well, Gina tells me you're a lovely person."

"Of course." She rolled her eyes at his careful reply, then took hold, again, of Gina's arm. "She's the lovely one, clearly."

"Both of you," said Duncan.

A brief silence fell over the group, which Duncan broke with an announcement that he needed the bathroom. The way Marina looked at him, the fact that he noticed and was pleased, set him on edge.

"Donovan, there's someone here you have to meet. Your future husband." With that, Marina pulled Donovan away, and Duncan and Gina were left standing together.

"Marina's high as hell," he observed to Gina. "I'm not sure I see any value in trying to talk to her tonight."

"Oh, she's always like this. She's chatting with you, it's going well."

Duncan shrugged and glanced over at Marina, catching her looking back at him. He headed off to the bathroom and took his place in the long line outside the door. After a moment, he noticed

Marina stepping away from Donovan and the other man, coming to join the line behind him.

"Oh, for fuck's sake, can't they open up another?" she griped, bouncing a little to suggest her need to go.

Duncan offered to let her skip ahead of him. Instead, when the room freed up and Marina darted in, she pulled Duncan along with her.

"I can wait," he stammered, but Marina had already locked the door behind them.

"I don't need the toilet anyway," she told him, and the next thing he knew, she was standing in the tub, hiking up her skirt.

"Jesus, what are you doing?"

"I told you the host's a bastard." Reaching for one of the silver soap dispensers on the sink, she unscrewed the top and began urinating into it.

"Marina, stop. Other people might use that. Not just the host, the party guests."

"Sssshh. You're making me mess up. Goddammit, you should do it. Women are useless pissers."

"I'm not going to do it."

A knock came on the door. "One at a time! What's going on in there?"

"Just a moment," Duncan called back. He wanted to get out of there, to unlock the door, but Marina wasn't done yet and the pressure in his bladder was intense. He unzipped his fly, relieved himself, and was almost finished when the door opened behind him. Apparently, Marina hadn't locked it properly and, to his horror, when Duncan turned, he caught sight of Gina standing just a few feet away.

She looked at him, confused and then distressed, and walked away. He caught up to her and drew her into a corner, out of Marina's sight line. "She just yanked me in after her. I didn't know what to do—that woman's crazy. You didn't tell me she was crazy."

"You might have kicked her out. Walked out yourself."

"I'm sorry. I didn't want to offend her. I guess I wasn't certain what to do, what you'd want me to do."

"What *I'd* want you to do? Were you really thinking about that?"

He nodded and her expression grew pained. In an instant she was crying. He was startled by her tears, wasn't sure what they might mean. He feared she might be terrifically upset with him, but then she took his face into her hands. "I'm the one who should be sorry. I've been twisting you in knots, haven't I? Thinking about what I want, making it all about what I want."

"I'll admit," he conceded, "this past week hasn't been easy."

"I know it hasn't. I got carried away, and I'm sorry. I promise that I'll stop now."

She had stopped too—quite suddenly, from then on, Gina stopped treating him like he'd hurt her, stopped talking of a child or of altering, in any way, his professional path. Over the next weeks and months, he continued playing piano at the studio, and giving lessons, and working on the same performance projects. The threat had passed, it seemed. He and Gina were at peace again and had returned to the pleasant pattern of their lives before.

In August, as Marina predicted, Gina was indeed invited to perform again in Vienna. Duncan had managed to escape another conversation about their future child before she'd left. At first he'd been grateful, but in the ensuing days of her absence—with phone calls even fewer and farther between than her last time in Vienna—he couldn't help but feel that he'd been too quick to assume their problems were resolved. Perhaps something larger had shifted in Gina, and between them. Perhaps this silence was her way of beginning to, gradually, let go—not of her dreams of motherhood, but of Duncan, of their shared future.

A week after Gina had left, Marina called, out of the blue, to ask him if he was still interested in composing for her film.

"Gina had told me you might be. And we're now in postproduction, so this would be the time to meet if you're still interested."

"To be honest, I'm not sure. I've committed to some other projects."

"I see. Well, up to you, then, but if you have some recordings, you might as well send them along to me and then, if I like them, we can discuss what I'm looking for and offering. I don't see the harm in that, do you?"

A voice in him warned that yes, there might be harm in that. After all, it was already suspicious that Marina was reaching out now, just after Gina's departure. Still, he'd never been much good at saying no, and all Marina wanted was a sample of his work. He sent this off and two days later Marina called again to invite him to talk. This time he conceded, meeting her at a garden restaurant near her home in Gramercy.

"I listened to what you sent me," Marina told him, after they'd exchanged quick kisses on both cheeks. "Obviously we wouldn't be here if I didn't think you have marvelous talent."

"Thank you. That's kind of you to say." He was being polite and careful, mindful, as Marina spoke, of the way she sat down in her chair so that her slender legs were stretched out to almost touch his, while the rest of her leaned back, appraising.

"Those were pieces for dance, am I right? And now you're looking to expand into film, is that true?"

"Thinking about it, yeah."

"I can't blame you. I'd imagine that in dance there's so little to be gained, so little money and recognition." She sipped her water. "It's hard to see why you'd even want to, except for Gina's sake."

"Actually, it's Gina who encouraged me to explore new possibilities."

"And do you always require her approval to explore new possibilities?"

"No, of course not."

Marina smiled, acknowledging her teasing, then grew serious again. "Though I would like to know that this is something *you* want."

"Right now I want some wine and a waiter to take our order."

They ordered, and while they waited for the food to arrive, Marina admitted that she'd done some investigating about Duncan, and had learned from her acquaintances that he was considered, at least by some, to be the best-kept secret among young classical composers. "You haven't done much and most people don't know of you, but the few that do admire you."

"That's nice to hear," he said, flushing a little. Marina might be exaggerating, but it was a rare pleasure for him, being offered praise. And now Marina was prepared to offer him money as well.

"Given the quality of your work, I'm willing to raise my music budget. How does sixty thousand sound to you?"

"Seems reasonable," he said, trying not to fall out of his chair. Sixty thousand was twice what he'd earned throughout the entire year.

"Good, good. So then we can start getting to the fun part.

There are a few musicians I'd like you to hear, artists who capture very well the tone I want for my film."

Over the next two weeks, while Gina was away, keeping busy, Duncan was kept busy by Marina. As he began composing, working every free moment he had, she invited him to several shows a week, some small bands at local venues, and some large orchestra performances. After one show at Lincoln Center, which she insisted was her treat, she introduced him to an elegant European couple.

"Duncan, I'd like you to meet Astrid and Riccardo. My mother and her fiancé."

He'd been caught off guard by this meeting with Marina's mother, and especially by the sly way her mother smiled at him. Still, he told himself that he was doing nothing wrong, that this was a business relationship—Marina was now his client, and paying him an awful lot, and so spending time with her this way was a perfectly fine thing to do.

He clung to this idea, even when she arrived at his door, two nights later, holding a bottle of wine and dressed in a blouse open far enough that he could see she wore nothing underneath it. He clung to this idea even when she put on music and flung herself across his sofa. Even when she was tipsy and again using this as an excuse for saying things she shouldn't.

"It's probably not my place to comment, but it honestly surprises me that you didn't accompany Gina to Vienna this time—I mean after the last trip."

"I've got projects I'm finishing, and this one . . ." He left it at that, not indulging Marina by asking her what she was alluding to about Gina's last visit. He recalled the name she'd mentioned before, Benoit—the man who would be crushed to hear Gina was married. "Anyway, I think it's a good thing for a couple to spend a little time apart. Miss one another."

"Not all men are so trusting."

"Gina's never given me a reason not to trust her."

"Oh, Duncan, you're too sweet. You really are. Gina is so lucky. Most men with your talent are egomaniacs, but you're as innocent as you are gifted. It's a good thing you've seen as little as you have. I mean a scene like Vienna, the conniving and exploiting. Gina can handle herself, of course, but that kind of thing would crush that pure spirit right out of you." Marina laughed and he tried to smile, though in truth he was shaken, reminded of the insecurity he'd suffered that past summer and which was now, in Gina's absence, stirred up in him again.

Duncan peered down at Marina, who was lying back on his sofa, now with her eyes closed. She was alluring, he couldn't deny it, stylish and worldly, and he supposed it flattered him that such a woman would see so much possibility in him. As much as Gina had encouraged him before, she'd also borne witness to too many of his failures to idealize him any longer. Lost in his thoughts, he continued watching Marina lying there until he wasn't even sure she hadn't drifted off to sleep. When the song ended, though, she sat up again and opened her eyes, looking at him boldly.

"It's an interesting piece . . ." He began to comment on the music, what little he'd had the presence to observe, while Marina stared up at him. An amused smile formed on her lips. Then she kissed him.

He didn't pull away—not at first. Sure, he'd been briefly stunned, if not surprised—but also he found himself excited, susceptible at that moment to interest from an attractive woman who wasn't his wife. Another alluring figure to mold and shape him.

He allowed her to open her blouse further, exposing herself, before he stood and backed away.

Just after he withdrew, Marina stood too and brushed past him, blouse still open, walking off to refill her wineglass in the kitchenette. "I shouldn't have done that. Gina's my friend. You're married. You must think badly of me."

"I don't. I—"

"It's just so obvious that you two don't fit together anymore. She's moved on to other things, and you really should too. But if you don't see that, it's not my place to insist."

Marina finally glanced up at him, but something else caught her attention. She looked over at the door.

The music continued to play, which must have accounted for the fact that he hadn't heard the sound of a key turning in the lock. He'd been too distracted too by Marina to notice the front door standing open. No one was at the doorway now, but Gina's luggage remained where, a moment before, Gina must have been.

He'd darted out to the hallway and peered over the banister just in time to see Gina two flights down, fleeing through the building entrance. What could she have seen or heard? He bounded down the steps, but by the time he burst onto the street, Gina was nowhere in sight. She must have slipped into a taxi and away. Later, after Marina had left with a flutter of apologies, he called up anyone he could think of in search of Gina, but she wasn't staying with her friends and no one knew where she was. He hadn't any idea how to reach her until a week had passed, when one of her fellow dancers let him know that Gina had flown home to Santa Fe.

All right, all he had to do was get Gina on the phone and explain himself—he hadn't slept with Marina, hadn't wished to sleep with Marina. He'd been indulgent with her, too indulgent, yes, but in the hopes of gaining a commission that would let Gina and him move forward in their lives together, do what they wanted. He'd come around to what she wanted. A child. He could be ready. No, he *was* ready!

Once she'd heard this, once she saw how sickened he was to think he'd hurt her, well, Gina would forgive him. Nothing unforgivable had happened.

"I just need five minutes on the phone with her," he told her father when he called their house in Santa Fe.

"I'm sorry, but she won't speak with you, Duncan. She's made it very clear that she wants to move on now."

"Look, Mr. Reinhold, I don't know what she might have told you, but it's all a big misunderstanding. If you'll let me explain, she'll see she's overreacting."

"It might seem like she's overreacting to you, but that's how Gina is. Other people, what they feel as a ripple, she feels as a tidal wave."

"But it's barely a ripple. It's a mistake."

"I'm sorry, son," said Mr. Reinhold, in a tone that might have suggested sympathy but was, Duncan was sure, bereft of any. "It's awful to lose someone you love," he said contemplatively, Duncan now growing angry that Mr. Reinhold would turn his grief as a weapon against him, "but I'm afraid that's what's happened."

Duncan hung up from the call in a state of baffled despair. None of this made sense. There must be some part of the story he wasn't getting, but he had no means of learning what. He turned to Gina's friends for understanding—perhaps her fellow dancers would have an explanation, but they were equally perplexed and frustrated by her disappearance. She wasn't speaking with them either.

It struck him then that she wasn't abandoning him only; she

was giving up on everything: her career, their apartment, her life in New York, that life she'd envisioned for them when she was just nineteen. She'd seen it all so vividly she'd made him fall in love with that life too, and now she'd just run off to Santa Fe, mysteriously, to let their life together die.

It all seemed so utterly unlike her, this behavior, as if she'd collapsed into some former, weaker, childhood self, dependent on her father, fearful and withdrawn.

A week later, Duncan received a call from the artistic director at PS 122. The man was calling to invite Gina to choreograph a piece for their festival that winter.

"Gina's paying a visit back home," Duncan told him, "but I'll be sure to relay the offer." He phoned Gina's house several times that day, but no one picked up his calls. Finally, he left a message on the house answering machine.

Two days later, having gotten no response, he phoned the artistic director to ask whether Gina had been in touch with him directly. After learning that she hadn't been, Duncan canceled his lessons for the next days and flew out to Santa Fe.

He arrived at the Reinhold house, unannounced, at 10 a.m. Mr. Reinhold came to the door and refused to let him in.

"I have something I need to say to Gina," Duncan let him know. "It's not only about me. A professional matter too."

The man stood and looked at him, breathing deeply, his broad chest expanding. He was larger than Duncan, powerful still. His red beard covered half his face, but Duncan could see his jaw was set. "I can't let you in, I'm sorry."

"Mr. Reinhold, she's had an offer from a theater that means a lot to her. It's the dance company that made her want to come to New York in the first place."

"Gina needs a break from New York for now."

"You mean she needs a break from me."

Mr. Reinhold made no reply, only stepped out onto the lawn and beckoned Duncan to follow.

"Listen," Duncan continued, walking beside him, "I didn't do what Gina thinks. I'd never betray her or disappoint her that way. That's the last thing I'd ever do."

Mr. Reinhold sighed, speaking slowly. "Duncan, a guy like you, you can't help but disappoint her. You're all promise and no follow-through; you'll say anything to please her, and even think you mean it, but you don't know what the hell you mean, 'cause you have no idea who you are or what you're about."

Duncan had always had a nagging sense that Gina's father didn't like him, but the man had never admitted it, or given any indication of the reason why. He'd had no proof that this was how Mr. Reinhold saw him, until now; he would need to work hard to keep his hurt from getting in his way.

"I'm about loving your daughter. That's what I'm about."

Mr. Reinhold's arms were crossed, his lips pursed, unyielding. But Duncan wouldn't back down either.

"With all due respect," Duncan went on, gathering his courage, "you don't get to tell me who I am or what I'm about, and you don't get to do that for Gina either. She's a grown woman. She should come out here and face me and tell me in her own words what she wants."

"I'm sorry you've come down here for nothing." Without another word, Gina's father turned inside, shutting the door behind him.

He should have pounded on that door, Duncan thought later. He should have camped out on that lawn until Gina came to see him, instead of walking away. Whatever was happening inside that house was wrong, he knew it was, that somehow Gina had lost her footing and her father had seized upon the moment to get her back—his daughter, who had always been his compensation for having lost his wife and whom he'd never wanted to let go. Thinking of Gina being kept here, he saw her for the first time as frightened, almost like the anxious, guilty boy Gina had spent the past five years saving him from being. It was his great mistake to leave her there, and for the next months, alone in their apartment, he was haunted by his failure.

Why had he yielded to Frank Reinhold? What sort of creature was he to be led around always by others? For most of his life, his mother had made decisions for him and told him who to be. Then he'd let Gina reshape him to fit as well as he was able into her vision for him, and when that went awry, and he failed to match her fantasy, he'd been intoxicated by the allure of something—someone—new, Marina, and his impulses upended the life he'd built and the only relationship that mattered.

Then—months later, that spring—chance had given him the opportunity to correct for all of this, when a stranger named Graham Bonafair had shown up at his door to remind him again of who he was and what that meant.

He loved Gina and understood that she was lost to herself, the way he once had been. Did he not owe it to her—and to them—to take control of his destiny and do whatever he must to bring her back to herself, to him, and her true home?

Eleven

Gina // Siena

July 1996

After a frantic drive to Hlavni Nadrazi station, Gina squeezing Duncan's hand at every painful pothole, they arrived with just minutes before the train to Vienna. Thankfully, there was no line at the ticket window, and, with a strained sprint down the platform, she and Duncan collapsed into their seats just as the train was pulling out. For some time after, Gina's heart kept pounding until at last she settled down and turned to watch the lovely, wistful city, even stranger to her now, rolling past her window and into memory.

Not since Berlin had she had such a feeling: that she was leaving a place a different person than when she'd come. The fog was clearing, replaced by a sharp sense of purpose. She wasn't yet ready to tell Duncan the cause, but she wondered if he felt a change in her. At times that morning he'd seemed to watch her with a puzzled look, and she supposed that it was odd, her insisting on this sudden trip, and that Duncan must be wondering about her motives. She imagined each of them at this instant, seated across from one another, silently guessing at the other's thoughts. Perhaps Duncan had formed certain ideas, but this, she told herself, shouldn't trouble her too much.

How wrong we always are, after all, when we believe we know the minds of those we love.

"I hope Violet won't be upset we left so quickly," she announced, breaking the silence, and her own reverie. She must keep on top of the situation—Violet would have her own theories on Gina's sudden disappearance, and it would be prudent to provide her friend with some answers.

Duncan hardly seemed to hear her: pale and worn out from his injuries, he was having trouble keeping his eyes open. Soon he was dozing, and Gina, meanwhile, fished her writing pad out of the suitcase and sat down again to write a letter to her friend.

Dear Violet,

I owe you an apology for leaving Prague the way I did, without explanation. It must be confusing for you—my showing up out of the blue, and then vanishing as fast, without reassuring you that Duncan is all right (he is) or stopping in to say goodbye.

There are things I could tell you about the past weeks— things I'd planned to tell you when I came to Prague. But then this morning changed all that. Changed my plans, changed everything. I should have suspected what was happening from my sickness yesterday, but I didn't know myself until I awoke today, tender in places that left no room for doubt. . . .

She left off there, distractedly, thoughts circling back to hours ago, when she'd left Duncan in bed and set off, in a tumult of feeling, to wander the Prague streets. Images had flooded her memory as she ambled about, losing track of where she was going, until, as if in a dream, she'd come upon this cottage-like building and had seen Duncan walking through the entrance. She'd been startled to find him—she'd left him asleep not long before—and had followed him into what she then recognized must be a temple. From the back of the room she stood and watched him, his head bowed and body rocking.

He was praying. Duncan, who did not believe in prayer. Duncan, rational Duncan, who'd so often put his pragmatism ahead of faith in what he loved—here he was, with such a penitent way about him that tears came to her eyes. She couldn't know what words he might be casting up to God, but she believed that they must have to do with them, that he must be seeking some means to keep them whole, to repair the harm they'd done each other. She'd left the temple knowing that what had happened between them was a blessing, her discovery that morning a gift of grace.

Now Duncan sat across from her, deeply asleep and oblivious to the fact that his prayer had been answered. He slept on like that, while she finished her letter to Violet and penned another, much the same, to her father.

In Vienna, they switched to the train for Rome, where they took a sleeping car for the overnight ride. It took Gina some time to shake off her thoughts and settle down to sleep, but she had slept, because soon it was morning, and Duncan was waking her to let her know they were approaching Roma Termini. As soon as the train halted, there was a great rush all around to catch the Siena train. A crowd had formed already on the platform, thick and loud and buoyant: young men and women flirted, rival fans taunted one another. Many passengers had brought along their lunch and sat down on the platform to eat; others poured glasses of wine. While Duncan waited among them, Gina went off to change money and buy the tickets and some food.

Rested and feeling better, Duncan devoured the sandwiches she'd bought, though all Gina could bring herself to eat was a slice of plain, dry bread. In Chiusi, they were required to change trains again, and for the last leg of the trip, the raucous passengers began to sing. The singing cheered Gina, reminded her that Prague was now behind her, and that what lay ahead was turbulent and unknown and, quite possibly, fantastic.

At Stazione di Siena, chaos was already erupting, people spilling through the front doors into the street in search of taxis. Without porters in sight, she and Duncan had to struggle with their luggage, and by the time they were outside, the line at the taxi stand was so immense, they despaired of ever getting into town. As they stood debating what to do, a young man in a cap approached them, asking in English if they wanted transit to the city center.

"*Sì, sì.*" Duncan nodded, and the young man took their bags and led them to a minivan filled with tourists.

The ride was hot and bumpy, but thankfully short, and soon the van pulled up along a brick wall with signs leading to parking lots and to the Piazza del Campo. From here on, the way was closed to vehicles, all but the few police cars that crawled among the throngs of pedestrians through the narrow, slanted streets. Vendors stood along the gutters selling mementos of the race and other items that might appeal to tourists—binoculars and hats, maps, bottles of water. An enterprising young man spotted

Duncan and Gina dragging their suitcases and offered his assistance.

"I can be guide and carry for you. Only ten thousand lire."

Gina insisted that they do it—Duncan was still in no shape for lugging bags—and the young man proved to be useful in other ways as well, full of information and advice. They would need to hurry to reach the *campo* by four, he let them know, because after that, only the entrance at Via Giovanni Dupré would be open. If they didn't already have tickets to the race, he would help them to locate the local men, *palcaioli*, who managed the wooden seats around the square.

The young man led them down one of the streets that radiated from the city center and soon they reached the square, paved in red brick and fronted by a circle of red medieval buildings and a palace with a tower casting its long shadow. At the center of the square, a great mass of people stood together, hemmed in by barricades. The narrow band of exposed ground between the crowd and surrounding buildings formed the track where the racehorses would run, and around the outside of the ring stood wooden bleachers, already packed.

After a long search, Gina spotted two free seats and their guide negotiated over tickets with the older man who manned the bleachers. For a hefty price, the man gave them tickets, but insisted the suitcases took up too much room and would need to be removed. Their guide suggested they try the Hotel Duomo, which might keep their bags for a fee, and he and Duncan started off then, leaving Gina on her own to hold the seats.

The time was half past three, the heat of the day was intense, and the red brick of the square blazed under the summer sun. As Gina stood amid the noisy, jostling crowd, breathing in the smell of sweat and dirt, she began to feel her eyes ache and her dizziness return. The scene around her seemed overbright: the fans dressed in the sharp colors of each district, blue and red and green. It was all so theatrical—the waving flags and pageantry, the picture-perfect ancient square—and for a moment, she couldn't quite believe that this was real, that this could truly be her life now, this mad adventure she and Duncan had begun.

All that day she had been running, speeding toward this race that would mark only the start of one much longer and leading who knew where. None of it felt possible, nor would it, she realized then, until she'd shared the news with Duncan. She felt seized by a desire to tell him what she'd been too overwhelmed and nervous to admit to him before, this secret she'd been holding, which she now felt the urge to name.

It was their future she was carrying, their future child.

Twelve

Duncan // Siena

July 1996

*I*t *took* some time before Duncan and the young guide reached their destination: an elegant three-story building painted a mint green, the Hotel Duomo. Inside, the lobby was teeming with people, some on chairs and others standing, all gathered around a television that had been set up to broadcast the race for those who lacked the inclination to get a seat on the square. The group chattered in Italian—locals, from the look of them, mostly older people who had likely seen the race dozens of times and didn't find it worth the risk of heatstroke to witness it live again.

Duncan walked past them and up to the man behind reception. He introduced himself, asked the man if he spoke English, and then inquired whether, for a price, he might leave his luggage in the hotel during the race.

"I'm afraid we only hold luggage for our guests, signore."

"Well, as it happens, my wife and I are also looking for a room."

The clerk sighed heavily. "And I'm also afraid rooms this week are booked ahead for months, signore."

"I see."

"Then, of course," the clerk continued, "private citizens do rent out rooms for a price to help tourists. I do know someone with a room, a neighbor, or I might, but sadly the police are against this practice. Understand I risk a fine, giving you this information."

"And how much would this fine be?" Duncan reached for his wallet, selecting a twenty-thousand-lira note before the man could summon a larger number.

The man accepted the bill and reached for his desk phone. "I'll call my neighbor now."

Duncan waited while the clerk negotiated with his neighbor in Italian and then announced that the cost of the room would be two hundred thousand lire—high, but not outrageous, and certainly worth it in these circumstances.

"And the room includes a meal, signore. You'll have trouble getting food any other way. The restaurants are booked like the hotels." The clerk paused to let Duncan take this in, and then handed him a slip of paper. "If I might just get your names then, signore. Yours and your wife's. I will copy from the passports, is fine."

Duncan handed over the passports, and after studying them the clerk looked up, surprised. "Gina Reinhold is your wife?"

The question caught him off guard. How could this man have heard of Gina? So much time had passed since Berlin, and he and Gina had come so far, that Duncan had felt safe enough to stop consulting the papers. If a story had run about them, if the search had widened, he might have missed it. "That name's familiar to you?"

"A man came in an hour before, asking after her. He said to call him if I see her."

"A man? What sort of man?"

"Maybe fifty years, with red hair, tall, American like you. He said his name was Reinhold too."

Duncan was trying to stay calm; this might be a mistake, another Reinhold or Reinhart or Reynolds. "Did he have a beard, by chance?"

"He did, signore, a short beard."

Duncan felt his face grow hot.

But could it really be? He tried to sort it out, how Mr. Reinhold could have discovered where they were and gotten here so quickly. Was it possible that Violet or Graham had discovered the travel agency by the hotel, then, after learning he and Gina were headed to Siena, that one of them had alerted Mr. Reinhold? Gina's impulsiveness he'd always attributed to her mother, but perhaps Mr. Reinhold had a streak in him too—would he not learn this news and immediately book a flight from Santa Fe that morning, cutting them off? It was also possible that Gina's father was already in Europe, on the hunt, and had flown here from Berlin or Zurich or wherever he'd picked up their trail. A feat like this would require immense coordination, which meant that if what he envisioned was in fact true, Gina's father was sparing no effort or expense to bring his daughter home.

"I should be getting back to my wife," said Duncan, thinking of Gina then, sitting in plain sight out on the campo. He was furious at himself for his complacency, for speaking of his plans so openly in front of the travel agent back in Prague and now for leaving Gina unattended. Thanking the clerk, he turned toward the door.

"Wait, signore? Don't you require the address where you'll be staying?"

"Yes, right, of course." He hurried back to take the slip of paper with the address.

"And what shall I tell this man if he comes back asking after Ms. Reinhold?"

Duncan paused at the desk, long enough to withdraw another twenty-thousand-lira note. "You might suggest he try some of the other hotels."

"Yes, very good, signore."

The clerk took the money, and Duncan removed another bill to offer the young guide, before parting ways with him and rushing off in the direction of the campo.

The beat of drums sounded in the distance. The parade must be underway. Duncan headed toward the noise, walking as quickly as he was able with the pain shooting through his ribs. On his way he passed a group of laughing men and women, smelling of alcohol and dressed in costume—one man had his face hidden behind a carnival mask. Soon after this, Duncan ducked inside a shop selling local paraphernalia and selected the mask closest to the one the other man had worn—Venetian style, with white and red and gold—then doubled back and picked another mask for Gina. Moving under cover from there on, he felt safer, but not safe. Police were everywhere, gathered to manage the crowds, and perhaps the authorities had been notified that Gina's kidnapper was here. For all he knew, his picture and Gina's had been circulated among the dozens of officers he passed.

At last Duncan came to one of the openings onto the square, but an officer stood barring the way.

Paranoid, even if masked, Duncan felt he had no choice but to find an unguarded entrance, so he stumbled along in pain and the heat, trying his luck at the various streets that radiated from the campo. Two officers blocked the next entrance, but at the third, whoever was on duty must have stepped away, and Duncan simply squeezed past the barricade and inside the square. It seemed no one had noticed him, but if police or anyone had seen him and yelled for him to stop, Duncan wouldn't have been able to hear them anyway above the drums and trumpets and the chanting crowd. The parade performers were ahead of him, men in blue and white medieval costume, followed by a cart driven by oxen. Duncan slipped in among them, emboldened by the mask, searching the bleachers for Gina.

Having come from a different entrance, he wasn't sure which way to go. Each side of the square looked the same and it took him some time, as he scurried along the edge of bleachers, lost in the din of the crowd, to position himself with regard to the clock tower and identify the right direction. The bleachers were packed and most of the people were standing, no doubt obscuring someone as small as Gina. As he proceeded, searching, the call of a trumpet stopped him. Seconds later, a charge of men on horseback thundered past, wielding swords. Duncan hugged the bleacher wall, the ground trembling underfoot. After the horses passed, a brief calm descended, and then came an explosion so thunderous and ground-shaking that it took Duncan a moment to still his nerves and realize from the atmosphere of hushed anticipation that the race was about to begin.

"Duncan!" He heard his name being called—not by Gina, as he'd hoped, but by a man. He turned to look in the direction of the shout, peering out at the crowd at the center of the square. A man stood writhing at the edge, pushing against the barricades, tall, red-haired, and bearded, looking so determined that Duncan was gripped by panic. Mr. Reinhold had seen him.

Was it possible? Duncan still wore his mask, but when he looked down at his shirt, he realized he'd worn one of the few he'd brought with him, a blue and green madras that Gina had bought him, and that Mr. Reinhold had once envied aloud.

Another explosion marked the start of the race, and ten horses went careening around the square, with brightly dressed jockeys clinging to their bridles. Duncan quickly jumped over the short wall that fronted the bleachers. His body radiated pain and he had to stop and catch his breath as people nearby grumbled at him. He turned back to watch the race just in time to see the first jockey fall, and men in white shirts and orange pants run to scoop him from the path of the other horses. Beyond, Duncan could make out Gina's father, watching him, bristling behind the barricade, waiting for the race to be over so he might leap across.

The race was only ninety seconds long; Duncan had no time to waste. He had to move, but couldn't think how it would be possible in the stubborn crowd. He began climbing, thinking that perhaps he might slip back behind the bleachers and find his way to Gina by walking underneath the seats. Moving upward, cursed and shoved by those he passed, he heard mounting cheers, and then a whinnying shriek followed by a collective gasp. When Duncan looked back at the track, he saw another jockey fallen from his horse, but this time a horse was down as well, and a second man lay on his stomach a few feet away.

The medics were already on the track attending to the injured as, on the far end of the campo, the winner was met by hoots and cheers. Holding his breath, Duncan watched two of the medics come to the man prone in the dirt and help him slowly to his feet. Duncan supposed he'd already guessed who the injured man must be, even before the figure was mostly upright, a head taller than the two medics who held him, his arms around their shoulders, his head bobbing.

Had Gina seen this? Her father trampled before her? The crowd had grown so rowdy now that Duncan had no hope of finding Gina until the square had cleared a little. He waited for people to begin descending from the bleachers, and finally, when the seats were half-emptied, he spotted Gina, standing still at the center of so much movement, remaining as he'd asked her to remain, in the precise spot where he'd left her.

He called her name and waved. As he approached her, she looked at him blankly, until he realized that he was still wearing his mask. He took it off and held it in his shaking hands.

"Are you all right?" he asked her, trying to glean from her expression what she might have seen. She seemed far too calm to have noticed her father, let alone that he'd been hurt. Looking back the way he'd come, Duncan could see the horse down on its side. From here, Gina would have been able to observe the fall, but not the details, not, he hoped, the faces of anyone involved.

"That was horrible," she said, clearly shaken, though the abstract way in which she said this confirmed for Duncan that she had not seen clearly who the wounded man happened to be.

He pulled her to him and held her, hoping she couldn't feel him trembling or sense his terror—Gina's father was here, and he was wounded, maybe grievously, because of him. It was too awful to keep from her, though if he told her, he knew this would be the end. All his hopes were collapsing. If he'd ever entertained the fantasy that one day Gina might finally forgive him for his lies, he knew that she would not forgive him what had happened on this day. So unsteadied was he by this realization that he was afraid he would trip as they climbed, side by side, across the bleachers. He recalled his injuries of the last day, his fever and his aches, and felt as if this new shock had made him ill again. When they reached the ground, he was sure it must be shaking still with the rush of hooves.

From the campo he stumbled on, borne along by the steady current of people that fed into the surrounding streets. He didn't bother giving Gina her mask, since the mood between them was too somber and he doubted anyone could spot them in the throng. For a time he simply followed the crowd without thinking, until Gina asked after the address of their lodgings, and Duncan withdrew the note he carried in his wallet.

"Via del Poggio," he read aloud.

"I think we've already passed it. We need to turn back."

They tried to do this, but going against the stream of people was impossible, so they were forced to wait until the flow had thinned enough for them to move against it.

Gina rang the bell of a simple brown brick house and they were greeted by their host, who introduced himself as Mauro. He was very large, with a big stomach, but a light way about him—someone, Duncan imagined, who'd gotten heavy only later in life.

"I expect for you," Mauro said, ushering them in and showing them to their room, which was on the small side but charming, with a window overlooking the street. Their luggage had just arrived, Mauro said, and pointed to the suitcases waiting in the corner.

"You're hungry now?" the man asked them. "My wife and I will make you dinner."

Duncan thanked him, and, after their host had left, explained to Gina what the clerk at the Hotel Duomo had told him—that all the restaurants would be booked and the city overwhelmed that night.

"Better to stay in," said Gina, "after all the traveling and heat and crowds. To be honest, my dizziness hasn't gone away and I think a calm night would be best."

Duncan gladly agreed, and after a shower and a change of clothes, they joined Mauro and his wife in the dining room. The meal was much too large: soup and pasta and fish, which Duncan ate slowly, occupied by his grim thoughts. Thankfully, Mauro distracted Gina with his chatter, only too pleased to make conversation with a pretty American girl.

"It's a pity my son can't be here to meet you. He lives in Rome now, or he did. Last month he left to Barcelona, chasing a Spanish girl. Who can know if he'll return?"

"Love has no respect for borders," said Gina.

"And no respect for fathers and their wallets," Mauro went on lamenting. "I am the one to lend him this apartment, and now it just sits there, empty. He doesn't pay even for maintenance."

"You ought to rent it out to tourists, then," Gina advised.

Mauro's eyes widened. "For the maintenance price *you* two could use this if you plan to visit Rome."

"Oh, I hadn't—" Gina looked to Duncan then, expectant, and he had to rouse himself to listen. "What do you say to heading to Rome next?"

"Why not?" He smiled at her as well as he was able, though the image he kept with him barred the way to thoughts of Rome or Paris or New York, or of any future anywhere. He was still seeing the awful scene on the campo, Frank Reinhold, forehead bloodied, that strong man dragged between the medics like a sack.

The image refused to leave him, was with Duncan still, even later that night, in bed, where he knew better than to hope for sleep to visit him. He couldn't keep the questions from coming.

Where was Mr. Reinhold now? How badly off was he? People died from accidents with horses—and if he had died?

Only a villain could go on by Gina's side without knowing if her sole remaining parent had been lost because of him.

Several times now on their trip, he'd snuck out in the middle of the night while Gina was asleep, but this time was surely the most dangerous. Tiptoeing downstairs, he'd been surprised to find Mauro awake so late, and told his host he was merely taking a walk, as he stepped out with the map from his guidebook to lead him to the hospital. The unfamiliar streets were mazelike and unsettling, populated by wandering drunks and lit only by dim lanterns. It seemed a miracle when he reached the limit of the old city and found a taxi waiting.

"Azienda Ospedaliera," he instructed the driver. "Viale Mario Bracci."

"Fifty thousand lire," the driver demanded; Duncan informed him he had only thirty.

They reached an agreement, though Duncan sensed he was still being overcharged, and worried how he'd manage to get back if he spent all his money now. He quickly dismissed the concern, unsure whether he ever *would* be getting back. There was so much that could go wrong. Gina's father might not be alone. If he and Graham were united in their search for Gina, Graham might be with him. Perhaps they'd brought police along and Duncan might be caught. As he approached the hospital, he understood that walking in might mean he'd never leave this building freely, and yet he rode on, in the vague hope that somehow matters would turn out all right.

The hospital was plain and modern. The line for reception

stretched nearly to the door, teeming with visitors, and every seat in the waiting area was filled. Duncan had a hard time getting anyone's attention, even after he'd waited his turn for half an hour.

"Does anyone speak English? I'm here to inquire about Franklin Reinhold. He was hurt in the race."

"Non capisco, " said the nurses, until an older nurse who'd been standing off a ways took notice of him.

"Who you are, then?"

"Frank Reinhold's son-in-law."

Duncan received no response. Instead, the older nurse muttered something to the others in Italian. *"L'Americano dalla corsa di cavalli. "*

As the nurses chatted, Duncan tried to gather whether he was their subject—*That's the one responsible, the criminal!*—and he began to fear he'd been reckless to admit who he was, though after a few minutes of being ignored, it seemed that he was less a wanted man than one who'd been forgotten.

"Excuse me?" Duncan asked tentatively.

"Reinhold, trecentoquarantatre, " said one nurse, and, seeing Duncan's confusion, scribbled the room number onto a piece of paper.

In the elevator riding up, Duncan braced himself for what might be awaiting him. Outside the room he paused to peer through the pane of glass, relieved to see no visitors, no activity inside. The room contained three beds, though he couldn't tell which belonged to Gina's father until he stepped in and saw Mr. Reinhold in the center bed, asleep. The man was hooked by monitors to a machine that beeped beside him, and a feeding tube was in his arm. In the eerie glow of the fluorescents, his skin looked yellow, waxy, deathlike.

Duncan had entertained the thought before that Gina's father might not survive, but as a sort of experiment, daring himself to imagine the worst—only now did it strike him as a real possibility.

As Duncan drew closer to him, Mr. Reinhold began to stir. His sleep was light, or else he'd merely been resting, because abruptly, the man's eyes opened and fixed on Duncan, shining with greater fire than it seemed that battered body could contain.

"That was *you*, in the mask." Mr. Reinhold addressed him, neither surprised nor frightened to see Duncan suddenly appear. For a moment, Duncan feared the man would shout for an orderly or the police, but the way Reinhold slurred and blinked his bloodshot eyes let Duncan know that he was fighting through a fog of medication. Possibly Reinhold wasn't sure whether this meeting was more than a hallucination.

Mr. Reinhold's focus remained squarely on Duncan, as Duncan searched for what to say. "I hope you know how sorry I am that you got hurt." He'd have gone on, but Mr. Reinhold appeared not to be listening, was craning his neck to see out of the room.

"You're here by yourself?" There was sadness in his face when he said it, as if in order to proceed he had to overcome the wish—as improbable as he knew it to be—that Gina had come too, and he would finally be reunited with his daughter.

"Yes, it's just me. Gina's fine, don't worry. But you understand I had to leave her back at our room."

"You're asking me to . . . *understand*?" Mr. Reinhold was struggling to sit up straighter in bed, but the pain of it led him to collapse back down again.

"I only mean that I wish Gina could see you, that there were some way for all of us to accept—"

"Accept that you've stolen her? Is that what you're . . . what you're hoping I'll do?"

The words were labored, and Reinhold's lids drooped, so that Duncan came to feel discussion was impossible. Even if the man calmed down and they made headway, anything that passed between them would likely be forgotten.

"This might not be the right time to explain myself—"

"I ought to wring your neck!" Reinhold bellowed, with such sudden fierceness that Duncan was taken aback. He could see in the man's raving expression that he was not under control, that his judgment had been overthrown by medication, pain, and shock. "I should have gotten rid of you the first time you tried to take her from me!"

"I didn't try to take her from you," Duncan replied calmly, hoping to bring him back to reason a little. "It was Gina's decision to come home to New York."

"New York wasn't her home! She was lost there and you just about wrecked her." Mr. Reinhold struggled to breathe. "She came running back to me in pieces. And then you had the nerve to show up at my house to try to tempt her away from me again!"

The man was speaking from a very different place than he had then, thought Duncan, on that day in Santa Fe when he'd stood on his lawn, surrounded by flowering cacti and bougainvillea, sounding like the responsible and evenhanded father, the caretaker with only his daughter's best interests at heart. A different man showed himself to Duncan now, almost barbarous as he went on, rasping, spittle forming on his dry, cracked lips.

"You think you've got her this time, but don't delude yourself. Once she knows the truth she'll drop you and come back home with me again. Graham told me what the doctors in Berlin had to say. She clearly doesn't understand what's happened, what a sick bastard you are. But I know, and I'll see to it you end up rotting in a jail cell, wishing you'd never dared to take her. I'll see to it that you do!"

Mr. Reinhold's face was red: Duncan could see a vein bulging in his forehead, the cords straining in his neck. Hatred was coming off of him like heat, and Duncan could find no words to calm him. He must have been startled by the man's rage, because only now did it occur to Duncan that their heated exchange had attracted attention. An orderly came charging in, addressing Duncan roughly in Italian. Security might be arriving any instant. Without a word, Duncan dashed past the orderly and out the door, pain bolting through him as he raced through the hall, voices shouting in Italian behind him. Bounding down the stairwell, his ribs throbbing, he burst into the lobby, where a pair of revolving doors was all that stood between him and freedom.

The walk back to the apartment took hours longer than the trip by taxi, punctuated by breaks to recuperate from pain. The way was dark, the street names hard to see, and twice Duncan became lost, absorbed in his distress.

It had been frightening, and pitiful, to see Gina's father in this state, the wishes hidden away in his heart laid so bare. In all the years he'd grumbled over Gina's father, suspecting the man might be against him in some way, he'd always assumed that their rivalry was of the common sort. Even as he'd lied to Gina, mere days ago, inventing an argument between Gina and her father, it hadn't occurred to him that the reality was worse than he'd imagined. He'd pretended Gina's father had wished to keep her, and now it appeared that was the truth. Their conversation had left him dazed, in part because the man's condemnation of him had landed hard, but also because the same accusations could be made of Reinhold too. All along, this man who appeared to want his daughter to live as a free spirit hadn't, in his heart, wanted her free. What Mr. Reinhold wanted—profoundly, perversely, maybe even more so than Duncan—was to keep Gina for himself. And so it seemed to Duncan that, through his selfish act, he might also have rescued Gina from a kind of confinement he hadn't even known she'd faced.

By the time Duncan arrived at Mauro's house, the night sky was turning blue. He came in silently and climbed the stairs to find Gina asleep in bed. Lying beside her, exhausted, achy, soulsick, he had the wish to take her in his arms, to protect her from all the forces, even those within him, that aimed to keep her bound.

But if this was really how he felt, and if he loved her the way he believed he did, he must tell her, immediately, what he'd done to make her his again. He must allow her, in full knowledge of the facts and with full freedom, to decide if she wanted him or not.

There in the brightening room where Gina lay peacefully sleeping, he reached out to tap her shoulder. She rolled over, opened her eyes, and looked straight at him, the way her father had done just hours before. He was afraid of what she was seeing, but lacked the composure then to pull himself together, to smile and fake the way he had been. He was convinced that Gina must know something was wrong, and yet the expression on her face was pure lightness, a kind of radiance he was startled by, transfixed. In that moment, as he was about to confess, Gina spoke first, silencing him with her two brief words.

"I'm pregnant."

Thirteen

Gina // Siena, Rome

July 1996

In the moments after she'd made her wonderful and frightful admission, she'd awaited Duncan's reaction, but had been met only with silence. He'd been stunned, and then, when he'd come back to himself a little, he'd kissed her and held her while they lay in bed, still speechless, as the sun brightened the shades over their window. After they'd risen, while they dressed, he finally began to talk, though what he had to say had nothing to do with his feelings, as she'd hoped. He expressed concern over the practical side of things. She ought to be seen by a doctor. There were tests that should be run, supplements she should be taking.

"I'm thinking in that case," Duncan went on, "we definitely ought to leave Siena and head to Rome."

"So soon? They do have hospitals here too."

"Small facilities that are bound to be swamped right now. No, no. We won't take a chance on that." His tone was firm. "You'll need a doctor who speaks English, which you're bound to find somewhere like Rome. Didn't Mauro offer his apartment last night?"

She was taken aback by the speed with which Duncan hatched this plan. "Yes, but he'd had a few glasses of wine. We can't be sure he meant it."

"So let's ask him." Eager to have the matter settled, Duncan pulled on his shirt and headed downstairs. After she'd also finished dressing, Gina caught up with him and Mauro in the kitchen, where Mauro was fixing their breakfast.

"He thinks Rome's a great idea," Duncan began.

Mauro picked up from there. "We'd love to keep you here with us, but truly Siena's not very nice now—too many tourists. And you can always come here again to visit. Only three hours on the train." As he spoke excitedly, Mauro fished through the kitchen drawers, pulling out a pair of keys. "For you, take these. The apartment is very pleasing. I can make you a promise you'll enjoy it."

"And are you sure paying maintenance is enough?" she asked him, though neither Duncan nor Mauro seemed especially concerned over the price.

"Enough, yes. Only look after it a little. I love this flat. I lived in it myself as a young man." Mauro paused, long-lashed eyes flashing, and Gina could see in the jolly old flirt the handsome youth who'd moved from adventure to adventure in that city. It might have been Mauro's nostalgia for his time there that stirred up longing in her too.

"Well, all right, then. I guess we'll be heading on to Rome."

Duncan reached for her and squeezed her. "Mauro says there's an eleven thirty train. If we're quick we can still catch it."

Once they were up in their room again, Duncan set about packing, hurrying around, tossing items into the suitcase, all the while focused on the tasks they would now be required to perform——they'd need to get more lire to pay for the room and for the taxi, then in Rome he'd call the hospital and see about scheduling an appointment. Gina watched him, struck by his busyness, and by what, through this sudden move, he was avoiding discussing. Since she'd made her big announcement, he'd still said nothing of his feelings.

Of course there was so much she wished to ask him. It terrified her not to know if this child she wanted dearly filled Duncan with joy or dread. But as much as she'd have liked to prod him, she told herself she must give him space at first to sort out his reactions, and so she resolved to spend the day not speaking of the pregnancy at all, if it came to that.

Around ten, they left Mauro's apartment and walked together with their luggage to a stand where they might find a taxi. There, they parted ways with their host, taking the keys to the apartment and a card with Mauro's number.

"Divertitevi a Roma!" Mauro shouted, waving, as the car backed out jerkily and raced up the steep road.

For three hours, they rode together through the Tuscan countryside, surrounded by patches of cultivated green, olive and cypress trees, vineyards. The day was perfect, blue sky and fleecy clouds, and from her first sight of Rome through the train windows, Gina found it incomparably lovely, belonging to some more perfect future, some life she now felt she was meant to lead. She gasped aloud, from a combination of excitement and fear, and finally had to stand and walk the aisles of the train to discharge the nervous energy inside her.

Mauro's apartment was on Via Mazzarino, in Rione Monti. The address turned out to be near the train station and very central too, roughly equidistant from the Trevi Fountain and the Roman

Forum. The street itself was quiet, with residential buildings no more than five or six stories high, and the occasional small restaurant with umbrellas and chalkboard signs out on the pavement.

They followed the street numbers to a great wooden door that opened with their largest key. Inside was a vestibule leading to an elevator and stairs. The small space was presided over by a very large statue, a male nude, as if sculptures of high quality were so abundant in Rome that they might be placed at the entrance of even minor buildings. The apartment itself was charming, with fans hanging from high ceilings, wooden floors, and a balcony off of the living room. To Duncan's delight, a small piano stood between the living and dining areas, and on the widest wall, across, stood a giant canvas containing a detailed portrait of a woman's face.

Gina stood observing her, this woman with a quiet smile, while Duncan phoned the hospital and returned to announce they would be seen if they could get there right away. There wasn't time to settle in, therefore, as much as Gina would have liked to, and, just minutes after they'd arrived, they were heading back to the Metro to ride to Tor Sapienza in the Municipio 4.

There, at Rome American Hospital, Gina was examined by a young obstetrician, a woman who'd been born to American parents and who narrated for her, in perfect English, the meaning of the image that Gina saw during her ultrasound. Duncan stood beside her in the room, holding her hand and kissing it to calm the nerves that wouldn't leave her until the doctor had told her several times that all looked well and the pregnancy was advancing normally.

"And how far along is it, can you say?" Duncan asked, while Gina turned to look at the wall.

"Hard to be precise about these things, but I'd guess under six weeks."

When Gina turned to face him, Duncan was nodding, relieved.

"A citizen of Europe," Gina piped in brightly, and shortly after, she and Duncan made an appointment to return in three weeks' time, which implied that they would still be there in Rome, a declaration, in effect, of their intention to settle, for a while at least.

That evening, back at their new apartment, they set about unpacking, and Gina had the sensation that now, after so many weeks spent in hotels, they'd arrived at a kind of home. The portrait of the woman overlooked them, and Gina wondered aloud to Duncan who she might be. "Mauro's first love? A daughter?"

"Our guardian angel," Duncan proposed, kissing her cheek, and at last she could see in him the delight she'd been awaiting.

Was it possible Duncan wanted what she wanted? That image she'd carried for so long, of the three of them, her and Duncan and their child, starting a home together—might it be here? In this city that had entranced her already?

Over the next days she and Duncan seemed genuinely happy, and she began to trust that he was as quietly pleased at the prospect of this new future as she needed him to be. Now and then she'd notice him smiling a boyish smile that wouldn't leave him, that reminded her of their earliest days together, back in school, when she'd catch him trying to conceal the grins that would suddenly overtake him.

They fell easily into a cheerful routine. In the morning, they ate their breakfast out on the balcony, then spent the early part of the day exploring the city. In the afternoon, when the heat was too great to be outside, Gina read and Duncan sat at his desk with his composition sheets or played the piano. He'd decided to try to get back to composing, since in Rome they were finally in no hurry, and conditions were calm enough for him to concentrate again. To get his mind back on his music, Gina bought them tickets to a performance at the Accademia Nazionale di Santa Cecilia, one of the oldest conservatories in all Europe.

The next day, she and Duncan took the train to Vatican City to visit St. Peter's Basilica. She'd been overwhelmed when she'd entered, and had to look down at the floor to get her bearings. The church was far larger than she'd imagined, dizzyingly so, and every foot of it contained such an abundance of artistry. In the past, beautiful things would often make her sad. They seemed to belong to the more beauteous realm of her childhood, and so recalled her loss. Here in Rome, though, her reaction was different. She felt instead a stirring hope that she might live beautifully again. They would both be better here, she and Duncan, away from the reminders of their former, lesser selves, now that Duncan had let go his fear and inhibition and she'd thrown off her own uncertainty about his readiness. Standing inside the basilica was like awakening to the fully alive existence she'd longed for since her childhood had ended.

She began to fantasize about a future there in Rome, and images came to her, solid and persuasive: of her pushing a stroller along the local streets to pick up Duncan from rehearsal; her coming to see him perform inside a grand concert hall, like the one at the Accademia Nazionale.

One morning, while Duncan sat down to compose at the small piano, she took a walk to the Accademia—the ancient and elegant stone building joined by modern structures, performance halls that, from the outside, resembled enormous silver disks. The grounds were otherworldly, the students passionate and serious, so much like Duncan, when she'd first seen him, that she knew he belonged here. She found her way to the admissions office and there spoke with a woman on the staff about the requirements: there was an application, and then an audition in the fall. The greatest obstacle to Duncan being accepted to the program was the language. He would need to be proficient in Italian. Gina collected the application materials and carried them home to give to Duncan.

His initial reaction was disbelief.

"You mean for me to apply? For us to stay in Rome. You're serious?"

"And why not?"

"We'd need money, for one thing."

"And we have it." He was perfectly aware that she had several hundred thousand left from her mother, which, if they took care, might last them as much as a decade. "And we can work here too, why not? You can give piano lessons. I can teach and, eventually, after the baby, start dancing again. We can compose, create new work, do everything that we did in New York before."

"Could you really go on this way?" he asked her, finally. "You wouldn't miss home?"

Even as the events of the past came to her more clearly each day, she by now felt so removed from her own history. At the least, she felt strangely little pull to return. Her colleagues in New York were getting on just fine without her. None of her other friendships rivaled what she had with Violet, and Violet was no longer there. The only person she would miss and who would suffer her absence, deeply, was her father. "There's just my dad, and he's across the country as it is. Plus, we're not on good terms, you say. That I've been wanting distance from him."

"Right, yes." Duncan spoke a bit too firmly, a bit too fast, but before she could press him further, he continued. "All I'm saying is, moving abroad is a big step. It can be lonely. I mean, I'm for it, I think *I* could do it. I don't need more than you. But I'm not sure that in your case it's the same."

In fact the prospect of such isolation did make her skittish, but she took pains not to show it. She could see the anxiety in Duncan's expression, the need in him to believe that she was equally content with only him, and would continue to be so, without end. "It won't just be you and me anymore," she pointed out. "You, me, *and* our child. I can't think how I'd need more than that."

Duncan reached for her and held her, apparently persuaded. Already the next morning, she'd found him at his desk, working on his conservatory application. She went off on her own then, to visit the Pantheon at the Piazza della Rotonda, a lovely square with the temple looming at one end. She'd been struck to see such an ancient building built on so grand a scale: columns as thick as five men standing side by side. Inside, a giant dome opened up onto the heavens. It was fantastical, really, to think that she might go on living in a place where a ten-minute walk brought her to a Roman temple, or to the Trevi Fountain, or to Trajan's Forum. So many wonders all around her, she might have gone on to see more, but she was feeling how her energy was fading and a small cramp was forming in her belly. She bought a bottle of cold water and walked slowly back to the apartment, where she found Duncan at the desk beside the balcony, so caught up by something he hadn't heard her come in.

She crossed the floor, wondering if he might be in the grips of a musical idea—but no, he was on the phone.

He wasn't speaking, only seated, his head leaning on one hand. His leg bounced tensely, and the phone cord was tangled around his forearm. When he saw her, he swiveled to face her and assumed a more neutral expression, but she had seen, in the instant that preceded, a look of despair. In her panic, she ran through the possibilities regarding what he might have heard. Could the hospital have phoned? Could there be a problem with her? With the baby?

"What? What is it? Was that the doctor?"

"The doctor? No, no." He set down the phone and rose to kiss her. "Don't worry. Nothing like that." Yet his face betrayed his distress.

"Something upset you."

He raised his hand to his forehead, massaging it, making the skin fold and straighten beneath his fingertips. "I didn't want to bother you about it, really. But . . . it's my mother, if you need to know." Reluctantly, he admitted that he'd phoned in for their messages. "She's taking it badly, my being away. Though I couldn't have expected any other reaction. But it doesn't change anything. The only place I want to be is here with you."

He sat down and pulled Gina onto his lap. As he held her, silent, gripping her tightly, she could feel him taking solace from her. She didn't assume that what he'd told her was the truth—it might be—but whatever he'd heard over the phone must have left him shaken.

"And was that all of it, then?" she asked him.

"All of it?"

"There weren't any messages for me?" She was pressing him a little, could feel him squirm beneath her.

"No, this time there weren't."

"This time? Were there other calls for me before?"

"No," he hurried to say, his tone hardly convincing. "People know we're away. There wouldn't be any reason to call."

"You're sure you're not protecting me from something? Maybe something unpleasant from my father?"

Duncan looked struck. Abruptly he stood, pushing her off of his lap, and began to pace the room. "I guess I can't blame you for being suspicious, since I wasn't straight with you before. But I wish I had your trust back."

"Relax, Duncan, you do." She smiled, choosing to relent, to put him at ease again. There was no point in pressuring him this way. She dropped the subject of her father after that, though privately she did find herself thinking of him, feeling that she couldn't let him go on without some reassurance. Eventually she'd have to tell him of her plans to stay abroad. She didn't inform Duncan of her intention to call home—he'd only object, and anyway, she didn't require his permission. The next day, she first tried her father from a pay phone in the Galleria Borghese, where she'd gone while Duncan stayed behind, composing, in their apartment. Having gotten no answer, she tried again the next morning when Duncan ran out for milk. Again, after four rings, her father's recorded voice came onto the line: *"You've reached Frank Reinhold. . . ."*

That morning she chose to leave a message. *"Dad, it's me. I'm sorry for not calling sooner. I should have, I realize. It's all been complicated, but you should know that I'm fine, really better than fine. I sent you a letter, though I'm not sure you received it. I hope you're all right. I've tried to reach you several times now and, well, I'm starting to get nervous. I'll try you again soon. Hope you get this. I love you."*

In bed, later that night, she found herself thinking back on a painting she'd seen in St. Peter's Basilica, a work by Raphael: Lot's wife turning to look at Sodom, burning, as she fled. There the woman stood, frozen, a pillar of salt, unable to move on with her family. This seemed to her a warning. Don't look back. Don't cry salt tears when you've been saved. She and Duncan were going to start a family together, an exciting new life in a great city, and he seemed so contented with this that he'd put his own concerns behind him. She'd heard nothing more about calls from his mother; he'd expressed no further doubts about continuing on as they had been. In the last week, Duncan had completed his application to the Accademia and contacted an Italian language school that ran through the summer—he'd missed three weeks, but if he hired a tutor to help him catch up, and with his background in French, the teacher was confident he'd manage.

Duncan was moving forward; she ought to do the same, and yet she couldn't get over her worries—especially regarding her father. Where was he?

It crossed her mind, rather darkly, that there was only one person who would know if her father was okay.

She waited before she made her move, knowing she'd be setting in motion something that would not easily be stopped. There would be consequences, and so for several days, she carried the number with her in her purse and periodically removed it, had a look, considered, then put it away again. It was a risky thing that she was doing, and on the morning that she resolved to act, she'd been up for the whole night, standing and circling the bed, unable to stop moving. Finally, at eight that morning, when Duncan went in to register for his Italian lessons, Gina withdrew the slip of paper and dialed the number she'd been given over the phone in Vienna, by the clerk at the Hotel de Rome—the number for Graham Bonafair.

Fourteen

Duncan // Rome

August 1996

On Fridays, Duncan and his fellow Italian students were let out early and would go walking together across the balcony that overlooked the courtyard, down the stone steps through the gate onto the sidewalk. The Italian course was run out of a small grammar school on Via Del Vaccaro, a lovely little cobblestone street with a passageway forming an arch between the buildings. There were several restaurants in the area, and on this afternoon, the students were proposing they go for lunch together.

"Can't, I'm sorry," Duncan told them, already backing away. But today his classmates were determined.

"Perchè no?"

"Come on, it's early."

"Who will mind if you stay longer?"

"Mia moglie," Duncan answered, making use of the phrase he'd learned that week: "my wife." This was the first time Duncan had pronounced the words, the first time among his

classmates that he'd acknowledged having a wife. It seemed a mistake as soon as he said it. He was, perhaps, growing too relaxed in Rome.

"You're married?" asked a Welsh girl with huge, pale eyes. He'd taken off his ring for class so as not to prompt questions about Gina. "We all just assumed you went home and sat in your apartment alone."

He laughed at himself, and even thought he managed to blush like the shy sort they took him for. During lunch break, when the others gathered in the courtyard, he'd go off to eat his sandwich and write letters on a bench. He liked his classmates well enough, but he didn't think it prudent to let them get too close. Whenever the class exercises involved answering personal questions— *Where do you come from? What brought you to Rome?*—he chose to make up stories. In the course of that week, he'd invented a whole fictional account of his previous life in Michigan, son of a factory worker and a nurse of Italian descent who'd aroused his curiosity about this country. He'd even chosen to go by his middle name, Maxwell, or Max. No one knew him as Duncan, and since he'd begun growing a beard, soon it would be hard for any new acquaintance to be sure that the Duncan Lowy of his old photos, were they to surface, was him.

"Max has a wife," the Welsh girl spread the word to the Spaniard. "He's just full of surprises, isn't he?"

"Is she for real, then?"

"She is, and she hates it when I'm late." He was in a hurry to leave, suddenly. He'd made a mistake admitting he was married. That might cause trouble for him in the future.

"Why don't you bring her back here? She can join us for lunch too!"

"Sorry, but she's even more of an introvert than me. Anyway, I've gotta run. Good weekend to you all. *Ciao!*"

Finally, he managed to jog off. He couldn't allow Gina to mix with these students, and now he'd have to keep making excuses for her absence. The unnecessary complication bothered him, but after he'd walked for a few minutes, his irritation faded. In general, he found it hard to be annoyed in Rome; everything was just too lovely. The light here was so vibrant, the streets so charming—paradise seemed to lie around each corner. Just then he was passing by a row of pretty ivy-covered houses on his left, and on his right a grocery selling pyramids of brightly colored fruit. He bought some yellow plums to eat on his way and couldn't recall, back in the States, ever tasting fruit so sweet.

Pleasure like this had its costs, he thought, and one cost of remaining in Rome would be holding himself aloof from people. As much as he might prefer to settle in, make friends, live a normal life here with Gina, he knew he couldn't take the risk. Not since he'd learned how much more was at stake. Gina was pregnant. The pressure upon him was twice as great now. An innocent soul hung in the balance. He must remain under the radar as long as there was still a chance that a story about him might run in the paper or crop up on TV, still a chance that the hunt for him might reach from Siena to Rome. If the past weeks had taught him anything, it was not to underestimate Mr. Reinhold's resolve.

He reached the flat around twelve thirty and found that Gina wasn't home. He'd assumed as much, that on a nice day like this one, Gina would be out sightseeing for several hours and he'd have use of the apartment to attend to his own dealings.

His first order of business this afternoon was to call in to his home answering machine. Lately he'd been checking in as often as he could, ever since the shock he'd suffered when, after a lapse, he'd listened to his messages during his second week in Rome.

One after another, everyone who'd played a part in his previous life—his employer at the dance studio, his landlord, Blake, his father—all of them had called him in a panic:

"Duncan, I've just gotten the most insane phone call about you. . . ." "Duncan, Gina's father called me. . . ." "Duncan, what's going on?"

He'd felt the breath leave him, though he'd tried to remain calm, to tell himself that such a moment was inevitable and must be faced. Stoically, he'd listened until he'd come to the recording from his mother.

"My God, God help me, what have you done? Is it true? Gina's father called from Italy. He says he's gone off searching for you. That you've taken Gina hostage; he says she's not well and that you've used her weakness to turn her into your prisoner. Her father even believes that you hurt Gina yourself. He's asked me to urge you to turn yourself in. He tells me if you don't, he won't be able to protect you from a prison sentence, which you'll have to serve in Berlin, where I can never see you. My God, Duncan, this is a nightmare! I think I must be going mad!"

His mother sobbed into the line, so that Duncan felt his insides plummet as he listened. This was worse than he'd imagined. Though he'd recognized something like this might happen—Graham had reached out to his mother, so Frank Reinhold might do the same—he'd assumed more care would be taken with an old woman who was innocent in all of this. Apparently Mr. Reinhold had spared her nothing, had been perfectly willing to inflict suffering if some part of that suffering would stir Duncan to experience anguish of his own, and anguish that Mr. Reinhold must have felt Duncan had caused him. His anger at Gina's father allowed for some relief of his own guilt. He wouldn't have been forced to do this thing if Reinhold hadn't kept Gina from him and made her a prisoner himself. And so he must resist manipulation, survive the man's crueler tactics, or else Gina's father would disrupt his peace so greatly that, if Duncan didn't simply cave, he would make some fateful mistake.

He'd called his mother later that night, while Gina was asleep.

"Mom, I swear, what that man says, it isn't true. Gina and I are back together, yes, but very much willingly. We've reconciled. And she isn't sick. The one who's sick is Gina's father. He's so enraged to have lost her to me, he'll say anything to bring her back to him."

"Duncan, are you sure? I wish I could believe you, but he's got lawyers, police."

"He's got nothing but lies and the money to back them up. He's trying to hurt you to get to me, Mom. That's what this is. Please, please listen to me. Please believe me and not that man and the stories that he'll tell you. I'm not in danger, nor is Gina. We're both happy—except that I can't be happy if I think that you're upset."

He was persuading her, he sensed, and supposed this gave him courage to press on. Or else perhaps what gave him courage was the rage he felt toward Gina's father. A spirit of defiance rose up in him, which wiped away all hesitations, the stickiness left by his guilt. His resolve was redoubled. Gina would remain with him.

"There's something more you need to know, Mom." He swallowed. "There's a chance that Gina and I won't return."

"What do you mean you won't *return*? To New York?"

"To America."

"For how long?"

"I don't know."

"You don't mean ever?"

"I guess. I don't know what I mean." He could hear the nervous strain enter his voice, and could feel the small part of him that wished to come to his mother like a child would, tell her he'd gotten in over his head and needed help. Instead, he quickly shored up his resolve. "It's possible that I'll live here. For a while, at any rate. But it will be fine."

"Live where? Where on earth are you, Duncan?"

"I'm where I should be—with Gina."

"Duncan, that girl is not the only person that matters, not the only person who loves you and deserves a place in your life. You can't just shut us out," his mother insisted, her voice becoming shrill. "Your father and I need to have a way to reach you. To get in touch."

"I promise I'll write you soon and explain more. Until then, please don't worry about me and I won't worry about you. You can handle this. We both can."

He hung up the phone, briefly relieved, but knowing this would not be the end. Every day he called in to his messages again, awaiting another from her, a next breakdown, some threat or tug upon his conscience. None came. Not from his mother, nor from the others he'd responded to with letters. The letters he'd sent out to his acquaintances offered much the same explanation: he and Gina had gone off together, and her father, unable to accept the fact, too possessive to let his daughter go, had spun a wild narrative to try to stop them. He'd written all these letters in the course of the week, during his lunch breaks at school, every letter except the one to Blake. Blake, he knew, would require a different argument.

Blake, he'd written finally, *I apologize for failing to call you and for the fact that I can't agree to meet. At the moment, a meeting would be too risky for me, for reasons I bet you can guess yourself. I can't be sure Gina's father wouldn't send someone to follow you, or that you wouldn't allow it, out of a sense of loyalty to me, and a conviction that you're saving me from making a huge mistake. I know you mean well, and so I hope you know that my failure to trust you isn't an insult. If at some point I think you've come around on this, I'll be glad to see you again. For now, all I can say is that I'm wishing you the best, and I hope you can find your way to wishing that for me—even if for me, that means being with Gina.*

When he'd read his letter over, he couldn't say that he expected Blake would be convinced. Nevertheless, it was the best he could come up with, and he'd chosen to send it, several days before, in lieu of no response at all.

Now, having skipped lunch with his classmates, Duncan was famished, so he stepped out to the corner store and bought some bread, cheese, tomatoes, and cured ham, along with a newspaper to keep him busy until Gina returned. Upstairs again, he ate his lunch as he read the major stories: the Summer Olympics had ended and America had taken gold in the decathlon and set records in the two-hundred-meter race. Meanwhile, in politics, Bob Dole had picked Jack Kemp as his vice presidential running mate. Duncan had nearly forgotten the election coming up in November. These stories of America felt so disconnected from him now.

Bored by the paper, he looked up at the clock. The time was half past three, around when he came home from a regular class day, and typically, Gina was back before he was. He put on music to relax him, and then, feeling sleepy, chose to lie down. Without intending to, he fell asleep, and when he woke again, the time was half past four.

It wasn't like Gina to be gone this long. If she knew she was going to be late, she'd have left a note or called. He checked the phone, making sure it was on its base, and then he went across the hall to ask the neighbor on their floor if he'd seen Gina at all that day or knew where she had gone. When the neighbor said he hadn't, Duncan made another quick trip to the small grocery on the corner, the same one where he'd bought lunch. "Have you seen *mia moglie?*"

"*Non l'ho vista da ieri.*" Not since yesterday, said the old woman at the counter. Duncan thanked her and hurried home, fearing that it would be in the time when he was gone that Gina would try to call. On his way up the stairs, he kept hoping to hear ringing. No one called, though, not then and not in the course of the next hour, as Duncan paced the apartment, by then unable to distract himself from thoughts of what might be wrong.

Another accident was possible—he returned to the horror of that afternoon spent in Berlin, in the lobby of the Hotel de Rome. He remembered that feeling of despair on the ride over to the hospital, of preparing himself for the realization that he'd lost her utterly, that Gina was gone. If he hadn't suffered such a shock then, if he hadn't felt the bareness of his life without her, he wasn't sure he'd have been able to do what he'd done next, pretend she'd never left him, cling to her through his elaborate lie.

And what if today was the day, he thought, that Gina had uncovered the lie? What if today a missing part of her memory was magically restored and she'd realized how her love and trust had been abused? Or what if the day he'd been fearing most had arrived? Mr. Reinhold had found his daughter. Duncan recalled now a particular morning when he'd woken early and stepped out to find Gina in the living room, holding the phone. He hadn't heard her speaking, and she'd hung up as soon as she'd spotted him.

"A wrong number," she offered. "I guess it woke you too?"

He'd shrugged, truly uncertain what had happened, only now the meaning of that small event shone clearly. She'd been on the phone with her father, plotting her escape.

His imagination was running wild. He tried to contain it, to convince himself that all that had happened was that Gina had lost track of time in a museum or gone to see a movie in a theater she'd walked by on her way home. There were a dozen stories more plausible than Gina's father tracking her down, and yet he couldn't stop himself from speculating how this could have happened.

Had Mauro led Gina's father to them? Duncan had been aware this was a danger as soon as he'd proposed they stay in this apartment—for the first time, someone from their previous destination knew the precise address where they'd gone next.

He'd been a fool to stay put for so long. He'd let his fantasies overcome his reason, and as a result, he'd lost Gina, maybe forever. She was gone and there was nothing he could do! He couldn't call the police. Gina hadn't been absent long enough to raise alarms and, even if she had been, he couldn't show up at the station and insist a woman already reported missing, who might be on file as having been kidnapped by him, was now missing from him. His hands were tied: he was stuck and would remain stuck. Gina's father would deliberately keep him in the dark, as Duncan had done to him. So days would pass with Gina gone and his not knowing if she was alive and well, if she still loved him or hated him, what would become of their infant. Until his not knowing would make him so crazy he'd bring himself to the police, and there be arrested and receive his due.

Five thirty and still Gina hadn't returned. Duncan was by then seated with an open bottle of wine, half empty. In the background, he played the local news on the rare chance that whatever had become of Gina was being covered in the press. As unlikely as he knew it to be, he kept imagining her face or her father's appearing on the screen, and more than once, he thought he'd seen them, he was in such a suggestible state. He was sitting this way, lost in frightened reverie, when he heard a key in the lock. He looked to the door in stunned silence, not sure what to expect, and couldn't quite believe Gina was back even when she stood again before him, smiling at him as if it were an evening like any other.

"Oh no, you were worried, weren't you?" She was taking in his ragged face, the wine. "I'm so sorry. I lost track of time." She came close to him and kissed his cheek. As she drew nearer, the scent of cigarettes wafted from her hair and clothes.

"You smell like smoke," he muttered, still in shock.

"Do I? I wonder— Well, yes, I stopped in a café. I didn't realize how late it had gotten. I'm sorry."

"You don't need to be sorry. I mean, you're free to do whatever. I just worried."

"I'm fine."

She smiled, then quickly crossed the floor to turn off the TV. Rather than rejoin him, she stopped at the balcony, looking outward.

"Gina?"

She turned back, trying to appear easygoing, but her distress

Robin Kirman

was palpable. Gina could never hide her feelings from him—this was one of the things he'd always loved about her, how passionate she was, and how transparent, by comparison.

"Something is going on, I can feel it. Whatever it is, you can tell me." He watched her slump her shoulders and slowly shake her head. When she looked up, she was laughing at herself.

"You're right, I'm a useless liar, aren't I? The whole point was not to worry you."

He came after her, trying to stay steady, reassuring. He took her hands in his, looking her in the eyes. "Please. I don't want secrets between us."

"Of course. No secrets." She hugged him tightly, her head against his chest, so that, as she spoke, he couldn't see her face. "I wasn't feeling well this morning, so I paid a visit to the hospital. It started after you left, cramps, awful ones. I wasn't sure how to reach you, and I didn't see any point in scaring you if it was nothing. Thankfully, the doctor said it was just dehydration, to be expected in the heat of a Rome summer. I just need to drink plenty of water and not exert myself too much. He let me go with this advice and a few pamphlets." Gina removed a stack of leaflets from her bag and set them upon the coffee table. "I should read them, but I'm too beat to do it now. I think I need to rest."

He walked her to the bedroom and she lay down on the bed. Duncan sat beside her. He was feeling a mixture of terror and gratitude—how fragile was his happiness, but he held on to it still. This woman he loved and the tiny creature forged out of that love—they were with him, safe. Or as safe as he could keep them.

He sat beside her, holding her hand and kissing it over and over, finding it hard to leave her side until, finally, Gina asked if he might close the curtains. The light remained strong into the evening, so he did his best to dim the room before stepping out to let her rest. In the kitchen, he filled a pot with water to boil pasta, and then recalled how Gina had said she ought to drink throughout the day. He reached for a pitcher, and the pot began to overflow.

He cursed, feeling his irritation. There seemed so much to manage at times, he couldn't think how he would do it—a child to care for, a new city to navigate, a home to make away from everyone they knew. And on top of all this he had his elaborate ruse to protect: from his parents, from Gina's father, Violet, Blake, Graham Bonafair, even his fellow classmates—the list went on. How would he ever manage to compose? How would he hold on to the person he'd once been?

Water had spilled onto his arms and shirt. He dried himself as best he could and returned, with the pitcher and a glass, to Gina's room.

When he reached the door, Gina was out of bed, standing by the window. The curtains had been drawn aside and she was looking down into the street. She quickly became aware of him and turned.

"Nausea. I needed air."

"Right, sure. And I brought you water too. That might help."

She thanked him and returned to the bed, smiling up at him sweetly. He set the pitcher and the glass down beside her, stroked her cheek and stepped away, choosing to say nothing of his misgivings, of his intuition, groundless perhaps, that as she stood staring out that window at the street, she was looking for someone.

Fifteen

Hours earlier, when Duncan had left for school that Friday, Gina had set off for the Metro, riding all the way to Tor Sapienza, where she exited and took the same walk she'd taken on her first day in Rome, when she and Duncan visited the hospital. She rode the elevator to obstetrics, chatted mindlessly with the receptionist—confirming her appointment for three days from now, asking a few very obvious questions she had in advance of the checkup—and then set out to do what she'd come to do. After thanking the receptionist, she stopped by the door to collect several pamphlets—on prenatal care, nutrition, and the like—which she'd need later to prove to Duncan she'd indeed gone to the hospital, that that was where she'd been all afternoon.

She left the hospital around eleven thirty, which gave her half an hour to reach the café where she would meet Graham Bonafair.

She was nervous walking over, uncertain whether she was doing the right thing. She couldn't help but feel that skipping off behind Duncan's back was a betrayal, and she couldn't anticipate what the outcome of this meeting would be. Reaching the café, she recalled how elated she and Duncan had been when they'd come here, after the hospital where they'd witnessed the miracle of the beating heart inside her belly. She stood to lose so much.

It was a typical Italian café, with a dark wooden bar and marble-topped tables, red wallpaper, and a checkered floor. Most of the patrons here were older, locals reading newspapers and chattering. The staff spoke no English; the menus were only in Italian.

Her heart was beating fast as she peered around the room, afraid to be faced with Graham after all this time and to discover what sort of feelings might be stirred, what memories revived. She'd recalled enough by now to make this meeting momentous. She was so tensely anticipating seeing him, was seeking his face so exclusively in the small crowd dispersed among the tables, that she didn't recognize, right away, who was seated there, waiting for her, instead.

He waved at her from a table in the corner. Blake Flournoy.

She was alarmed. How had Blake come to be here? Was he traveling with Graham? She tried to think what it could mean, what sort of setup she'd walked into and if she ought to simply turn around and leave. Blake continued to watch her. He was dressed in a pink button-down shirt and jeans, his legs crossed casually, and he was drinking an espresso, which he swished around in its small cup. Nothing about his manner suggested confrontation, yet she knew Blake well enough to be wary.

"This is a surprise," she said, taking a seat.

"I'd guess it is," Blake replied, grinning.

He was still handsome, but his straight blond hair, slicked back, was starting to thin, and there were bags under his eyes. He'd aged since she'd last seen him, over a year ago. Even when Blake had still lived in New York, he and Duncan had typically met without her. None of Blake's girlfriends ever lasted long enough to warrant outings as couples, and she was perfectly grateful for this, as she imagined Blake was too.

"Graham told you I'd be here?"

"He did, yes. And I asked his permission to speak with you first. I assured him I'd help explain things to you, so you'd be better prepared for meeting him."

"I had no idea you two had ever spoken."

"Thanks to recent events. He'd reached out to me, along the way, for clues as to where Duncan might be. We've all been trying to pin you down, but you haven't made it easy." Blake was watching her closely, a faint smile on his lips.

Just then the waitress came by to get her order. Gina asked for an orange juice, Blake for another espresso. Once the woman had stepped away, he continued. "Graham's been knocking himself out to reach you, as I'm sure you know, and I've had a hell of a time getting in touch with Duncan. I've left him ten messages on his machine but he hasn't been responding. I'd been trying to fathom why, until recently, it hit me. That machine used to be both of yours. You must know the pass code too."

"You say *used* to be both of ours? Isn't it still?"

"Right. Right. You've supposedly no idea about all that, all forgotten. That's what Violet's been saying. Just tripped and forgot. That's what I'm meant to believe."

The situation was becoming clearer to her now. They must all be in communication at this point, Violet, her father, Graham, and now Blake as well. She looked across at him, this man who had always sought a reason to condemn her and must be thinking he'd found one now. Just how much of the truth had Blake managed to guess? There was a bitter quality in his expression, a tightness around the mouth, even as he smiled.

"So you're doubting my brain injury?"

"I'd doubt any story that came from you."

She had to think how to handle this, how much she must admit to recalling in light of her choosing to reach out to Graham. "I can assure you that losing my memory was very real, and very scary. There's still a lot I can't remember and a lot of what's happened I can't make sense of either."

"Maybe we can fill in some blanks for one another. For example, I'd like to know how, in your disorientation, you were mindful enough to erase all the messages I left for Duncan. All the arguments for why you're a lying manipulator bent on ruining his life."

"Does it occur to you," she replied calmly, "that this could be why Duncan doesn't call you back? He has your number. He's a free man. If he hasn't called, he must not want to." Catching a flicker of irritation in Blake's expression, she pressed on. "Maybe it's finally hit him that your mistrust of me is pathological. And maybe he finally realized that he doesn't need a friend who insults the woman he loves any chance he gets and accuses her of the craziest things."

"I've only begun accusing you," Blake said, leaving off as the waitress returned to lower Gina's juice and his espresso onto the table. "*Grazie mille,*" he said flirtatiously, with his fading charm. He didn't look well, Gina observed, and she had the thought that Blake's self-concern and isolation had already started to corrode him. Love was what kept a person young and fresh, but Blake stood contrary to love, at least where she and Duncan were concerned. She'd wondered about this in Blake, whether his own desires for Duncan might lie, unacknowledged, in him. Possibly this was why, from the very beginning, he'd set out to destroy the love between Duncan and her.

It calmed her to recall that today's allegations against her were hardly his first, and yet, in all these years trying to stain her reputation, what progress had Blake made? He'd perhaps learned she'd told a few lies as a child—stories to conceal the state her mother was in, or other fantasies she'd invented for her own escape from pain. Or maybe he'd reached the conclusion that Gina had pushed Duncan to want the things she wanted. Well, if Blake believed that any of this would turn Duncan against her, he wouldn't have hesitated to share it. That he hadn't done so meant he'd known that Duncan would side with her, and he'd come off as the jealous and untrustworthy friend.

"Did you read Violet's letter?" Blake demanded as she took a slow sip from her juice. "Is that the point at which you knew?"

"I never received any letter from Violet. I don't know what you're talking about."

"Oh, come on now!" Blake was growing impatient. He banged his fist on the table. "I know what I'm talking about. Violet and I went over it. She knows I'm here, and believe me, she's about as eager to confront Duncan as I am to have it out with you. She and I may not have anything else in common other than wishing to see you two separated, but I know she's not lying to me. You got that letter." He stared but Gina's face did not waver. "She left it for you at your hotel in Prague, right before you suddenly insisted on leaving. And then you wrote Violet that letter of your own. You gave her an address in the South of France. You were trying to throw her off your trail, weren't you? While you and

Duncan headed to Siena. And all this time she's worried sick and you haven't even spoken to her. Some friend you are!"

"I really don't know what you're after. Duncan and I changed our plans together. We started for France, then heard about the Palio."

"But obviously you were trying to get Violet off your case. You told her you couldn't handle seeing her; you gave her this whole story about how you were pregnant."

"Did Violet tell you *that*?" It surprised her and frankly hurt her to think that her best friend would betray her confidence—with Blake of all people, and on such a delicate matter. "That's really none of your business."

Blake seemed to recognize her genuine annoyance. "Jesus, it's not actually *true*, is it?"

"Who would lie about a thing like that?"

Silence stretched between them, Blake clearly taking this in, what this would mean for his friend. "You're serious. You're going to have a child like this? Under these conditions?" He began to laugh mirthlessly. "You really are insane."

She could feel her temper rising—nothing about her choice to have this child was insane. At times, it seemed the only clear and good motive she possessed. "I don't need to sit here for this. Why don't you get Graham to step out from wherever he's hiding? I didn't come here to explain myself to you." She began to stand, but Blake took hold of her arm.

"Oh, don't act so shocked. It's not as if you haven't heard this before. I laid it all out for Duncan in my messages."

"I've already told you that I didn't listen to them." She spoke with such conviction, such indignation, that she might almost have believed this herself.

"That tape ought to be full by now. Someone's been erasing."

"And why not Duncan?"

"Because if Duncan heard the things I'd said, he couldn't go on with you the way he is!"

Blake was becoming exasperated. The other café patrons were looking over and she hoped someone would soon come to inquire if she was all right. In fact, she hoped Blake would go further and provoke a stranger to intrude, at which point she would tell the person that she didn't feel safe, that she was pregnant, returning from the hospital, and that she felt threatened by this gentleman whom she'd never before met.

It began to concern her, her exit from this meeting. She wasn't sure how she'd get rid of Blake if he refused to let her go, or if he should insist that she take him to see Duncan. And there was still the matter of Graham.

Reaching into her purse, she removed a pen and began writing on her napkin. "I'm done here. If you have something more to say, say it to Duncan. This is the phone number where we're staying."

Blake let go of her arm to take the paper, folding it up and stuffing it inside his pocket. From his other pocket he withdrew several bills and laid them on the table. "Let's you and I take a short walk. I saw a pay phone on the street. We'll try this number together." Blake rose from his seat and stepped over to pull out her chair.

"Oh, for God's sake. Is this a test? I can't guarantee that Duncan will be home and answer."

"I'm sure you can't."

She peered around her, considering her next move. There were two young men seated, smoking, by the window—maybe she could enlist them in her defense. She doubted Blake would talk as tough with men his own size. For the moment, she felt safer staying here than venturing outside.

"I've had enough of this meeting. I think you should go."

"Not without you," Blake spat. He stepped closer to her but then halted—he was looking behind her, his attention frozen. She turned and saw the man moving toward them, taller than she recalled, every bit as handsome and gracious. He paled when he caught her eye, and his step slowed.

"Hello, Gina," he said, drawing up beside her. She felt so relieved at his arrival, and so moved to see him after everything that had happened, she had to restrain herself from throwing her arms around him.

"Hello, Graham."

She and Graham walked together along Via Collatina on the way back to the train. The road was plain, suburban, with boxy, modern housing, a road that might have existed not in Rome, but on the outskirts of almost any city, even Santa Fe. Strolling now alongside Graham, she had recollections of such walks in the fall and early winter of that year, when she was still dwelling on her mistakes, struggling to keep her thoughts from drifting into dark regions she'd lingered in too long.

"I'm sorry I let Blake meet you alone," Graham offered, head hung in apology. "He said he just needed a few minutes in private, that he was concerned about Duncan and wanted to find a way to help you both. He was awfully persuasive."

"I'd imagine Blake would be."

"But believe me, Gina. I had no idea he'd be aggressive with you. I never would have predicted . . . But then, there's been so much lately that I couldn't have predicted."

Sweet, innocent Graham. She chose not to respond to this, not to address the events, in all their complexity, that had intervened since she and Graham had last been together in Berlin. She couldn't know how much of the story he had gotten or pieced together on his own, if Blake had told him Violet believed Gina was pregnant, if he understood how radical her new plans were— to start a family with Duncan, here in this foreign place, cut off, indefinitely, escaping from the life she and Graham had planned before. Right now she meant to keep their conversation focused on the motive that lay behind her contacting Graham to begin with: "I need to know about my father. If he's okay."

Over the phone, Graham had already told her of the accident back in Siena, reassuring her that her father was on his way to a full recovery—he'd called Graham from the hospital and relayed his encounter with Duncan.

"He's doing much better," Graham assured her. "Of course he wanted to come with me to meet you, but I told him what you said, that you'd be returning with me and that he shouldn't risk his health."

She nodded, avoiding Graham's gaze, guilt-struck. The feeling stirred up memories of so many guilty moments in Graham's presence, times when her affection had felt forced or when, in bed, she'd been distracted by his difference from Duncan, put off by his eager, overly direct touch. And now all her past remorse was compounded by the new hurts she had caused and would cause next. Graham still imagined he might leave Rome with her. Her father was awaiting her imminent return. But she would not be going anywhere.

She felt at a loss for words, but thankfully, anticipating such a moment, she'd written a letter, which she removed from her purse and handed to Graham now. She'd spent several days trying out phrases, explaining herself without overexplaining, and above all trying to persuade her father to stop persecuting Duncan. Graham took the letter from her, and she felt both gratitude and sadness, thinking whether she ought to have written an explanation for him too. How gentle Graham was. At times she'd thought him too even-tempered—there were depths of emotion she'd been sure they'd never reach—but in the days they were together that had seemed a gift.

She remembered clearly now her father's private art showing—how he'd so obviously brought her and Graham together. She could recall the painting on display of her and Duncan, and how, as she'd stood before it fighting back tears, this other man had come up beside her, while someone, maybe her father, had taken a picture of them from behind. She'd looked over at Graham, who was handsome with light eyes that sparkled warmly. He'd introduced himself as a friend of her father's.

"Graham Bonafair. Your father's said a lot about you."

"Has he?" She'd been annoyed at the transparency of her father's motives. He thought her too absorbed by her feelings for Duncan at that time—doubt, pain, regret—and this pretty friend was intended to distract her. She'd had an urge to be unfriendly to Graham, and had avoided him that afternoon. A few days later, though, Graham had come to the house, bringing by some canvases he'd picked up for her father. They'd spoken for a while in the living room and she'd learned that Graham had taken a teaching position in the university art department. He'd moved, he said, after a breakup with his fiancée, and she supposed that her father must have told him of the breakup that she had just endured.

It had all felt very contrived, but though she'd resisted at first, she found she enjoyed Graham's company. At first she felt perhaps he was a stand-in—another object for her to invite into her private world, draw into her hopes and dreams. But Graham brought his own cheerful disposition, so much easier and more hopeful than Duncan's, such a relief after so many grim months. They started taking walks, usually into the old town of Santa Fe, among the red adobe buildings, or else they'd drive out to Abiquiu Lake or Jemez Falls, swimming together, as she and Duncan had never done, floating on their backs under the huge blue sky. It wasn't necessarily that her feelings for Duncan had vanished—they'd just grown paler in the light emanating from this brightly smiling, unfamiliar man before her.

At times she spoke of staying on in New Mexico. After four months at home, she'd taken a job at the dance studio where she'd once trained, and Graham began to encourage her to audition for the larger troupes in Albuquerque. A new fantasy began to form—of their moving somewhere together, finding work, sharing a house. But no matter how many details she might assemble to make such a future sharper, it remained lifeless. Her work in New York far surpassed anything she could find there, and her past with Duncan had more vibrancy and reality than any moment ever did with Graham. Each time she awoke in Santa Fe, there was always a first instant when she expected to be waking in New York, with Duncan, and then the disappointment when she realized all of that was gone. She thought maybe this would pass—and she indeed tried to will her affections for Graham to bloom. But there was always the thought that dogged her—that at any moment she'd gladly erase her present to be back in her past.

"I hope you know I never meant to have this happen," she told him. "For you to be forgotten."

"Oh, I know you didn't." Graham was smiling. She recalled his tendency to smile, especially when he was hurt, that affability that had, toward the end, begun to feel slippery. Just how deep were feelings that could be graciously brushed aside?

If she'd needed someone like Graham for a time, these past weeks had proved that her connection to him was one born out of a rather short-lived need. She found, now, that need—for stability, for comfort, for his ease of emotion—was no longer there. Someone else—someone who had always been in the background of her mind, if she was being truthful—had stepped back into the picture and usurped Graham's power.

"It just happened to you," Graham went on, overly kind to them both. "It wasn't about me."

"No, definitely not," she agreed. All of it made easy by Graham's avoidance of the insult. "The whole year was wiped out. More, even."

Graham paused, briefly wondering. "Did you feel the gaps at all? Or did you not miss what wasn't there?" Obviously such thoughts must have plagued him, and he must now be curious to hear how it had been. As uneasy as the subject made her, she felt that she owed him some answers.

"I had a sense that certain things were missing. More recently."

"And how did it come back, then? Was it gradual?"

"At first, yes. There were flashes here and there. An image as I woke in the morning. Sometimes, even, I'd find myself thinking or saying your name. But no more than that until a sudden shift. One morning in Prague."

"Violet told me she left you a letter. So you did read it?"

"That's right," she said, a painful admission—for Graham to hear her admit she knew the truth and had decided to run from it anyway. She wondered if he was coming to understand this now. While she'd been careful with her lies with Blake, it seemed to her that Graham deserved the truth, or at least a half-truth. She *had* gotten and read Violet's letter at the hotel in Prague—though by then she'd already known more or less what it contained. Graham didn't require the whole story, though; all he had to know was this. "It was a shock and I was furious at Duncan at first. Only then I had to admit that I'd been happy with him. That my feelings for him were still alive and strong. "

"I see." Graham looked off and she waited for him to take in the meaning of what she'd said. "I think I understand now," he muttered sadly. "You won't be coming back with me."

"No, I'm sorry, but I won't."

He nodded, with more equanimity than she had imagined. Deep down, she thought, perhaps he'd known she hadn't loved him. Perhaps he'd wondered at how easily her memories of him had been erased, and this news that she was choosing Duncan surprised him less than either would have guessed.

"I can't say it makes sense to me," he said after a moment. "But I suppose you know what's best for you."

How very decent he was being, and how grateful she was for it, and yet this behavior only confirmed her choice. Despite all these weeks spent worrying and chasing after her, Graham was prepared to respect her feelings and simply walk away. Faced with losing her, Graham was rational and steady, whereas Duncan had been reckless and desperate. Love, she believed, had nothing sensible about it.

The Metro station was just up ahead and she was already late to meet Duncan. He would be worried and full of questions for her when she returned. As difficult as that return might be, she was eager for it, to be away from here and back with Duncan in their home.

"Goodbye, Graham," she told him, and he leaned down to kiss her, lightly on the cheek, before turning away, the long, lean back of her memories fading into memory once more, this time for good.

Sixteen

Duncan // Rome

August 1996

Later on that evening, while Gina rested, Duncan prepared dinner and set the table in the dining room. A cool breeze blew in from the balcony and the setting sun cast a gold band on the back wall, which formed a halo over the face in the giant portrait. The woman—faintly smiling, with deep-set, thoughtful eyes—peered back at him from the wall. A guardian angel, he'd called her when he and Gina had first arrived, and though he'd been joking then, more and more he did believe it.

He still wasn't a religious person, had never had faith in higher powers and certainly not in angels, not in anything like the fat cherubs he'd been lucky enough to see in person on the Sistine Chapel ceiling. Yet despite his doubts, now that he found himself living so beautifully, being so fortunate, he had the distinct sense that someone must be looking out for him. He had no other explanation for why fate had gone his way so often in the past weeks—no other way to understand why, scarcely an hour after he'd gone into the Prague synagogue, certain that Violet would reach Gina and expose him, Gina had announced an urgent desire to leave the city that very morning. Nor could he explain how it was that, in Siena, at the precise moment he meant to confess to Gina what he'd done, she'd chosen to cut him off with the news that she was pregnant.

Since then, the child bound him to his course. He hadn't known it would be this way at first—he'd felt, on the contrary, that he couldn't allow a baby to be born under false pretenses. But then he began to recognize how much Gina wanted this, and wanted him to want it, and he understood it would be cruel to be honest with her now. The time for such a confession would have to be in the far future, once they'd become parents and they'd built a solid life together, and she'd learned that he really was capable of giving to her what she wanted; then he could admit the deception that he'd found it necessary to maintain at the beginning.

"I know it must seem awful, what I did," he'd say, falling upon her mercy. *"I took advantage of you, I went against the wishes you'd expressed in the past. All I can say in my defense is that when you looked up at me in the Berlin hospital that day, I felt that you had chosen me, that this strange act of fate was precisely what was needed to bring us back to our feeling for each other, precisely what was needed to erase all the mistakes and all the rancor. I faced this moment, this impossible temptation: the paradise that I'd been longing for more than I'd even admitted to myself, and all I had to do was acquiesce, not deny it. So I didn't. And from there, messily, with plenty of wrongdoing, but all done out of love for you, we arrived here."*

When he recited this speech in his head to future Gina, he was quite persuaded by it. Put this way, and with years of good history between them to lessen the harm of what he'd done, it might almost seem romantic. See what he'd been willing to go through, what knots he'd twisted himself into to keep that one going?

My God, you really do love me, he knew Gina would think. Not all women might feel that way, but Gina of the grand gesture, Gina who considered her father's obsessive devotion the hallmark of true love, didn't she crave precisely this sort of madness? Wasn't that what she'd always wanted from him, to stop being so cautious and to lose his head a little? So now he had, that much was certain—he'd ceased to be the timid Duncan of the past and had lost his head.

The meal was ready, and Duncan set it onto serving plates, which he carried to the dining room. The places were set. A small bouquet he'd picked up stood in the center of the table. The curtains blew in from the open balcony, and he could hear the muffled sounds of the city: the honking taxicabs, the whirring Vespas, shouts in Italian. He peered down into the street, seized by the fear he'd had the night before: that someone might be outside, watching them. A man walked by with a dog. An old couple passed under the window, holding hands. Not Gina's father, not Graham, not the authorities, not God. Only maybe, somewhere unseen, his guardian angel. He felt the urge to laugh.

He was going to get away with it.

"Duncan, what did you do?"

He turned to see Gina, who'd stepped out into the living room and was admiring the table. She was wearing a white dress, her face aglow with sunset light. He thought he'd never seen her look more beautiful than she did then. Such freshness and innocence— that he should be awarded this, after all his lies and failings, it wasn't fair, it wasn't just, but he would at least never take for granted this gift that he'd been given.

"You did all of this for me?" Gina, smiling, came up beside him.

He wrapped his arms around her, his hands upon the belly with the tiny heartbeat inside it, which, one day, would beat more strongly than his own. "I did this for all of us."

Seventeen

Gina // Rome

August 1996

On her train ride back from Tor Sapienza she had a fearful sense of how narrowly she'd escaped Graham and Blake. After being careful for so long, correcting for Duncan's recklessness, she was the one who'd been sloppy this time, by agreeing to meet Graham without considering the risks. Naturally, he might be contacted by Blake, or others might use him—sweet, simple Graham, who was too kind and naïve to realize it—to get to her. Still, she couldn't rid herself of the fear that Graham hadn't successfully chased off Blake, or any others he might have tipped off to their meeting. Every few minutes, she rose and walked down the center aisle of the train, looking at the passengers in the neighboring cars, seeking Violet or Blake or her father. None of them appeared, though, and after a time, she calmed down enough to take her seat.

She ought to relax, really, prepare herself for meeting Duncan, and yet she couldn't get past the agitation Blake had caused her. She'd been stunned by him, not only by his ingenuity in

persuading Graham to let him meet her but by all that he'd managed to deduce from the information that he'd gathered. He'd
been right about so much: how she'd pretended not to have read
Violet's letter but left it for Duncan to read, how she'd come up
with the visit to the Palio after calling the train stations and learning that getting there would require their leaving right away. On
the trip, she'd written to Violet and given her the French address
to throw her off, as Blake had guessed, and after sensing that
Siena wasn't safe for them, she'd encouraged Mauro to offer up
his place in Rome so that Duncan might accept it. Part of keeping
the game going involved letting Duncan believe, at every point,
that he was the one to manage their escape.

She'd been so expert in this, really, that Duncan seemed completely unaware of her efforts—all the more reason it shocked her
to hear, on one of the early mornings before Duncan was awake
when she'd called into their answering machine, that Blake had
figured out so much.

*She knows everything, Duncan. Her memory is coming back to
her, if it was ever even gone at all. She knows she left you, knows
you're lying that you're still a couple and that people are after you to
stop you. I can't say if she's always known, but at the very least since
the day she got you out of Prague. Think about it and you'll realize
I'm right. You'd have been caught by now, if Gina weren't helping
you. There's too much that can't be explained any other way. Why did
she lie to Violet about where you were headed? Why didn't she ever
insist on calling her father? Why haven't you ever called me? I keep
trying you, though a part of me knows she'll never let me reach you.
She won't let you hear this, and you don't want to hear it either—
you're determined to see Gina as some innocent being, when that's the
last thing she is.*

This final insight of Blake's struck her the most. What a relief it had been for her to find Duncan convinced of her innocence, so convinced that he managed, for a time, to convince her of it too. For their first weeks together in Europe, she was the Gina of their pure past with him again, and, once she'd known the feeling, she'd known this was the only Gina that she ever wished to be. She chose not to see this as her being false, but as her returning to the person she must be—cheerful and loving and without guilt—to be a proper mother to her child.

For the child's sake, she'd done what she had to do, she told herself, and in a way, the real agency in all this wasn't her own, but belonged to this creature deep inside her. As if in some fairy tale, she'd slipped into forgetfulness so that the child could be conceived, and then, after it was, it had wrenched her back into full consciousness again.

It was the pregnancy that brought the past back to her, the sensations lodged in her body's memory. She knew with certainty that she'd felt this way before—tired, dizzy, tender. Suddenly, waking in her Prague hotel room, the details of that time returned to her: Vienna, the festival, the dinners out with her fellow dancers and the Frenchman, and the night she'd felt so ill that the Frenchman insisted he take her to a doctor. At the doctor's office the next day, she was given a test that left no doubt what was happening. She'd purchased a plane ticket to New York that very day. There were five shows left to perform, but she couldn't tell Duncan this news over the phone.

She hadn't informed Duncan she was coming. At the time, she'd hoped to make her arrival part of her surprise, though in retrospect she wondered at this choice. Might she have been afraid to tell him the news? She and Duncan hadn't discussed any changed feelings over having a child, but they'd taken fewer pre-cautions in the weeks before her departure. She'd been testing his resistance; she thought he might want this, but she hadn't had any means to be sure. And yet, for all her nervousness, she'd run up the stairs, eager to see Duncan, not suspecting that anything could be wrong.

The lights were on in the apartment, though low, and music was playing, loudly enough that Duncan must not have heard the door open. Duncan was by the sofa, looking distractedly toward the kitchenette, where Marina Du Bellay was standing holding a wineglass. Marina spotted her first and, lowering the wineglass with a clink, stared back at her, her lipstick smeared and her shirt open, looking so pale and guilt-stricken that Gina knew at once what sort of scene she'd interrupted.

She'd left her bag and run out of the apartment before Duncan had even noticed she was there. Outside she'd darted into a taxi and had gone to stay at a cheap hotel near her dance studio. All the next day, she'd stayed in bed. She had the feeling like she'd lost her adult self, like standing in the doorway witnessing Dun-can's betrayal, she'd become again the little girl standing before her fallen mother, suddenly so frightened and alone. What she'd done next had felt like a necessity. She could not trust Duncan. She could not trust herself to have the baby on her own.

She found the clinic, endured a short interview, and was given pills. This had seemed the least violent method. She hadn't counted on the blood. Yes, at the clinic they had said there would be bleeding, but in the night when she had woken up on bloodied sheets she'd been so horrified she'd spent an hour in the shower, and then another hour washing herself again after she'd cleaned up the mess, shoved all the sheets into bags that she set out with the trash.

She'd left for Santa Fe with the conviction that there could be no coming back. That pain, the blood, the guilt—it had all been too terrible to bear remembering. She'd done this mad, impulsive thing in a moment of rage, which, had she considered more deeply, she'd have known was bound to pass. She knew Duncan didn't love Marina, that Duncan didn't wish to leave her. This wasn't the danger she faced—the danger was in allowing herself to become hopeful, the danger was in becoming a mother, and loving anything as much as she would love that child, as much as she had loved her mother, only to know she might have it torn from her.

In her panic she'd destroyed that hope. Duncan she could forgive, but she could not forgive herself, and that meant punishment, eradicating all that made her happy, all that she'd been able, with Duncan or since her mother's death, to give herself: a thrilling career, a loving life with Duncan—all that she'd said goodbye to, so that she might embark on a new romance that was empty from the start. In its emptiness, she was able to hide. Graham knew nothing about her, and it had been far easier to be someone else with him, flat and new and without fault. A man like Graham was too kind, and too uninterested in the truth, to bother to ask more. With Graham, she began to invent a new half-believed-in future in which Duncan had no part.

Possibly that future might have come to be, and the past with Duncan might have been truly erased, if not for the strangest twist of fate. Everything she'd worked so hard to forget had been simply and effortlessly erased for her.

In those first days following the accident, when the past was emptied from her mind, for all that it had been scary and unsettling, she'd also felt so very light. She'd loved Duncan without restraint. She'd had no reasons not to love him. Here was this sweet and caring boy doing all he could to please her, to take her mind off of anything that troubled her—and what could she want more than that? Maybe her mind had known better than to recover, maybe some part of her recognized that this happiness hadn't been with her before and should be clung to, and she could have stayed in that state of naïve bliss forever if she hadn't woken in Prague to that sore, gnawing, nauseous feeling that she was sure she'd had before.

That morning when she'd woken inside the Prague hotel, she'd lain in bed, on her back beside Duncan, the room around her spinning, and all the memories and images that had been cast loose had begun falling into place.

She'd stepped out onto the Prague streets, feeling as if she no longer knew what was true and what was false. The brightly painted houses looked like toys. Nothing was as it had seemed, not her loving Duncan and not her own lovable self. A letter from Violet was waiting for her in the hotel lobby, and she knew her friend would be meeting her in an hour or so, at which time she'd be rescued from Duncan, and this mad hunt that she'd unwittingly been caught up in would end. After today, she might never even see Duncan again.

She continued her walk, heading into the old city. Her thoughts were too much of a maelstrom for her to do anything but meander, half-blindly, until she ended up in front of a house that looked even stranger than the rest: the little old-fashioned cottage with the Star of David out front. She might have been hallucinating—for an instant she imagined that she was—how could it be that Duncan stood before her, like a ghost?

Had she not seen him then, so humbled, eyes glassy with tears, would she have gone on to meet Violet? Would she have run off with Violet, rather than escaping Violet and running off with him? She might have—yes—she'd felt so insulted and betrayed. He'd preyed upon her weakness; he'd exploited her affection; he'd destroyed her yearlong efforts to get past him and be free.

How it had surprised her, then, when she'd seen Duncan and felt a shift, a sudden strange urge to laugh, right there on the sidewalk. Duncan, how in the hell could you have done this? You wily bastard, how did you dare?

She was moved then by the magnitude of what he'd done, the many details that she'd disregarded earlier, but which attained their proper meaning now: the missing address book, the wedding band that slid too easily off of her ring finger, the sudden move out of Berlin. For her, to get her back, he'd schemed and risked almost everything he had: his career, his connections to friends and family, his reputation, his safety. He'd tossed aside every other commitment, drowned out every moderate objection— he'd thrown himself off of a balcony, for God's sake—for her, for their love!

All those voices in her that had doubted him for being seduced by Marina, or insisted that he'd lose his faith and disappoint her, were silenced, on that day, by what Duncan had done. Her cautious, pragmatic Duncan, whom she always feared lacked the madness required for great art and great love—he was crazy to the core! Weren't they meant for each other? Duncan was just the liar that she was, and Duncan's love for her was just as true.

When the train reached the station nearest to their apartment, the time was nearly five. Gina was almost two hours later than she'd intended and surely Duncan would be home and worried by now—with questions. On the walk home, she had to keep herself from hurrying and growing flushed, and, at the apartment, she took the elevator up rather than the stairs, so as not to appear breathless at the door. She must seem pale and slow moving when she entered, since the story she'd prepared involved her feeling ill. She'd learned early that, with lying, the key was to remain attentive to the smallest details, and to inject into the lie as much truth as possible. For this reason alone, she'd arranged to meet Graham near the hospital, and had collected the leaflets she'd present Duncan, as evidence, before announcing she was tired.

In fact, she wasn't tired in the least, was very much the opposite—she was coursing with adrenaline, too restless to stay put. She still felt compelled to come and look out of the window to be sure she wasn't being watched, checking whether she recognized a face hidden away in a parked car. She was standing by the window when Duncan entered, carrying a pitcher of water, looking on from the doorway.

She stammered that she'd been feeling off, and Duncan led her back to bed and poured her a glass of water. He was starting dinner, he let her know. "Do you feel well enough to eat?"

"Well enough to try."

Dinner was set out for her with flowers, and she was relieved, seeing this, that Duncan must have believed her. During the meal she ate less than she might have, in light of the story that she'd given. Since she'd claimed to be tired before, she suggested they go to sleep early, and they awoke at dawn the next morning, when the sun began shining in and the room warmed, until she found herself shifting in bed, searching for cool spots in the sheets. It would be a hot day, so she advised they get up and out before the heat became too strong. She wanted to walk a bit, since they'd done no sightseeing together all that week. She proposed a stroll down Via dei Fori Imperiali, the road that had formed the spine of ancient Rome, running from Trajan's Forum to the Coliseum.

She'd made the trip several times herself, moved both by the grandeur of the way and by the poetry of the ruins. The road was wide, with paths for pedestrians to pass under the umbrella pines so common in the city. Statues lined the way, and at the bottom of the road the Coliseum rose like a great sun on the horizon. Walking at dusk, as she sometimes did, she would see the light hit the amphitheater so that it seemed to glow.

Trajan's Forum was the least preserved of the famous ancient structures, but it was the one that drew her most. Nearly all of the original marketplace was gone, and what was left were excavated foundations and grassy paths with columns planted in rows, or fragments lying on their sides. She hoped Duncan wouldn't find it disappointing. To her it was mystical, walking on ground where ancient Romans had walked before her, taking in the columns standing where a building had been, where a single stone marked a wall that had contained inhabitants of another rich and complete world, now vanished.

These ruins felt close to her. She'd grown up inside a ruin. Her mother was a ruin, her father and her house. Every corner, word, or look was a fragment left of some better time. And she, too, accumulating losses of her own, had become her own barren space, a field of fragments and absence. Only now something in her had shifted. The emptiness had filled. She contained a life. An extraordinary life—this creature that had willed itself into being. She would be a mother. She would raise a child with Duncan, and he'd go on to write music and she'd return to dance, and their lives would unfold in perfect collaboration, in a way even wilder and more romantic than she might have imagined on her own.

Duncan came to stand beside her, with his arms wrapped around her. There they stood, under the cloud-shaped trees that shaded a brick wall, peering out at the excavated ground.

She placed her hand over her belly, unthinkingly, and leaned back against him. Duncan was bound to her. She knew this now. It had taken her discovering his madness to be certain, but today she felt it in his grip. However battered, however deserted by family and friends, however like a ruin they might become, she and Duncan would endure.

"I love you," he said, squeezing, hands laced over her belly.

She entwined her fingers with his. "And I love you."

Duncan would never let her go, she thought. Not with her to help him. She'd never let him let her go.

The End

Acknowledgments

My deepest gratitude to the wonderful team at Simon and Shuster, who did such beautiful work on behalf of the book. Special thanks to Adam Eaglin, whose vision and encouragement have guided me for years and made this novel happen in the first place; to Zack Knoll, the most talented, dedicated, and generous editor a writer could wish for; and to Sylvie Rabineau, whose faith in me has fueled my creativity and expanded my sense of what's possible. Thanks also to my daughter, for her patience and radiance.

About the Author

ROBIN KIRMAN studied philosophy at Yale before receiving her MFA in writing from Columbia, where she also taught for several years. Her curiosity about human psychology has led her to combine work in psychoanalysis with writing fiction. Her first novel, *Bradstreet Gate*, was published by Crown in 2015, and her television series, *The Love Wave*, is currently in development.